CONVERGENCE

CONVERGENCE

BRIAN W. CLASPELL

This is a work of fiction. The events that unfold within these pages as well as the characters depicted are products of the author's imagination. Any connection to specific people, living or dead, is purely coincidental.

Library of Congress # 2017908491

Cover and interior design by Maria Fazio

ISBN: 978-1-947315-00-6

ACKNOWLEDGMENTS

For Anna who believed in me - Always.

. . .

For my children who had patience and great love.

. . .

For all those who read, edited and commented
on this manuscript.

. . .

For L.D. Beyer for his advice and experiences he shared.

. . .

For Maria Fazio who created the cover concept and
formatted the book.

. . .

For Charity Bradford and Amy Hancock who are just as
passionate about writing as I am.

. . .

For my parents and extended family, they are all great.

. . .

Did I mention, for Anna, who I believe in – Always!

CONTENTS

Prologue

DURING THE COLD WAR

It was a chance that the CIA could not pass up. The opportunity to get an agent involved in the Ministry of Knowledge in the Soviet Union. The Kremlin was actually unwittingly inviting an active CIA agent to participate. The fact that one of the CIA's best modern day linguist and interpreters of ancient languages had a second job as a professor of antiquities at the University of Maryland was a beautiful streak of luck. Professor Samuel Thomas was CIA true and proper. He was the agent that had cracked many of the Eastern Block codes that had given the United States a considerable intelligence advantage in the 1980s.

Now the Kremlin through an extreme stroke of luck had found an archeological dig in northern Russia. They did not have the expertise to interpret some of the things they were finding. Their exhaustive search led them to less than a dozen candidates. Professor Samuel Thomas was second on their list. The first man, a much younger choice, lived in England and had a young family. The younger professor was reluctant to get involved in a project where very little information was available and would put his young family far behind the Iron Curtain.

Professor Thomas was a single man. He had married young, but that had not lasted very long. He then had a live in girlfriend for many years but that passed also. He fancied himself a lady's man and was often known to take on a new girlfriend every few weeks. He seemed to be the epitome of the "one night stand" of the pre-AIDS era.

When asked by the Kremlin to come to Moscow for a "special project" that could last six to twenty four months, he was not excited. He was in the middle of an operation called Contra-connection that would disrupt the activities of some of the South American drug cartels. It was an off shoot project of the Iran-Contra operation. Professor Thomas was heavily vested in this project. He was on the verge of deciphering one of the largest cartel's forms of communication in Columbia. They had been able to track the profits from accounts in the Bahamas to accounts in Switzerland. This had all come together perfectly. Professor Thomas was working on correcting a recent snag in the operation that once fixed would pull it all together. It would make their many long years of work worth it.

The team called the Fabulous Five, who had worked so hard on this project; thought that there was no way Professor Thomas could, or would, be pulled from this assignment. But the news of this offer made many of his superiors salivate at the prospect.

Officially, the US State Department objected to the offer of an ordinary American citizen being invited into the USSR for a "fuzzy" purpose. They pushed the Kremlin for more disclosure on the project. The Kremlin refused but said it was "purely historical and archeological in nature" and they would "share results and give Professor Thomas appropriate credit". This, of course, made the CIA salivate at the opportunity even more. If it was top secret, the CIA had a lot to gain. If it were really just a historical dig, then Agent Thomas would at least have connections with the Ministry of Knowledge and might be able to leverage those in the future. This seemed like a no lose proposition. The US State Department relented on the objections when the Ministry of Knowledge agreed to let Professor Thomas report back weekly on his work and his health. This, of course, would be a somewhat controlled message but it would be regular sanctioned contact from a CIA operative from behind the Iron Curtain.

The chief of the CIA would claim that President Ronald Reagan himself made the call for Agent Thomas to take the assignment. That could never be proven, but it was made high enough in the hierarchy that Agent Thomas was surprised when his mid-western vacation was cut short and he was escorted immediately for reassignment. He was not even given a chance to turn his work over to his colleagues or even debrief. His sole focus was to prep for his new assignment behind the Iron Curtain.

Less than a week later he was being briefed in Moscow on the project. The briefing was short and focused more on security protocol and how his communication with the States would be handled. There were no specifics on the assignment only a description of an elaborate archeological find. He was then taken north-east of Moscow in a military truck. How far he was taken, he was not quite sure. As he traveled, he considered that his team on the Contra-connection project might make some progress, but he was needed to complete the project. He knew that they could not complete it without him. This he was sure of. This assignment in Russia would be great; it was a chance to be a real "spy". He had done this type of thing a few times early in his career, but not often. It was the thrill of this concept that attracted him to the CIA in the first place.

The archeological site was less than had been described to him. The ruin was a small village, but not a lot had been uncovered. There was a make–shift modern village of hastily constructed buildings on the far end of the dig site. He was taken to a barracks like building. When he entered the building he noticed there were about thirty double bunked beds, about cot size. At the end of the barracks were two small rooms. Professor Thomas was led to the one on the left. It was barely big enough for a single cot and a small shelf for clothes. There was also a single light dangling from a cord and a space heater on top of the shelf.

The soldier that took him to the spot said in broken English, "It is our best–for you".

Professor Thomas answered in Russian, "спасибо (thank you)" and then explained to the soldier that he could speak fluent Russian. Professor Thomas did not eat dinner but went right to bed. He vaguely remembered hearing people coming into the barracks.

There was a regimented wakeup call in the morning. He instinctively came out of his small room to a bustling barracks. Standing to greet him was Sven Choski, the head of the dig. Sven was a stout man who worked in the Ministry of Knowledge. In any western country he would have been a well respected educator at a fine university. In the USSR, being connected to the Kremlin in anyway was even more prestigious. Next to Sven stood Commander Blootov, the senior military leader and overall official leader of the dig. Sven greeted Professor Thomas and insisted that they go to the main artifact room immediately.

Sven was almost as giddy as a child waiting for Christmas. They entered a building that had cement block sides and a canvas-tent like roof. There were several long tables with a few artifacts scattered amongst the tables. The artifacts were clearly in various stages of the process of cleaning, evaluating and cataloging. At this time of day though, the room was empty except for the three of them and a single guard at the far end of the structure. The academic side of Professor Thomas came to life as he started walking along side these tables. He stopped and looked at an artifact, a weapon that set on a table. He stood thinking for a moment, going through his own personal catalogue system in his mind. Then it came to him, "I have seen one of these in the Smithsonian vault–I believe it was from the eastern Mediterranean area."

"Yes, Samuel, yes" Sven said in anticipation and building excitement.

"And you found that in this dig sight, some place in northern Russia?" Professor Thomas asked seeming somewhat surprised.

"Interesting, isn't it?" Sven picked up a similar piece from across the table that had already been catalogued. "We have been working for a year and have several finds like this. Not just weapons though, but other things also. Many are fully intact."

At the end of the large room there stood the guard in front of a locked cage. Sven had the commander and the professor sit at a table near the cage. He unlocked the cage and brought a box covered with a canvas sheet and placed it in front of Professor Samuel Thomas. Sven was smiling, barely able to hold his own enthusiasm.

Professor Thomas slowly pulled the canvas off of the artifact. In almost an instant, the spy in Samuel Thomas was gone and the academic explorer was in full control, at least for that moment. "You found a bronze plate?" The plate sat in a wood frame and had been sealed to the edges with wax.

Sven had a satisfying smile, "Yes, and writing—looks like some form of Egyptian or Hebrew or some combination. But that is why we need you."

"Are there more?" Professor Thomas was now eager for more.

"Not yet, but we hope to find more." Sven said confidently.

"It will take a while to figure out a basis for translation." Professor Samuel Thomas set stunned, carefully studying the artifact. Without looking up he said, "I cannot believe it, ancient writings on a bronze plate clearly from someplace in the Mediterranean basin found here in northern Russia."

Sunday
Chicago Time (Modern Day)

CHAPTER 1 – THE AIRPORT

"That was nice of you to stick around and visit with me." Darcie said as she sipped her last few drinks of the cocktail in anticipation of needing to say good bye so that she could catch her plane.

Jacob knew that his sister-in-law had routed her travel through Chicago so that she could see him. There were other alternatives to get from Atlanta to New York City. Coordinating a schedule like this with the ever changing security measures since 9-11 was difficult to arrange. However, he was glad to see her. Sandy blond hair, light skinned with a reassuring smile exerting confidence - she looked so much like her older sister that he almost cried when he saw her. The pain was still almost unbearable, even after nearly a full year. "I am just glad your plane came in close to mine." Jacob responded politely.

The conversation dragged longer than it should have and Darcie might just miss her plane if she didn't get moving soon. Then the announcement came over the loud speaker as though it had been directed right at Darcie. "This is the last boarding call for United Flight 678 to New York City. Please make your way to the plane immediately if you have not yet boarded."

Darcie got up. Jacob did also. They hugged each other and Darcie said, "You can come out for the holidays if you would like."

"I might." Jacob responded as the embrace took him back to his long embraces with his wife Carol. It was not the same, but the memory lingered and haunted him. Jacob sat back down to finish his soda before he went to get his luggage. He watched Darcie disappear into the hallway with the terminals and pondered his last goodbye to Carol.

Almost immediately after Darcie disappeared, a man walked up next to the table and set a metal silver brief case on the table. "I will be done in a minute and you can have the table." Jacob said not even looking up at the man. His mind was still reminiscing about a time he went on a business trip and his wife had hidden cookies in his suitcase. The cookies did not travel well but he had eaten them anyway just so he could tell his wife how good they were.

"Please, hold this suitcase." The man just walked away as quickly as he had approached. Jacob did not even see his face. A sense of realization came over Jacob almost instantly. This was the airport. A man he had never met just left him a suitcase that did not belong to him. He immediately began to scan the airport with his eyes to find a security officer.

Before he got too far, a woman sat at the table across from him. She was a beautiful woman with brunette hair that was pulled back. She looked sophisticated and very educated. Her skin tone was a slight olive color and was smooth. She was clearly a few years younger than Jacob was. "If anyone asks, you are Mr. Conrad, Mr. Jim Conrad."

"Who are you?"

She quickly showed what appeared to be some type of law enforcement identification as she said, "I am with the CIA and we need your help right now." It wasn't as though she were asking, she was sort of insisting.

Before Jacob could get another question out of his mouth, a Latino American looking man approached the table. "You are Mr. Conrad, yes?" He spoke in clear English but with a distinct Latin–American accent. He was young, probably in his early to mid twenties.

"Jim Conrad, and you are?"

"You are a hard man to find. Some believe you are a figment of the CIA's or MI6's imagination. But I see that you are real." The man said as he quickly studied Jacob and the lady across from him.

Jacob said. "I do like to keep a low profile. So, who are you?"

"I am an associate of Mr. Martinez. He is looking forward to your personal visit this evening at the Drake Hotel–your usual place to stay while you are in Chicago."

The young woman spoke-up, "Mr. Conrad will call Mr. Martinez with his intentions later. Whether he comes or not, let Mr. Martinez know that we appreciate that the invitation was brought by his son. That shows respect."

"Very well then." The man turned and walked away. The table had become a haven of activity that seemed to center around Jacob. He was ready to be done and looked at the lady across the table. "Can I go now?"

"You need to go with me. We are likely being watched and you leaving in another direction would just cause suspicion. Grab the suitcase and your carryon bag and come with me." She put twenty dollars on the table to more than cover the bill and then she grabbed his arm and quickly ushered him through the airport. He was not quite sure why he followed her through this seemingly harmless adventure.

As they stepped out of the secured area, Jacob asked, "What about my luggage?"

"We will take care of it." They went directly to the curb side pick-up area where a finely dressed man stood with a sign that read

"Mr. Smith". She directed him to that limo. "I thought I was Mr. Conrad?"

"Mr. Conrad, you do like to keep a low profile. It is better to travel under an assumed name sometimes." The driver shut the door.

The young lady looked at Jacob, "Open the brief case." She spoke matter–of–factly and without any sense of emotion.

"Okay, but you know my many names and I don't know even one of your names."

It was almost like a light came across her face. She realized that she had been so routine about the operation that she hadn't considered what Jacob must be experiencing. "I am Jenny." She said with a slight grin that could have been construed as friendly or sinister.

"Is Jenny your real name or just a name for the charade we just played out?" Jacob said as he opened the brief case.

"It is both, easier to remember that way." She said with a slight smile on her face.

The brief case had several passports, credit cards and a considerable amount of cash. As Jacob opened up the first passport, he was surprised to see his picture with the name "James Smith." As he quickly went through the brief case, he saw several other identities including a "Mr. James Conrad". Each had corresponding credit cards, driver's licenses and other pieces of identification.

"You will need to check into the Drake as 'Mr. Smith'. I will explain more as we get to the hotel." Jenny told him.

"But how long…"

Jenny anticipated his question before he even finished. "You should be able to stay the night in the hotel and checkout in the morning. You should never have to even leave the hotel room. We made up additional identification just as a precaution for the airport. If Mr. Martinez' son had asked for identification, he would have expected to see several different identities."

"But won't Mr. Martinez expect to meet with me tonight?"

"I will explain more when we get to the hotel, but Mr. Conrad never meets with anyone. He will hope that you meet with him, but he will expect to meet with me. I handle nearly all of Mr. Conrad's business."

"So who really is Mr. Conrad?"

"That you really do not need to know. For tonight, you are Jim. Now change into these clothes before we get there." She pulled a nice set of slacks and a nice shirt from a hanger in the limo. She also handed him socks and designer shoes.

"In front of you?" Jacob asked.

Jenny laughed and said, "I will avert my eyes."

It was a bit awkward changing in the limo, but Jacob managed to remove his slacks and shirt and put on a much more expensive set of clothes. As requested, he handed his identification and credit cards to Jenny for safe keeping. Well before they got to the hotel, Jacob had transformed himself into Jim. And for the check-in procedures that night, he would be Mr. Jim Smith.

CHAPTER 2 – ENTERING THE DRAKE HOTEL

Jim (Jacob) had lived in Chicago for years, but had never been to the Drake Hotel before. There was a bellman, but Jim and Jenny had no luggage. They entered through the revolving doors the room opened up to a staircase. Jim scanned the room to familiarize himself with the surroundings realizing that Mr. Conrad had been here before. The ceiling had fine woodwork and crown molding. Making their way up the stairway, Jim noticed the intricate patterns, chandeliers and art work. It was almost a scene out of the roaring 1920's—perhaps a scene familiar to Al Capone or other notorious fellows. He took a right and went up another short set of stairs that led them to the front desk for check-in.

Jim stood just behind Jenny near the check-in counter of the hotel holding only a metal briefcase. The check-in clerk said, "Ah, Mrs. Smith, your suite is ready. I have provided you and Mr. Smith with the normal amenities. We are pleased to have you back."

Without another word, Jenny turned and headed for the elevator. Jim walked next to her. They had to use the key card in the elevator to access the floor that the room was on. Jim knew that meant it would be nice.

Two men were in the room as Jim and Jenny walked in. One looked at Jenny and said, "It's all clear. You can talk freely in here." Then they left.

Jim reminisced about the suite he and Carol stayed in for their anniversary a few years before. It was a nice room but this room was incredible. The bedroom was in another room. In the middle of this room was a table with a chilled bottle of wine and a few appetizers. There was also a fruit bowl. This was not the presidential suite, but it was very close to the best suite in the hotel. It certainly was better than any Jim had ever stayed in before.

"You did well." Jenny said as she started to make her way around the room. Jim wasn't sure if she was checking for something or just familiarizing herself with her environment.

"There wasn't really much to do, I just followed you in." Jim stated simply as he looked out of the large window at the stunning view of Lake Michigan.

"You kept your mouth shut—that is almost always the right thing to do." She made her way to the closet and opened the door. Jim could see a few nice men's suits and a few very sophisticated dresses. Jenny paused for a moment, as if something must be wrong, but then continued and went through the bureau drawers.

Jim followed her around the room. "So what next?"

"I will need to run an errand, you can wait here." Jenny instructed Jim.

"Is Mr. Martinez a drug dealer?" Jim asked inquisitively.

She looked at him a little impatient, but decided that he should know at least a little bit about their predicament. "Sit down." There was a small couch with a coffee table next to it. A couple of other elegant chairs were on either end. Jim sat on the end of the couch and Jenny sat in the chair closest to him.

She looked at him, clearly pondering what she should tell him. The she began. "Ricardo Martinez deals in 'exotic goods'."

"He steals art and antiques." Jim concluded.

"He doesn't steal very often, but does trade in rare artifacts that he then sells on the black market to rich investors who want a private and unique collection. His father was Cuban and his mother was Mexican, both deceased. They were both connected to drug trafficking in the 1980's and 1990's."

"But Ricardo, does he traffic drugs?"

"He goes by Ric, and no he does not traffic drugs. Shortly after his father was killed he stopped that part of the family business. Nobody knows exactly why he stopped. He is a fairly well known criminal but has eluded the law for many years."

The hairs on the back of Jim's neck were starting to tingle. His interest peaked and he was getting a rush of adrenaline as they talked. "So you are pulling a sting operation to finally capture him?"

"No, the CIA cares very little about his trafficking of stolen goods. We are more concerned with national security." Jenny corrected.

"So why him?"

"Many of his clients sell weapons and information. We need a relationship with him to help find some of them." Jenny responded.

"So how are we going to do that?" Jim inquired.

Jenny stood up. "You have almost completed your part. The rest will be up to me. Now I need to run my errand. Be ready for dinner in about one hour." She continued to walk to the door as she talked. "Wear the black tux on the right side of the closet."

She was then out the door. Jim sat dumfounded wondering what he had gotten into. It was a little exhilarating. He was just glad that this had not happened while Carol and his children were alive. He would never have wanted to be part of an adventure like this with his family to take care of. Of course, he would have traded this entire adventure for just one more afternoon with his wife and children.

CHAPTER 3 – DINNER

The closet had precisely six men's outfits. They were all neatly pressed and hung in the closet at equal distance from each other. There were also three pairs of men's shoes on a nearby shoe rack. Two of the outfits appeared somewhat of a classy casual look. Each had a jacket, similar to the one he had put on in the limo. These outfits would look fine with or without the jackets.

The next two outfits were a little more formal. The final two outfits were black tuxes, very formal. Jenny had asked him to dress in the very formal outfit. He figured he better try it on just to make sure it fit well so there would be time to adjust it if needed.

The tuxedo seemed a perfect fit. He was pleased. Then he began to wonder if the other clothes would fit as well. Jim carefully tried on each outfit in the closet and then those in the drawers. Each fit as though it had been custom made for him. This made him a little uneasy. Just as he was putting on the tuxedo once more, Jenny walked in. Without a beat she stepped up to him and finished tying his tie. "There, that looks sharp. You look fitting for a rich man with large assets in Swiss Bank accounts and a desire to remain under the radar. Shall we go to dinner?"

Jim started, "Are you going to change?" But before he could finish his sentence she had pulled her dress off and started to get another out of the closet. "She has no inhibitions," Jim thought to himself as he picked up a magazine and sat in a chair so as not to face her directly.

She was ready in a matter of moments. They headed to the elevator to go to the restaurant. The métier d' did not recognize Jim and Jenny, but once he had their name they were seated at a private table that was away from any other table in the restaurant. It was the ideal table placement, privacy and a view to most of the restaurant.

"Mr. and Mrs. Smith, we are pleased that you have come down to dine with us. Can we start you with your usual bottle with the jumbo shrimp cocktail on the side?" The waiter had no pen or pencil, but seemed to know their preferences. He handed each of them one of the menu's.

Jenny started to speak, but Jim stepped in. "I believe the jumbo shrimp cocktail would be fabulous, but we would like a bottle of water please." Jim wasn't sure if the waiter's look was surprise or displeasure. He was sure that Jenny was not pleased.

Once the waiter had walked away, Jenny quietly whispered, "We have been coming here quite a while and always have the same room service order on the first night. It is tradition." Her voice was calm and her tone persistent.

"Well, Jenny dear." Jim continued in as polite a voice but just as persistent. "You may remember that I no longer drink alcohol"

"Not even for national security purposes?" She said very quietly.

"Not even if my beautiful wife insists." Jim said with a satisfying smile. "And please pass one of those rolls."

Jim did not alter the rest of the dinner, except for the after dinner cocktail. He ordered a non-alcoholic version of that drink. Jenny did the same.

Jenny said, "Do you know who that is across the room?"

"Yes, he is the mayor of Chicago sitting with one of our fine senators." Jim could recognize the senator even with his back to him.

"And the table over there?" She indicated a table a few down from the mayor's table with a gesture of her eyes.

"No, who are they?" Jim asked.

"That is a table filled with three CEO's of fortune 500 companies. And the table in front of them is a known crime boss from Chicago's north side."

"And I see our friend from the airport behind you." Jim responded.

"Yes, with his father." Jenny noticed them before they sat down.

Jenny observed as Ricardo Martinez stopped to visit with the reputed crime boss and then also spoke to the mayor and the senator. All seemed friendly and content with the interaction. As Ricardo left the dining room, the métier d' brought a note to Jim.

Jim set it on the table so that they could both read it.

"Anonymity is a price to be cherished. I expect both of you this evening or do not bother coming at all. Regards, Ric."

Jenny concluded, "This is not good."

CHAPTER 4 – PLANNING THE ENCOUNTER

Jenny didn't say a word all the way back to the room. There was a brief nod to a gentleman in the hall that would have gone unnoticed by a less observant person. Jim noticed it and figured it was some type of communications.

By the time they entered into their room, another man was already seated on one of the chairs next to the coffee table. He was smoking a cigar and had a glass of wine sitting on the table next to him. Before Jenny even said a word, and it was clear she wanted to, he jumped right in and said, "We have to send him in or years of work are down the drain."

"But this is too dangerous to put an untrained civilian into." Jenny fired right back. "Jim, however handsome and charming as he might be, is a novice and just here for looks." Jim felt a pat on the back and slap on the face all in one sentence. However, it was quite accurate.

"It's a conversation and a negotiation. You negotiate and he can just indicate approval. Keeps his position very powerful and doesn't compromise the grander scheme." The man countered.

Jim quietly sat at the edge of the couch near the gentleman and started to read the Chicago Tribune. He didn't say a word, but listened to them argue for about 10 minutes. Finally, when there was a brief pause in the conversation, Jim looked up at the gentleman in the chair near him and said, "Hello, I am Jim Conrad–and you are?"

Jenny chuckled slightly. The man looked at him and said, "I am Deputy Director Frank Warner. I am pleased to meet you Jim."

Jenny jumped in, "And Jim, do you have an opinion on this."

Jim thought for a minute, at least he pretended to think–he had been thinking about this ever since he walked into the room. "I figure that I am here all night anyways–as long as it isn't too dangerous I do not mind going."

"You are a character Jim." Jenny concluded. It was clear that Frank was pleased. Jenny was just intrigued.

"But I want to carry a gun. You can't do that legally in Chicago, but I figure that someone like Jim Conrad would carry one–just for safety." Jim continued.

Frank almost jumped out of his chair, but realized that he might just lose the upper hand he had gained on Jenny if he objected. Jenny appreciated this and quickly agreed to give Jim a gun.

Frank's objections were short lived and he finally relented so that the evening plans would not be spoiled. The conversation shifted to discuss and plan the evening's events.

CHAPTER 5 – THE CASTLE VLADEEMAN

Somewhere near the heart of Romania sits a quaint town on the edge of Transylvania called Brasov. There is a church in the middle of this town called the "Black Church" which had been used as refuge during many invasions from the east and the west. It was burned, attacked and revered, but still stands for over five hundred years after being built. The town has been an historical crossroads for invasions.

Just north of Brasov is the famous Bran Castle, revered castle used in the Dracula legend. It is not as ornate or as splendid as the early Dracula movies would lead one to believe, yet it was still an important part of the history of Romania and particularly that area of Transylvania.

Almost exactly 70 kilometers west is a less known castle built during approximately the same era and about the same size called the Castle Vladeeman. It is less known than the Castle Bran, even by the locals. A shorter pudgy man, Dragos Sabir, who normally resides in Brasov owns the castle. It has been owned by his family for several generations. Dragos is a low key individual that stayed under the radar even during the communist rule in Romania.

Dragos' castle has become, over the years filled with antiquities that he and his family had collected over many generations. Many of these were collected from the Romanian aristocrats shortly before World War II to be kept safe from the Nazi's and then kept after that to be safe from the Communist. Dragos' father convinced many of the neighboring countries' aristocrats to move their wealth into the Sabir families' remote location as a safe place for their wealth from the "common good" of communism. To the Sabir family's delight, many of the original proprietors had died and not passed the knowledge of the secret treasures onto their children. The Sabir family now claimed any of this unclaimed hidden treasure as their own.

Dragos also obtained treasure in many other ways, some legal and some a little more shady. He had come upon the two etched plates of bronze by accident. He didn't know if they were authentic ancient writings or just a more modern piece of work. He had no way to validate the story he had been told or translate them without bringing in additional experts. He felt this might be too risky since he had pulled the bronze plates from a dead Russian who happened to also be a former KGB agent.

CHAPTER 6 – REPORTING UP

Frank sat in a small room with a double bed. It was in the Drake, just below where Jenny was staying but the room was certainly not of the same caliber. He had stayed at much worse but he had a slight resentment that one of his subordinates was in a much nicer room. But it was still the Drake Hotel. He was senior enough to get his own room. He had returned to his room to make a phone call.

He didn't like the idea of having to call his superiors and inform them that the civilian they were using was about to get intimately involved in a major CIA operation. Sure, his boss knew about using the accountant from Chicago as the face of Jim Conrad. He even approved and encouraged the "real touch" to Jim Conrad. However, including him in the heart of the operation was not how the CIA operated and he knew he would get a lot of pushback from his superiors.

He also knew that in order for the total plan to work, Jim Conrad had to be a real person that could be seen and had to be met by some shady characters. The CIA had invested a lot of money in this operation and wanted to see it successful. Frank had invested a lot in this personally and was equally anxious to see the scheme play out.

Deputy Director Frank Warner would call his boss, Sr. Director Tom Sportsman, after Jim and Jenny had entered Ricardo's room. That way there would be no way to say no.

CHAPTER 7 – LONDON TOWN

Sir Arthur Borden and his wife had just taken in the London Eye with Arthur's college friend from the states. It was well after midnight. The London Eye had been kept open all night to celebrate England's success in recent international football competitions. One would have thought that they had won the World Cup, but any international success by England was reason to celebrate at this time. Sir Arthur Borden grew up in the states and was a US citizen but had learned to be a strong soccer fan since he moved to England. His favorite team was the Manchester United.

Sir Arthur Borden was actually knighted nearly forty years earlier when his young family moved to England. It was a "tragic happening that we are pleased was bestowed" became the official statement from the monarchy after accidentally bestowing the title of "sir" on a young professor from the states.

Arthur had taken a professorship at Oxford so that he could be close to London to observe and study all of the ancient manuscripts from the Middle East and Egypt that came through the museums in London. Paris may have been his first choice, but he spoke only

English. However, he was considered an expert on many ancient languages.

His friend, a controversial professor of political science over the same period of time, had come to London for a conference to speak. He was the keynote speaker on "English Aggression manifested in Modern America." The lecture was based on a few papers and an upcoming book. He connected with Arthur and his wife on the few occasions he came to London. They did not share the same political view, but enjoyed the banter and reminiscing of old times together.

On the way to the tube, Arthur's wife took the arm of the old college friend to help her down the stairs. It was half way down the stairs when a man in a hooded shirt stabbed the old college friend and Arthur's wife. The perpetrator quickly disappeared into the night.

CHAPTER 8 – MEETING RICARDO "RIC" MARTINEZ

Jenny entered the room cautiously. Jim followed just one step behind her. Jenny scanned the room as they entered. The room was not as big as Jim's room. It was still bigger than most hotel rooms. It had a bed in the main section as they came in the door. The bed had not been slept in. Jenny surmised that they only got the room for this meeting. She knew that Ricardo lived in Chicago and did not need a hotel room. In an adjacent room there was a working table for a meeting and a desk. She also checked the bathroom. There was no adjacent suite where a door could be opened. In the room were Ric and his two sons. Jenny knew that he also had a daughter, but she didn't expect to see her. This was Ric's most trusted inner circle and no one else.

Ric, his younger son Victor and Jenny sat at the table. The oldest son, Ricky, stood behind Jenny. He was smaller than his younger brother–but looked rougher. Jim pulled a chair away from the table and sat positioned so that he was looking directly at Jenny and to the left of Ric. Ricardo was anxious to meet Jim and to do business with him. He had heard of Jim and his reputation and knew that the prestige of working with someone like Jim would also raise his own prestige as a businessman.

Ric got straight to business. "So Mr. Conrad–you are looking for something to add to your collection."

"Mr. Martinez, you can call me Jim–and Jenny will conduct my business for me." Jim said in short.

"Thank you Jim, you can call me Ric. This is my son Victor and my oldest boy Ricardo Jr. We just call him Ricky." Ric then turned to Jenny and continued. "You are looking for something specific."

"Jim has a small collection of old books, manuscripts and the like. He is looking for something unique…"

Ric interrupted. "Anything in particular? Original Shakespeare? A Gutenberg Bible?" He sat anxiously but in a quiet tone waiting for her answer.

She looked at Jim and he gave a nod. It really meant nothing, but gave the illusion that he was in charge. "Well, Jim is looking for something unique to display his collection in, something fitting from a royal renaissance time period." The plan had been to get some type of rare manuscript. However, Jenny decided to bait him with something different.

"We can look and maybe we can also find some literary classic that would also catch his fancy." Ricardo responded hoping to entice additional business his way.

"Perhaps, why don't you see what you can find and we can talk. However, an antique desk or bookshelf would be the most desired item. If you can find a manuscript Jim would like something, shall we say, that is 'unique'."

Ric's oldest son, Ricky, jumped in. "We are not stealing something just to find out you aren't buying." The oldest son was unpredictable. Ric always thought that he might need to give the business to his younger son and find something else for his older son. Ricky spent too much time with some of the older business acquaintances and developed a short temper–a necessity from the old business, but not needed in Ric's new empire very often.

Jenny physically turned towards the older son and said. "I didn't ask you to steal anything. Just find out what some people may be willing to sell and give me a shopping list." She quickly turned her back on him and faced Ric again.

The son took this as an insult and quickly grabbed her by her hair pulling her head back. He had a gun to her head in a matter of seconds.

Jim did not hesitate; he pulled his gun and put it to Ric's head. "No one puts a gun to my Jenny's head."

Jenny looked horrified.

The younger son didn't move. His father gave him a stern gesture to remain calm. Then Ric said. "Jim, I cannot find you your treasures with a gun to my head. But being a practical man, I suppose you cannot remove the gun without the gun being removed from Jenny's head."

"I think I will like doing business with you Ric." Jim concluded as he lowered his gun.

It only took a look from Ricardo and his oldest son reluctantly lowered the gun. As he did so, Jenny swung out of the chair, grabbed the gun from his hand and had him pinned to the wall with her fingers around his neck. "If you ever pull a gun on me again, I will kill you. A shot to my head won't stop that." She then released his neck, handed him the gun and turned her back on him once again.

They spoke for the next hour. Ric always liked to keep a record of his interactions so he took a photo to "commemorate their friendship". Jenny and Jim were not aware of this gesture and Jenny certainly would have never allowed it.

"I will contact you in a few days and let you know what I have found." Ricardo already had things in mind, but wanted to set the expectation a few days out in case the prospects in his mind didn't work out. If they did work out, he knew he would be calling much sooner

"You have my cell number," Jenny responded.

CHAPTER 9 – LONDON POLICE

Sir Arthur Borden cradled his wife in his arms. She was dead but he continued to cuddle her. Arthur sat in shock and disbelief as to what had just happened. Holding his wife he knelt partially over one of his oldest friends that was now lying dead in the tube of London. All he could think about was calling his children to let them know what happened.

His children both lived near Washington DC with families of their own. His mind crossed over to a discussion his wife had with their daughter the day before about visiting the grandchildren. Both his wife and daughter were excited at the time. These were now just shattered dreams. He did not even notice the police and the other authorities come until they pulled his wife's bloodied body from his arms.

The police spent about an hour talking to him and cleaning up the stairs to the tube. It did not appear to be robbery, but a deliberate murder. The police seemed to conclude that this was an "opportune murder" of the controversial American professor that happened to get Arthur's wife in the mix. The thought did cross Arthur's mind that he was the intended target, but he couldn't figure anybody that would want him or his wife dead.

The police dropped him off at his office at Oxford. He couldn't convince himself to go home. He would sleep on the sofa after calling his children. He called each of them and explained the situation as clearly as he could and told them he would call back tomorrow morning their time to talk more.

It only took a matter of minutes until he cried himself to sleep on the sofa in his office.

CHAPTER 10 – THE WINDING ROAD TO BUCHAREST

Dragos was now involved in an extreme early morning drive down the long and winding road to Bucharest from Brasov. He knew a friend at the university that he thought might be able to help translate the bronze plates. He thought that his friend might just claim his etched plates for the national museum. The last artifact that he brought to "Bucky" had been confiscated and put into the national museum. Of course, the last item happened to be a shield that had likely been used by Vlad the Impaler.

Dragos' mind was not on his friend Bucky or even the legend of Prince Vlad, but on the events the evening before. He did not intend to get in the middle of a KGB gun fight. The KGB agent, Daniel, had come to Dragos for help. He was Romanian by birth and had gone to Russia at a very young age because of his aptitude for learning languages. This made him a very desirable candidate for the KGB. He was indoctrinated early but never forgot his roots in Romania.

His father knew Dragos' father and told his son to look up Dragos' father if ever he needed anything. Dragos' father died and the former KGB agent now looked to Dragos for that help. Ever since the fall of the communist Russia regime, the KGB stayed intact to some degree and still functioned in many of the cold war tactics, including some of the internal Russian affairs. Some also formed or become part of the Russian mob–a name that indicated a single unit. It is not. Nor can you always tell the KGB from the mob, sometimes they are the same.

Dragos got a call in the middle of the day and he agreed to meet Daniel, the former Romanian KGB member, at the Aro Palace. The Aro is a hotel in the middle of Brasov. It is considered one of the more elegant locations in the town.

The Aro is a beautiful hotel with a large foyer. It was open with a few couches in the middle. It did not as of yet conform to the "no smoking" policy that most of the rest of the world adhered to. When Dragos entered the hotel there were several individuals huddled together smoking.

There were many small meetings being carried out in the lobby. These were conducted in either Romanian or English. Dragos sat in a chair facing the entrance near an American and Englishman, he surmised. They were talking about touring a local chocolate factory. Dragos knew the one.

Daniel was easy to pick out of the crowd as he walked into the Aro. He wore a long coat with a fur collar, maybe standard issue for the KGB. He carried a backpack and had a distinct haircut. He walked more upright and alert than the average clientele of the Aro. The typical crowd was a little more like Dragos– average and slightly plump, or a little more in his case.

Dragos pushed himself up and walked to meet Daniel. After a few minutes of quick introductions Daniel asked for a more quiet location to talk. Dragos knew just the place. They walked a few blocks down a back road until they came to the town center. Dragos led Daniel down one of the roads off the main square and then into a narrow offshoot. They went into a door and then down the stairs. He spoke to the owner and they were escorted to a private, secluded section of the restaurant. There were two tables but Dragos was assured that the second one would not be filled that evening.

Dragos and Daniel ordered a few drinks and a small dish each and asked not to be disturbed. This was not the first time Dragos used this room to conduct business. It was also not the only room he had that he could arrange like this. However, this was his favorite. Something the cellar setting reminded him of "spy" work. And he considered his line of business the equivalent of free enterprise "spy" work.

Once the food and spirits were served and a complimentary shot of brandy, the small room quickly emptied, Daniel opened the backpack he was carrying. He pulled out two bronze plates with something etched into them. Each was encased in a similar wood frame with wax around the edge to seal the plate to the wood. The plates looked old, except for the splatter of blood on one of the plates. They looked bronze, but could have been any number of metals.

"What are these?" Dragos certainly had an inclination that this might be important or better yet, valuable.

"Professor Blovaski felt that they were ancient plates, perhaps written in a form of ancient Egyptian or ancient Hebrew or some combination." Daniel went on to explain that Professor Blovaski sent pictures to a colleague that might be able to interpret them. He estimated that only a dozen or so could actually interpret them quickly. Another couple of dozen linguists might take years. Professor Blovaski focused on the one he knew best, albeit from reputation only, from the shorter list–Sir Arthur Borden.

"What are you doing there?" Dragos asked Daniel.

Daniel explained that Professor Blovaski was a Jewish linguist, primarily for ancient languages. He only survived because he had been so good at what he did. He had been assigned to him while he was young to help learn more languages. Daniel spoke nearly thirty languages, most fluently and he spoke many of them as though they were his own tongue. He just happened to show up the night the professor got the plates.

"Where did he get them?" Dragos pushed.

"He wasn't sure where they came from." Daniel explained that he got them from one of the ministers in the government and was asked to just authenticate that they were ancient records. He assumed that one of the archeological digs in northern Russia was the origin, but he had no idea for sure. He explained that he was given explicit instructions not to share with anyone, but just authenticate that they were of ancient origin. He was afraid that someone found out he sent photos of the plates.

"We were chatting when a bullet came through the window and killed the professor. I do not even think they knew I was in there until I grabbed the plates and ran."

"Do you think he was killed for the plates?" Dragos asked anxiously.

"I don't know, but he was troubled and he told me that these may have value beyond just monetary value. He was only part way through his story when he was shot."

Dragos' gut was telling him by this point that he ought to just leave, but the story kept him intrigued. Daniel showed him the plate again, this time he could see a clear writing on the tablet in blood "Король 1131". Daniel said, it was the last thing he did besides hand me the plates and point for me to leave.

"He just didn't tell you what it meant?"

"He was shot in the neck and couldn't talk." Daniel had paused to let it sink in. Then he continued, "But 'Король' means 'King'."

"King 1131, but king of what country? Who wrote it?" There was no easy answer. Dragos was now anxious to return to his house to do an internet search on Kings in Russia or Europe or even the middle–east around the year 1131. It would have to wait.

It was about that time that a man came into the same secluded section of the restaurant as Dragos. He stood upright and was dressed in a long coat with a fur collar. The coat was open as he started to pull a gun. Daniel quickly became aware of the situation and pulled his gun. The guns were identical; the technique for pulling the guns was identical. The strange man, however, started to draw first and that was enough time to get his shot off first. It didn't kill Daniel, merely incapacitated him. It would take a second shot to finish him off.

For Dragos that was enough, he wasn't as quick or as elegant— but he managed to pull a taser gun that he purchased from an American citizen and shoot the man in the chest with it.

The man went down in convulsions. Dragos grabbed the bag and put the plates into it. He hurried past the Russian. He knew that it would only buy him minutes if that. He was sure that this guy was KGB and probably would recover far quicker than the average man. He was right.

Dragos didn't waste time with going by his house. His car was parked between town and the Aro Palace. He made his way to the car and did not bother going by the house. Maybe the stunned KGB agent would spend some time looking into his properties in Brasov before realizing he left town. He headed straight for Bucharest to the only man he knew might be able to help translate these plates and help him understand what he had inherited.

"Bucky will help. He must." Dragos said as he started down the mountain.

It was raining as he came down through the mountains from Brasov. A usually scenic and pleasant drive was muddled with the early morning darkness, rain, and the events of the evening before.

CHAPTER 11 – THE DEBRIEF

Jenny laughed as they walked into their room "'My Jenny'–that is so precious." Frank, who was already in the room, was not impressed. Frank was a serious man who was always focused on the task in front of him. It was his biggest weakness, so focused on delivering results that he didn't enjoy life enough. Not many years from retirement, he knew that would change.

He would be even less impressed as he learned that Jim had pulled the gun on Ric. "You did what?"

Jenny gave another condescending laugh. It was one of those laughs that indicates that she was enjoying his frustration–a laugh that somehow also made her aloof from any real attachments. She used it only around her circle of friends, never in her under cover role. It served its effect of annoying the likes of Frank and other agents. She liked Frank, but this allowed her to avoid getting to close to him. She even used it on Jim. However, Jim found it strangely appealing. He saw it for what it was–a defense mechanism.

Jenny didn't really want to debrief in front of Jim. However, this room was the only one that they could be sure was 'safe' and couldn't be listened to by any outside party. They were certainly not going to let Jim out at this point–could be dangerous. It would also seem rude to shove him into the other part of the suite. So they let him just listen to the debrief.

Jim found this intriguing. He had found a new world he only read about or seen at the movies. Some things played right into the stereo-types and others were just routine procedures that would have made any novel a very boring read. He enjoyed it even though he knew that in the morning the whole thing would be just a memory.

Frank interrupted, "You have him looking for a piece of furniture? We specifically agreed to a manuscript of some type–something unique."

"We will get to that." Jenny said with her little laugh.

"He can find furniture on eBay. You could find furniture at Ikea. I can get an ancient desk from my mother's den." Out of the corner of Jim's eyes he could see one of the two other agents in the room hold in a chuckle. It almost made Jim laugh but he held his cool. He was enjoying this and did not want to give them any reason to remove him from the room.

Jenny said in a completely straight face. "I told him we would consider a unique manuscript."

"And he is going to look for that too?" Frank asked.

"Oh, he wants our business. The furniture he knows he can find. If he gets an ancient manuscript or old book that we want he knows he will have our business for a long while." Jenny was smug, but did not use her laugh. She knew she had played it right with Ric and had kept enough suspense in the retelling of the events to capture Frank's attention.

"I guess that may be nearly brilliant. He will look for something unique." Frank leaned back now looking more content.

"And the more unique, the more likely we will get connected to some real criminals. We might be able to snag the French guy or we could get Mr. Patel or Steve and maybe even Yuri." Jenny followed his lead and leaned back in her chair. Jim was still obviously leaning forward in his chair intently listening to every word.

"Yes, that too–maybe even Yuri." Frank seemed much more satisfied. "And when was the gun pulled?"

Jenny thought for a moment, "My tone of voice implied that we would only consider an artifact if he could find the right thing. That made his son mad."

"Ricardo Junior, I assume." Frank interjected.

"Junior, of course it was him. So he pulled a gun on me. Jim just reacted and pulled one on Ric." Jenny paused for a minute, just for effect and looked in Jim's direction saying "and Jim said 'don't pull a gun on *my* Jenny'." She gave her little laugh.

Trevor, the other senior agent in the room spoke up, "How endearing." This caused a little laugh from Frank. Frank and Trevor had worked near each other for years, but hadn't been on the same team or assignment until this one. It was a clear stepping stone for Trevor, he would replace Frank when Frank retired which might occur at the end of this multi–year assignment.

Frank volunteered for this assignment hoping to make it his last. Trevor quickly joined his friend hoping to be able to step up the ladder in the process. In fact, Frank had a lot of input into what this operation was going to be.

Trevor's interjection was appropriate, but he knew enough not to take the lead on the conversation. That was Frank's job and he was masterful and getting what he needed from people, even his agents. That is probably why Jenny played him the way she did. It was almost a game between the two of them. Frank actually liked the challenge as long as it didn't really challenge his authority. Frank continued on behalf of Trevor, "Endearing, but an unloaded gun wouldn't have done much good if you had decided to use it anyway.

"What!!!" Jim only thought it. He had put himself in character and didn't even react. Jenny was real impressed that Jim held his cool. Trevor had to ask even if his fellow agents ignored the obvious, "Jim, no reaction. Aren't you the least bit annoyed?"

He was, but he wouldn't give Frank the satisfaction for Jenny's sake. He also wouldn't give Jenny the satisfaction, "I haven't shot a gun since I was a teenager. And that was a rifle of some type. I probably would have missed at point blank range. In fact, I still had the safety on. I was just hoping Ric wouldn't notice."

Frank pulled the gun from the table and looked at the safety. "Sure is. Safety on and an unloaded gun. Ric was certainly safe from gunshots tonight."

The debrief lasted for a little while longer. They had told Ric they were off to Paris early in the morning and then off to their Château on the beach. He could call Jenny with any updates.

Jim assumed he could probably head home when they all left for the airport. He could then resume his life as Jacob. He would go back to his mundane job as an accountant with a renewed respect for those that defended his freedoms.

Frank, Trevor and the other agent left discretely.

After they were gone, Jenny asked if Jim had fun. "It is a night I will never forget."

"You have been a lot of fun too." Walking towards the bathroom, she dropped her dress and undergarments. It was a quick action. Jim saw her silky smooth dark skin glisten in the semi-lighted room. He could see part of her breast before he averted his eyes and sheepishly went to the dresser for some pajamas. He changed while she showered.

Jenny came out of the bathroom wearing only a t-shirt that just barely covered her rear end. It was evident that she did not have a bra on. She gave her little laugh as she saw Jim curled up on the couch. "You know, if you are interested, we could make love."

Jim had anticipated something like this—although he wasn't sure how it might be said. He knew that Jenny had little inhibitions but wasn't sure how straight forward she might be. He was flattered. He hadn't been with a woman since his wife and that was nearly a year ago. "Interested isn't really the question. Not that you are not beautiful and very tempting, but my religious belief prohibits me . . ."

"Your religion doesn't let you have sex?"

"No, I mean, my pastor teaches that sex outside of marriage is wrong. And well, we aren't even married in our roles. And I choose this; choose to follow this that is." It was clumsier than he wanted, but it at least didn't put the blame on her as a person. And it shouldn't have. If ever there was a reason to break his vow, it was with a woman like this.

"Well next time I will have to make sure we set up the undercover arrangements differently." Jenny wanted to tell him that she didn't sleep with just every guy she met, but she did really think he was different. She also figured that she might not ever see him again so she thought tonight would be the night. She didn't show it, but she was genuinely disappointed. Instead, she said the most polite thing she could, "Jim, you can share the bed with me. I won't try anything I promise. I respect your beliefs."

Jim had not really expected that and had not prepared a response. So he said the only thing he could, the truth. He turned to face her to say it. She looked really good and he almost relented in what he was going to say. "Jenny, I believe you. But I would not make it all night next to you without giving in. I better stay here."

Jenny saw that he was sincere. She simply said "okay." She turned the light off and lay down in bed. She faced away from where Jim was and a tear came to her eye as she thought about her childhood and the dreams she had then. She had some of things that she always wanted, but the cost to some of the other dreams she had still bothered her a little, but never enough to change.

CHAPTER 12 – MESSAGES AND PHONE CALLS

Before going to sleep, Ric would make a few calls personally and then send key emails to a few other people. He knew where he would get the furniture. He had already promised it to a collector in New Orleans–but would find a suitable replacement for him. He knew that party's needs and already had a plan to replace the desk.

Ric knew that the desk would impress Jim. He also wanted a unique book for Jim. This he had no leads on. He knew of several items that were great, but he wanted something really special. Most of his phone calls were about trying to find this item. He was hoping to have at least one recommendation by the end of the next day. He called Mr. Raju Patel. Raju had connections to many nefarious folks from the Far East. Raju had him call his daughter Seema who actually dealt in antiquities from China, India and the surrounding areas for museums on the United States east coast. He also tried "Steve", no last name known. Steve seemed to be into a little of everything and had a knack for never getting into any trouble. There were several others that Ric was familiar with that he reached out to using phone calls, text messages and a few cryptic emails.

His backup plan was to at least offer Jim an original Gutenberg Bible. He knew of one down at Indiana University. It was not complete, but had a fascinating history. His daughter had gone to that school and he had seen it on a visit there. He was even tempted to steal it himself–but thought that it would be better to give one of his associates a "hint" and let them perform the act.

Ricardo's intention was to give Jim the desk and find a unique manuscript to sell him before he would consider any other contact. Ric wanted to be his sole provider of these unique items. His son Ricky challenged the logic of this whole scheme.

Ricardo answered his son. "This is the infamous James Conrad– if we get his business we will be connected to one of the most elusive billionaires in the world. The additional connections we would make would be worth it even if we didn't make a penny on Mr. Conrad. And I intend to make more than a penny from him."

His son felt they could still make considerable money and build a relationship.

Ric was unaware that James Conrad was actually "Uncle Sam" and had been allocated a yearly budget of less than a million dollars, a few properties and a Swiss bank account that looked much larger than it was. This is what it took to build the character over the years and use him sporadically. This sting would take some additional funding, but not anywhere close to even 10% of the first billion. Most of this money would revert back to Uncle Sam proper once the sting had run its few years and netted what it could in capturing arms dealers. Ric also did not know that Frank's boss had selected Ricardo Martinez to be the last victim of the scheme.

CHAPTER 13 – RECEIVING END

Dragos was down the mountain. The previously beautiful mountain sides had drifted into endless fields. The morning air had a slight stench of farmland, but was a welcomed addition to what Dragos had been through in the middle of the night in Brasov. The light of the day had just started to come up over the fields of corn. He was a little distance from Bucharest, but not far. He got a text message. "Dragos, I am looking for something unique. This is a great opportunity. Call me. RM."

Dragos thought to himself "I don't have time for this."

Somewhere else, Yuri got a text message forwarded from a friend. Yuri was as elusive as Jim Conrad. Very few people had ever met her. In fact, most people didn't even know that Yuri was a she. In her line of business, less exposure was better.

The text message read: "Yuri, not sure if you know of anything. My sources tell me this request originates from that man, you know who I mean. Look at the attached." The attached read, "Steve, I am looking for something unique. This is a great opportunity. Call me. RM."

Yuri figured this was probably the note she had been waiting for even if it wasn't from the person she had expected it from. It might be her chance to finally meet James Conrad. She wondered if her friend, her "secret contact" in Russia, had come through for her. She hadn't heard yet and that usually meant a problem. Yuri had learned to walk away from snags, the cost usually ended up high. But this was different, this was potentially very big.

CHAPTER 14 – ARTHUR'S OFFICE

The sliding of the London Times under the door woke Sir Arthur Borden from his sleep. It took him a minute to focus and recall why he was in his office sleeping and why this was not just another ordinary day. His eyes slowly opened and he saw the thick old oak door. The gap at the bottom was large enough for the times to fit all the way under. He then glanced across at his desk. He was in a slightly larger office than most because of his tenure and his title– "Sir". As his eyes continued to focus reality began to set in. He was alone, his wife was dead. He did not even know how to start a day like this.

There was a stack of papers still needing graded on the corner of his desk. He had a papyrus scroll on the wall in a frame. It was part of the Dead Sea scrolls find from many years ago. He was one of the foolish professors to purchase it from a local. This only caused them to tear the scrolls into more pieces so they had more to sell.

He, of course, allowed his personal piece to be photographed and logged – but he kept it on the wall to remind him to be more careful in his archaeological endeavors in the future. Caution seemed to be wasted on archeology, he thought to himself as he considered his wife's fate and that of his friend.

He could not fathom a future at this point. Had it all been a dream? He didn't think so. He instinctively went to look at the paper to see if there was a story. The front page did reference the festival in London. Nothing about a murder in the tube though. He flipped to the obit page and nothing there either. He knew it had happened, but he needed to see it in print to make it final, to assure that it was not just an illusion.

Then it hit him, the paper was probably printed too soon to get the story. It actually had happened in the early hours of the morning. "Maybe," he thought, "the online version might have something." He quickly brought his computer to life. It was slow to boot so he always left it on just so he could get right to work when he came in. For some reason it was off this morning. The secretary or cleaning lady must have shut it down, he thought. He turned it on and walked down to the break room to get a coffee. He had never really got the "British Tea" thing and didn't really understand the whole European "special coffees". He had adopted a lot of British traditions and mannerisms, including the accent over the years. However, his coffee was still made black. Over the years, the first person in the building always made a pot just for him. There was a little sign in front of it that said "Sir Coffee", a play on his title.

"Darn it, no coffee. Maybe I am just the first person in." Since he never had to, he did not even know how to make the coffee.

He just headed back to his office and shut the door. It took a few more minutes for the computer to boot up and then he went to the London Times website. He did not have to look far. The top headline read "Prominent Professor and Wife Killed in Tube."

Can't even get my wife's death right, he thought to himself. Then in his mind he figured he had probably died in the tube also. Not literally, but without his wife he was as good as dead. Maybe they got it right after all he thought.

His email was downloading from the university server. There were the usual bulletins and then a message from Professor Alto in Egypt. He received an email from Professor Blovaski the day before with pictures of an artifact that had intrigued him. But with his old college buddy in town he had just sent it to one of his colleagues and decided that he would get back to it later. He sent on the note to Professor Alto who was quick to respond.

Professor Alto was Egyptian by birth but schooled in France, Japan and the United States. He picked up a stray dog while in the US and named him "Tenor". He originally went to school to sing and quickly saw patterns in ancient writings that mirrored patterns in music. It was a match for him that became his passion and the love of his life. He still sang, but became a renowned expert on ancient languages. In fact, Professor Alto and Sir Arthur Borden had attended a retreat together when they were younger. Professor Alto's dog died over twenty years earlier. However, he still signed all of his correspondence "Alto and Tenor". After school he moved back to Cairo to teach and settled there for good. He was one of the few people in the world who might be able to interpret the writings.

Not really having any other thing to do, he decided to check out what Professor Alto thought of what he sent. He opened the email:

Arthur at the round table,

It is good to hear from you old chap. No, I haven't received my funding yet. But it is looking good I may know in the next few days. Thanks for asking.

I am intrigued at your assessment that these writings might be ancient Hebrew or Egyptian. I would love to see them, but you really must include the attachments before I can comment. Please resend with the attachments.

Regards,
Alto and Tenor

That is odd, he thought. Usually if he forwards an email it keeps the attachment. He checked his sent folder and sure enough there was no attachment. Then he checked his in box for the letter from Professor Blovaski. Hmm, must have deleted it and the deleted folder is empty.

He figured that he might be able to get one of the IT guys to find it for him. He had deleted one before where they were able to recover it. He sent a quick email to the IT guy to recover his mail from the last couple of days. It wasn't what he should be doing on this of all days. He figured, though, that a purpose driven day may be his best approach anyways.

He went back to his email and saw a second one from Professor Alto,

Arthur at the round table,

I just got the news. It is too bad about Professor Blovaski. What are the odds, you forward an email from him and then, you know. It is tragic. Do you think we will ever see the mythical plate (or the pictures of it)? Maybe when things settle down we can call the university in Moscow and see if we can go look at the plate.

Regards,
Alto and Tenor

Arthur scratched his head. He quickly did a Google search on Professor Blovaski. He did not need to read Russian to understand what the story said and to at least confirm that the professor was dead.

"What are the odds?" he thought. Then it occurred to him. In the tube, maybe they were not after the outspoken American professor, but that he had actually been the target. He froze and then started to think about what his next course of action should be.

CHAPTER 15 – UNIVERSITY OF BUCHAREST

Dragos pulled into a lot and decided to take a short nap before going to the meet with Bucky. He was not as young as he once was and an all-nighter was not as easy as when he was in his youth. He figured he could get a quick fifteen minutes and then go in to see his old friend. A little over four hours later he woke up. In a panic he looked for the bag, it was still on the front floorboard on the passenger's side. Glancing inside, the two plates had not been disturbed.

He knew the office, but when he got there the professor was lecturing to a 300 level class on the other side of campus. His secretary knew Dragos and let him in the office. She offered him some coffee.

He kept the plates hidden. After thumbing through some books, he decided to Google "Kings in 1131". There were nearly one million references. Only most were of addresses and locations and not actual kings. He did find that the king of England at the time was Henry I Beaucler, but didn't think that had anything to do with it. At the same time there was a rebellion by Antioch and Tripoli against the Kingdom of Jerusalem. The professor where

Daniel got the plates was Jewish, maybe there was a connection. Then there was King Louis VII of France who became king in the year 1131.

His mind was turning, he had read about the Knights Templar and the Crusades in the same timeframe and there strong connection to France.

He even looked towards the Old Testament. It seemed that most Bible scholars he could find had the first king of Israel coming to power around 1100 BC. That wasn't far off and King Saul was a pretty powerful name in history.

He spent hours waiting for his friend and looking at just about every angle he could think of in his searches. In the end he realized he was just passing the time, just grabbing at straws. He had no idea what reference the departed professor had intended.

Monday
Chicago Time

CHAPTER 16 – MORNING PAPER

Jim rolled over long enough to see the back of Jenny walking towards the bathroom. It was a nearly 8 AM and she was still in the same shirt. She had made just enough noise as she got out of bed to cause Jim to be barely awake. As he watched her walk towards the bathroom and then shut the door behind her he thought to himself that he must be crazy. There is not likely a woman as good looking as her that would even consider sleeping with a man of his age and average stature.

He knew that his belief in God prevented him from taking such a rash move. Then he thought that he at least owed it to his wife not to jump into bed with someone he barely knew, but she was a totally hot woman. She was also a woman he was starting to like.

He could hear the shower in the other room as he slowly sat up to gather his thoughts for the day. He sat for a moment contemplating this interesting plight of a beautiful woman inviting him to compromise his values, a plight he would probably think about the rest of his life.

He decided that it was one that he had contemplated long enough this morning so he went to the door to get the morning paper. It was sitting on a tray that had a breakfast spread on it. He rolled the tray in and opened the covered plates. It was a fabulous spread of smoked salmon, fresh fruit and two coffees. There was a small note next to another plate that said, "Mr. and Mrs. Smith, the Chef has created a new pastry she hopes you will enjoy"–obviously made to the normal order with the addition of the pastry.

Jim opted to wait to eat until Jenny joined him. He started to glance over the paper while he waited. The front page was typical Chicago news. There was murder on the near north side that was likely gang related. Speculation was that the mayor would call for greater gun control from the surrounding counties. "Hmm, should have asked him last night at dinner," Jim thought to himself. Next story was about a number of layoffs at a local manufacturing plant.

Jim had finished the front page and started on the second page by the time Jenny came out of the bathroom. She came out fully dressed and ready for the day.

"It is your usual Mr. Smith," Jenny said with a slight smile pointing to the breakfast spread. "By the way, I thought about it last night and in the fake character being played by the fake character we are married." She laughed a little.

Jim smiled, "Guess it is a good thing we didn't think about that last night." He knew she was just kidding and he was too, at least mostly kidding. "So what is the plan this morning, off to find bad guys while I head into the office for some more exciting accounting work?"

Jenny grabbed the paper to glance as she said, "I suspect Frank will come by shortly and let us know how we will get you home."

Jim was looking at the back side of the paper that Jenny had picked up. Jenny must have caught Jim's look out of the corner of her eyes. She had seen him cool and collective over the last day since she had met him but he looked disturbed. "Jim, what's the matter?"

"Don't tell me you didn't know." He was clearly thinking through the situation and determining his next course of action. He was at least observant enough to notice Jenny's dumfounded look on her face and realize that she might not know. Of course, she might just be a good actress – would have to be as a spy. He grabbed the paper out of her hand and slammed it on the table so the side he had been viewing was side up. "There." He said pointing to a picture of a partially burnt out, wrecked vehicle.

The vanity license plate could clearly be seen, "MS CAROL".

Jenny said, "You know Miss Carol?"

Jim was almost too angry to cry, "My wife is Carol and I miss her. I had a license plate made in her honor."

Jenny's jaw dropped slightly, "Oh." It was only a moment later when the realization hit her, "OH!" The article clearly called out that Jacob had been in a wreck on the Eisenhower after flying home from a business trip. He was in a coma at Northwestern Hospital in a secluded ward. "I need to talk to Frank."

"Jenny, this had to be done by someone in the CIA–maybe Frank. Where did you put my wallet and credentials? I think I should just walk out of here."

Jenny searched through all of the scenarios and thinking out loud said, "There has to be a reason."

"Maybe, but not one I signed up for. I am an accountant not a spy. It has been fun but this isn't my life." Jim folded his arms and sat back to hear Jenny's response.

Jenny would not have a chance.

CHAPTER 17 – FRANK'S EXPLANATION

Frank opened the door and walked in unannounced as though he owned the place. He surmised that they probably already saw the accident as reported in the paper but was prepared to share the news if needed. He walked in with confidence. Trevor followed right behind him. Frank knew that he had to assure both Jim and Jenny it was in the mutual interest of all involved to keep Jim in the operation. It only took about three seconds for Frank to realize that they had seen the article. Jenny took one step on the couch next to Jim and leaped over the couch. She was across the room pinning Frank to the wall before he could shut the door behind him.

Trevor quickly shut the door. He knew better than to interfere with Jenny and Frank.

Frank was bigger than Jenny but she had mastered the technique of taking her opponent (or opponents) off balance better than nearly anyone in the CIA regardless of their size. Trevor had been the only agent to best her in simulated combat in the last four years. Frank had not ever won against her. He was older but still very skilled. However, he was now pinned against the wall with a very uncomfortable neck hold and Jenny looking at him directly in the eyes. "What do you think you are doing? This man has a life." Jenny's eyes were blazing with anger, both on behalf of Jim and because she was not informed of the plan ahead of time.

Frank had thought about his words and the impact they might have on all of those in the room. They were intentional and precise. "Jim has a choice. But we need him for this operation to work out fully. He lost a lot of his life about a year ago. His life is what he chooses right now."

"You could have asked instead of having him in a fake coma." Her grip relaxed slightly, but not enough for Frank to get an upper hand.

Frank was not interested in the upper hand physically. He wanted the upper mental hand. "I know, but last night's ride home was about the only time we could have pulled off an accident like this. If we waited for rush hour today there would have been too many witnesses." Frank paused to let the words sink in.

Jim listened from across the room intently. He was still mad but there seemed to be a bit of logic.

Jenny tightened her stranglehold just to make it a little more uncomfortable for Frank and said, "We debriefed last night. You should have told us then." Then she released her hold slightly.

Frank continued, "Jim still has a choice. He can recover from his coma as quickly as today or he can recover in a few weeks." Frank didn't really believe there was a choice. He knew that the plan needed Jim as a real person in order to be fully executed. "Jim will be paid well for his service to his country, $50,000 dollars for a couple of weeks. If it extends, $25,000 a week or until he has had enough and then he comes back to Chicago." Frank knew that two weeks would probably be enough. He had permission to promise more money from his superiors but he knew how much Jim made and $50,000 would be a nice addition to that salary for two weeks' pay.

Jenny released her grip. "I think it is a load of crap. I can't believe Langley bought off on a scheme like this. I guess it is up to you Jim." She paced a bit by the door.

Jim looked up from the chair and saw Jenny's frustration. He observed Frank's anticipation. "Is there any danger?"

Frank looked. He knew he had him now. "It is safe. You will deal with Ric pretty much and we will trace what we need to. We will provide any additional support to authenticate antiques you buy and set a price. We already have a bank account set up in Jim Conrad's name that you can use for expense money, including making any purchases we agree to. Besides, Jenny will be with you the entire time."

Jim continued to look at the players in the room. "My own antique road show and I get paid."

It was clear to Jenny that Jim had decided to be part of this scheme. She also realized that the nature of this scheme was fairly safe. If something did happen, then Jim (or rather Jacob) would simply be reported as having died while in a coma at the hospital after a tragic automobile accident. She was not thrilled with this or with the fact that she had not been consulted on the plan. She, after all, would be tasked with his safety.

"Travel and expenses paid. Remember you told Ricardo that you were going to France. The plane leaves later today." Frank pulled out two tickets from his suit pocket. "First class, of course"

"Not a private jet for a billionaire?" Jim asked.

"Remember that you travel under assumed names. Sometimes private jets get more scrutiny than traveling commercial." Frank walked over to hand the tickets to Jim.

Jim took the tickets. "I'm in."

"Unbelievable!" Jenny walked across the room and grabbed her purse. "I need some fresh air." With that she quickly left the room. Frank followed her.

CHAPTER 18 – SEARCHING

Steve sat back in his chair in an office in Amsterdam. He was an international salesman for a small Midwest medical supply company. This allowed him to travel unnoticed around the globe to do "other" business. Steve, of course, was not his real name but the name he used for this "other" business. He was careful how he transacted this business so that it could not be traced to his visits as a medical supply sales rep.

He had reached out to Yuri to give her the opportunity to find something for Ricardo and more specifically for Jim Conrad, but that did not mean he would not also be looking for an item to sell. His connections were tight and he knew that he could get just about any item in the world if the price were right. And for him, it was about maximizing profit. He had made it his life's work to get as much money as he could. He earned a lot and kept out about 5% for his living expenses. Based on this 5%, he was a very wealthy man. The rest he split between an offshore Grand Cayman Island account and his favorite charity the "Friends of the World Charity Fund".

He would not enter the arena with Ricardo and Jim until he was sure that he could deliver. His reputation demanded this and he would not let that reputation be harmed. Steve was precise and to the point. After the message from Ricardo, he went directly to the internet and Googled "rare books". He had a short list of about fifty in a matter of thirty minutes. Then he shortened the list further by eliminating those that he thought would be most difficult for him to acquire and those where he thought the challenge was less risky. Several made it on the list because he had connections at institutions that actually owned these manuscripts. Some of those connections were as Steve and some were as a medical supply salesman–but they were people he could leverage to get at the rare manuscripts.

He came to the final two by determining relative value and risk of obtaining the item. The first item on his list was the "Cosmography" which was printed in about 1477. This was a world atlas created by the Greek astronomer Ptolemy.

The second, Steve's favorite, was a copy of the Magna Carta, created in 1215. He thought it would be brilliant to steal a manuscript that was one of the founding documents that defined individual rights and freedoms of the people. He might be tempted to keep this document for himself. To him, these fundamental freedoms of the individual have been missing from modern culture.

Steve already had teams looking at how they might obtain each of these and what the cost of this acquisition might be. He already knew the payout for the "Cosmology" would be over four million dollars, one had sold in 2006. The Magna Carta would fetch well over $20 million dollars. There were no known copies that were still in private hands.

Seema Patel had ignored the late text message from Ricardo. She also had ignored the first phone call from her father and finally answered on the third phone call. It was late in New York and she was sort of estranged from her father. She kept in contact with him primarily because of the contacts he had to help bring eastern culture art into the United States. For her, it was all about the "greater good". She convinced herself that was the only reason she even tolerated a man that she considered a terrorist for supplying weapons to dissident groups around the world.

She benefited from the spoils of this life style–a nice college degree, a nice stipend to start her business, a great dowry when she married an American man and of course the connections across the east. She enjoyed many of the benefits, but despised his work especially after 9-11. She was living in New York and had even had lunch in one of the towers the day before the planes went into the towers. Her friend that she had eaten lunch with was one of the victims the next day. Intellectually, she knew that her father had nothing to do with this attack and would not condone it. But it was people like this that he did business with. She vowed to not take another penny from him after that date. She had not, but she still leveraged his connections.

Reluctantly she listened to her father's conversation about finding a "unique item". Her father assured her that he would not get involved in the transaction unless she asked him too. She could use any money to fund the arts in New York if she wanted. Seema finally agreed. She hung up the phone and went back to sleep. In the morning she started to put a few simple feelers out to see if there were any unique eastern manuscripts that might be for sale.

CHAPTER 19 – JENNY'S INSURANCE POLICY

Frank quickly caught up to Jenny in the hallway and grabbed her arm. "Jenny, where are you going?"

"Oh I will be back. But this isn't the place or time to talk and you know it. Walls have ears." With that Jenny walked down the hall and out the back stairs.

Frank would not have her followed. He knew that if she wanted to be elusive she was well trained and could get away. He also knew that it might draw attention to their situation. He would just let her blow off steam and she would be back soon enough.

When Frank returned to the room he told Jim, "Jenny is just frustrated we didn't clue her in on the plan. She knows it's the right thing to do. She will get over it and be back."

Jim figured he was probably right. He figured Frank knew Jenny better than he did and things would be fine. He decided to read through the paper.

Jenny was mad but her thinking was clear. The threat to Jim's life was minimal but still real. She knew his fate if something were to happen. The local paper would report of a man in a recent traffic accident had died while in a coma. Jenny was determined that Jim would not suffer such a mundane fate. She decided that she would ensure that there was a record of the sacrifice he would make for his country. He may have signed up for this operation but he didn't sign up for the service as a career. If necessary, he would be remembered for his service to the country and not shuffled under some bureaucrat's desk as though it never happened.

Once she was sure she was not being followed she stopped at an ATM and took out several thousand dollars. She then made her way to another bank and opened a safety deposit box where she placed the money and Jim's wallet that contained his real credit cards and driver's license and a brief note. She had the banking attendant notarize and date her note.

Even though she was nearly absolutely sure it would never be needed, she had created her own little insurance policy for Jim. With her mind clear and her little policy in place, Jenny started back for the hotel.

Jim was reading a quip in the gossip section about the mayor and his dinner at an "exclusive downtown hotel restaurant" when he heard the cell phone on the coffee table vibrate. The ringer was not on and Jenny was still out. He instinctively picked it up and answered. He regretted it as soon as he touched the talk button, but by then it was too late. He knew that this was beyond protocol and both Frank and Jenny would not be thrilled. He also realized that hanging up at this point would probably only make the situation worse.

So he answered, "Hello, this is Jim."

"Jim, I thought this was Jenny's cell phone."

Jim immediately recognized Ric's voice on the phone. "This is her phone. She is occupied at the moment but I figured it was you calling."

"And I suppose you know why I am calling too." Ricardo added.

Jim thought he should at least guess at this. He was supposed to be brilliant and a great judge of people. He also figured there was only one reason Ric would call this early, he must have something already. "Ric, we selected you because we know you know how to get things done. You have found something for me."

"I have." Ric knew it was a good guess but he was really impressed Jim would even venture the obvious guess instead of just being illusive. "You are going to France this morning?"

"Yes we are." Jim admitted.

"Good, then meet me at the Louvre when it opens tomorrow morning. I think you will be pleased." Ricardo said in a confident and sure voice.

"I am looking forward to it." Jim hung up the phone just as Jenny came back in the room. She saw him setting down the phone, "You didn't make a call did you?"

Sheepishly Jim looked up, "Uh no, I uh just answered one call."

"You answered my phone." Under threat of life and an undercover assignment over the last day, this is the first time he had seen her uneasy with him. Even when she had it out with Frank, she seemed controlled and deliberate. "And who did you talk to?"

"I just made arrangements for us to meet Ricardo at the Louvre tomorrow morning." Jim proclaimed.

"Us?!"

CHAPTER 20 – BUCKY

When Bucky finally walked in, Dragos had already pulled himself from the computer and was just reading a book. It was a dated text book from the communist rule period. The views were very contrived and directed at directing thought instead of opening the mind. Dragos was at least trying to stay interested since Bucky's office was filled with academic books and trade publications. There was no real literature that was for purely mind numbing amusement. Dragos could have used something lighter than an academic library after his night.

Bucky was a taller, very athletic looking man. He had received his nickname because he was from Bucharest (it seemed close to Bucky) and the fact that he went to the University of Ohio for his masters and doctorate degrees and was a "Buckeye" by affiliation. With those two references, he got the nickname early and now nearly everyone calls him Bucky, including his wife.

His wife was almost an arranged marriage. He married the daughter of a senior communist party member just before the fall of communism in Romania. He was a rare person that had been allowed to go to the United States to study and then return to his home country. He had always been a nationalist that loved his country. And even though he did not speak out publicly about politics, he favored the free enterprise system as opposed to the rigid communist regime.

He was surprised to find his old friend Dragos in his office. They went to undergraduate university in Bucharest together. Happened to be roommates and Dragos had helped Bucky with a research paper on the history of Romania. It was a positive piece on the whole history and also spoke positively of the regime in power at the time. The paper got international acclaim and earned Bucky a scholarship to Ohio State.

Dragos had taken Bucky to his secluded castle which had more history in it than any museum in all of Romania. Dragos' father was furious. Bucky agreed to keep it secret and also told Dragos that he would like to see most of the items in a museum. Under the regime at the time it was more likely it would have been distributed between elites and never seen by the common people.

Bucky has put more pressure on Dragos to turn the artifacts and other items over to the museums in the country since the fall of communism, but Dragos holds out. It is a slight bone of contention but has not hindered their long standing friendship.

"To what do I owe this privilege?" Bucky asked his friend as he walked in the door and sat on his chair.

Dragos was across a small table from Bucky. Dragos didn't say a word. He placed the backpack on the table and slowly pulled out the first tablet and then the second tablet.

"What is this?" Bucky asked as he eyed the curious bronze plates.

After getting the full story, Bucky was a little intrigued by the prospects of what these plates might be. However, he was not the adventurous type. "Dragos, these are poison. You should get rid of them as soon as possible. They have blood on them; recent blood and it could be yours soon if you aren't careful."

Dragos was frustrated; He had hoped his friend would have better advices. "You think I should just wait for the Russian and say 'here you go'?"

"Dragos, I would not even be on the long list to try to figure out what these are. They aren't Romanian so I don't have an interest in getting you to turn them over to a museum, at least not one of our museums. Maybe you should just call a museum . . ." He caught himself in mid thought. He didn't know which museum to call. They came out of Russia. However, from the description that Dragos had they could be Egyptian or Israeli. Picking the wrong one there could be a bad idea in and of itself. "What about the professor that you mentioned, the one that the Russian Professor had emailed?"

"Yes, Sir Arthur Borden."

Bucky pulled up a directory of scholars that he thought might have the contact information for Arthur Borden. He surmised the Professor Borden was British based on his title. He found a home phone and an office phone, no cell phone number was provided. They rang the office number hoping they would catch him in the office.

CHAPTER 21 – THE PROFESSORS CONNECT

Arthur still set dazed but focused enough to contemplate what he should do next. The death of his wife had still only barely sunk in. The realization that he might have been the target still seemed farfetched, but plausible. After much deliberation, he decided that his best course of action was to seek help from the authorities. He had nearly resigned himself to this conclusion when the phone rang.

He anticipated that the office secretary would pick up the phone until he realized he had not even told her he was in. He glanced at the caller ID hoping that it was the police. It was not. The readout was "Romania +40". "Who in the world?" He thought to himself.

He answered the phone, disguising his voice a little and said "Hello".

In clear American English with a distinct Slovak accent the voice on the other end of the line said, "This is Professor Bucky Christianson from the University of Bucharest. I am with a friend of mine Dragos Sabir. How are you Professor Borden?" Bucky had not even considered that it wasn't the professor. He had the speaker phone on so that Sabir could hear the conversation also.

"Do I know you?" Sir Arthur asked with a bit of skepticism.

"No, but I am calling about a matter I believe that you became aware of a day or two ago." Bucky responded.

Arthur was not really ready to talk, but he had the politeness of an Englishman and the directness of an American. "It really is not a good time, perhaps in a few days."

"A few days may not be good, you see we have come across some bronze plates . . ."

Arthur had to cut in, his mind now racing. They didn't say they knew about the plates but that they came across the plates. He also noted that there was more than one, the Russian's pictures and text had not really indicated that. "Have you seen these plates?" He quickly responded.

"We have seen them and have them in our possession." Bucky knew he had him hooked. He knew that Professor Borden at least knew of the plates and had an interest in them. "Shall we bring them to you?" Bucky knew that however they handed the plates over to Sir Arthur it had to be somewhat public so that they trail would shift from them to Sir Arthur. Besides, if it were public then the danger might become less. He envisioned an official handoff in Oxford from the Romanians to the British.

"Here is not good, I am planning travel to mainland of Europe today and can come your way as my first stop." He was now thinking and acting on the spur of the moment. He had unwittingly decided against going to the police until after he got the plates in his hands. And he did not feel safe anywhere near his familiar settings.

Of course, Bucky feared that the Russian would catch up with them long before Sir Arthur made it to Bucharest. "Perhaps we can meet you at your original travel location?"

"I will be in Paris later this evening." It was a lie, but it was the quickest place he could think to go where he could "get lost" for a few days.

Sir Arthur lied again when he told them he didn't have a cell phone. He took Dragos' number down and told them he would call to meet for dinner on the next night in Paris. As he hung up, it occurred to him that perhaps they were the people doing the killing. He checked the directory for the University of Bucharest and found a Savor Christianson. He called the switchboard and asked if Savor Christianson was in the office. The lady on the other end of the line said in broken English. "Bucky, yes–would you like me to connect."

"No thanks."

CHAPTER 22 – TO THE AIRPORT

The morning chill had worn off as Jim made his way to the limo with Jenny. He was carrying only the small metal brief case as the door was opened. Jenny climbed in and Jim was right behind her.

They could see Frank and Trevor get into a black SUV across the street. "Seems a bit stereotypic, the black SUV," Jim said as he picked up the Wall Street Journal that had been neatly folded and laid out for him. He noticed a pre-poured glass of juice and it occurred to him that it was still morning, even if it were late morning.

"Well I suppose, but they have to drive something and all of the big white Fords and Chevy's were already taken by the Chicago PD."

Jim could see Frank texting on his phone. He figured that it was an update to Langley or a note to his wife–if he was married.

Frank was simply sending a text to his superiors, "We have Jim on board. The operation is a go." Frank got a text back a few minutes later, "The operation was already a go."

As the limo pulled away from the curb Jenny said, "Okay, it is safe to talk in here. The driver is CIA and the car was swept." Jenny figured that Jim had lots of questions about the operations and that they might not have a chance to step out of character for a long while once they left the limo.

Jim seized on the opportunity, "Are you married?"

It was not the question she was expecting and certainly wasn't what she thought would be top of mind. "Jim Conrad, are you going to hit on me now?"

Jim never liked the non-answers when they came from someone else. "I do not think you answered my question. Are you married? I mean if we are going to work together for a while it would be nice to know a little bit about you."

Jenny was about to give another coy remark but instead decided to try to change the subject by giving him the 30 second life story with no details. "I am not married, never have been. I am glad that I am not in my home where I grew up – nice home and nice family but very ho hum. I left home for a scholarship to the east coast. Then I went into West Point on a special scholarship for the last two years of college. From there I went directly into the CIA for immediate work in the field. Trained by some of the best on missions I cannot talk about. Then, finally my life's dream, I took this assignment to meet you." She ended with a bit of sarcasm.

"Are you trying to pick me up now?" Jim said playfully back.

"I already know that you are mine for the next two weeks, even if you do sleep on the couch." Jenny said with a slight grin.

They both had a chuckle and talked for a few more minutes until Jenny got serious. "Jim, we are only a few minutes from the airport. Do you have any questions? After we get out of this limo it may not be safe to talk freely for a long time."

Jim thought for a moment. Then he spoke, "Can I get a gun and learn how to use it? Can you show me?"

"OK." Jenny pulled a gun from her purse and looked at Jim. "My Glock, here is the safety. You can turn on the safety by hitting this and pulling out the clip." She pulled a bullet from the clip explaining how you would load it if needed. She then added a few comments about safety. "Then you aim and shoot. The bullet goes in the direction of the barrel, so don't aim it at anything you don't want to shoot." She continued, "Especially me."

"So can I get one?" Jim asked anxiously. He was not a gun user, but figured that being a spy (albeit for two weeks) he should carry his own gun.

"We will figure that out in Paris. It wouldn't do well for you through security at the airport anyway. Anything else?" She was all business now. She had had a little fun but knew that time was short.

"What exactly do you want me to do when we meet Ric?" Jim asked.

"You are a natural at this. Just remember that we are waiting to meet criminals. He knows them and that is why we are getting to know him. Have an interest in what he offers but always take time to think about it and get back to him. You may be a billionaire, but the project has a budget and we are only going to buy certain things. Buying everything would make it appear as though you were overly anxious. That might draw suspicion and would at least hurt your persona." Jenny looked in the mirror to make sure she looked her best and then adjusted Jim's shirt and fixed his hair so that it was not out of place.

"I have a persona?" Jim asked.

Jenny laughed. "I didn't give it to you but I will have to live with it." The limo pulled to the curb at the airport. "I will teach you a few self-defensive moves tonight at the hotel just in case you need them. We should be able to go through some basics fairly quickly."

"Sounds fun," Jim responded. With that the door opened and Jenny stepped out. Jim followed. Jenny took his arm and they headed into the airport to catch their flight to Paris.

CHAPTER 23 – BUCKY'S LAST GIFT

Bucky remarked on the slight color changes on the plate with the blood. He suggested that Dragos go to the lab and clean it off. "I want to photograph the plates. I will take pictures of this one while you clean that one."

Dragos knew the lab and he was an expert at cleaning artifacts carefully as to not affect the condition. Most people know that cleaning a car before selling often brought a slightly better price. Dragos understood this about cars and artifacts. Most of the cleaning he had done was to increase value as opposed to protecting an artifact out of a duty to preserve history.

Dragos was off to the lab and left Bucky with the clean plate.

It was only a moment later that Bucky glanced up to see a man in a long coat with a fur collar. He shut the door as he pulled a gun and pointed it at Bucky. It had a silencer attached. In broken English the man said, "You have the plate I see."

In a flash, Bucky realized the man may not know of the second plate. "Yes, you can have it."

"And where is this Dragos Sabir?" The Russian asked in a calm voice.

Bucky hoped his friend Dragos would not return and that the Russian would take the plate and leave. "He, he wanted nothing to do with the plate. He gave it to me to put in the museum. But you take it. It is not even Romanian."

"I will." With that, the gun went off and Bucky lunged back in the chair and then slouched forward with a bullet to the center of the head.

He took a moment to text a message in Russian. "Yuri, I have the item. I will provide at the pre-agreed to location." He then left.

Dragos stopped at the restroom on the way back. He realized he had gone all night and well into the day without a break and without much to eat. He was feeling a little relaxed, but still anxious about the situation. He returned to Bucky's office with the cleaned bronze plate. Opening the door he saw his friend slouched over. There were a few blood splatters. He was not going to stick around to see if the second bronze plate needed cleaned. He grabbed a green bag from Bucky's office to stash the plate in and then left immediately, taking a taxi to the airport to find a way to Paris.

CHAPTER 24 – YURI

The first text message, that the plate had left Russia and not in the hands of who she wanted, had bothered her. Yuri preferred excellence. She nearly demanded excellence. The text she had just received was much more to her liking. The ex-KGB agent had the plate and was on his way to Cairo. Yuri was just a few blocks away from the university and the professor who would have the ability to translate the plate.

Yuri was a loner; she had been since she was very young– back when she was Stephanie Baker. Her short blond hair kept her young looking even though she was nearly forty now. She could have passed for her late twenties. She was an American, but nobody really knew that. She almost forgot what country she was born as a citizen. Her parents were "attachés" at many embassies as she grew up. She later learned that this meant her dad was CIA and her mother a marine officer.

Yuri was born in Germany, moved at young age to Japan, then to the states for a few years. Before she was 15 years old she had lived in France, Germany, Amsterdam, Moscow, Pakistan and Japan.

At age fifteen, her crucial period, she lived in Hong Kong. By this time she spoke seven languages. She was also well versed in the use of firearms and self-defense. Her parents had trained her how to survive because that is what they knew. Her parents were patriots. She was on her way to learning that also.

Then, shortly after her fifteenth birthday her parents took a diplomatic trip to Beirut. She heard the news on the Armed Forces Network before anyone made it to the house to tell her in person. Two American diplomats had been killed in Beirut by a car bomb. There were suspects, but it was clearly a terrorist act.

Yuri grabbed the stash of cash she knew her parents kept and the passports her mother had. She left the base before anyone got a chance to speak with her. The US government still classifies Stephanie as missing in Hong Kong and presumed dead. For all practical purposes, that part of her life was dead. She had a necklace with a non-descript key with the initials DMW on it that her mother gave her and that was it. But she didn't let that part completely die until she found those responsible for the death of her parents and invented some imaginative torture techniques. They were not necessarily new, but Yuri had never seen torture before and dreamed up the most imaginative thing she could think of at the time. There were still unanswered questions concerning her parent's deaths, but those that she felt were guilty had been judged and punished.

She had no loyalty to any country and the only family she had really ever known was dead. Her allegiance from that time forward was survival and then to making enough money to thrive. She developed a network of operatives and connections that kept her in the loop but distanced her enough from any real activity that she had gained a reputation but was nearly untraceable. By her early thirties she was independently wealthy and could walk away and never work again in her life. Instead she decided to dedicate her life to arms deals.

To the rest of the world she was an evil arms deal maker that provided many of the top terrorist organizations with weapons and bombs. She knew that many of the weapons she brokered ended up killing innocent people–a causality of war in her mind. She made deals when she primarily was able to pit one terrorist organization against another where they would kill each other. It was brilliant, calculated and effective. It was her last revenge on behalf of her family. Her personal restitution for the other ills she had personally committed over the years since her last happy year as a child.

But even this was getting old. She was in the process of leaving this work behind and settling somewhere in Europe to live out her life, maybe even date and marry if the right guy came along. Then a phone call changed her retirement plans. The person, he called himself "Captain", had a simple favor. Her answer was "no" until the rough voice on the other end of the phone said, "But Stephanie, I was hoping we could do business like I used to with your father."

The Captain knew her name and was somehow a connection to her childhood. She had no choice but to accept the simple job. Yuri tried everything she could to find the source of the invitation but had been unsuccessful. Her task was simple, get a bronze plate out of Russia that had ancient writings on it. Then take it to a professor in Egypt and have him fully translate the plate. Once translated, kill the professor and give the translation and the plate to a third party. It was that simple. Her pay was hefty, over seven figures plus all expenses. However, the cream on the coffee was meeting the voice on the other end of the line. That was the piece of the deal that she was most interested in. First, how had someone figured out who she was? Second, did this person really know her father and what could she learn about him?

Yuri knew that there was more to this than the simple task of stealing a plate from Russia and translating it. However, that was her task and she knew how to get that done. She would have to figure out why this person wanted her specifically later. For now, she would use her network of former KGB acquaintances that could get the plate out of Russia and bring it to Cairo.

So far there had been some obvious disappointments and a few more unnecessary deaths that didn't really help get the job done. Yuri knew that her contacts in the former KGB would be rougher than needed, but it was her only real option for getting that deep into a country that was still riddled with bureaucracy.

Now though, the plate was in the hand of her contact and the KGB member would be in Cairo tomorrow to meet one of Yuri's associates. The next few days would need to be played very carefully to ensure all of the conditions of the agreement were met.

She started with a text, "Steve, tell RM I will have something very unique in the morning and will be looking for bidders."

CHAPTER 25 – PLANE TO FRANCE

Jim was relieved to have gotten the whole safety lesson from Jenny when he got it. However, after letting it soak in he began to wonder if this might be more danger than he had anticipated. For Jim, he wasn't sure if he cared that much. His family was gone and he hadn't done much but sulk over his loss over the last year. He went on a date or two in the last months, but those seemed empty to him. Risking his life, if he was even really doing that, didn't bother him that much. Having a side benefit of helping his country wasn't too bad either.

He would have lots of hours to contemplate this during his long flight to France.

Jim had traveled to Europe a few times. He was not an executive at his company, but was high enough in the finance department to be afforded the privilege of flying business class, at least on international flights. Now he was in first class. He had to act as though it were second nature to him. Jenny sat in the chair next to him. Each chair fully reclined. There were multiple choices for meals and a more personalized selection of entertainment. Jim knew he could get used to this. His company had an office near Paris, so he actually knew a little bit about the city.

Frank sat in the back of the plane with a few others. He was not happy. Frank didn't like traveling coach on an overseas flight but this was too important to let out of his sight.

Jenny closed her eyes and considered the sting she was a part of. She knew this would catapult her career. She could choose a supervisory role if she wanted. But she liked the adventure of field work. Perhaps she would run a small sting herself or join Trevor in his next operation. Her aspirations for adventure would likely make the latter more interesting.

In this operation though, Jim and her would flush out arms dealers by dealing in "acquired goods". This would establish the criminal's method of operation. Then a second team would contact that criminal for an arms deal. The trap would be set and they would penetrate the operation as much as possible before making arrests and hopefully slow the flow of weapons to Hamas, Al Qaeda and other terrorists' organizations around the world. Jim was supposed to be a fictitious character, but Jenny didn't mind Jim as a real person. She knew that he would soon have to go back to his life—but she was growing attached to him for now.

Frank contemplated the plan also. He had been involved in a few stings before. This one was going exactly as he had planned it. His mind went back to an earlier operation, operation contra-connection. It had been interrupted when a key agent was reassigned. Once the agent was reassigned, he only saw him a couple of more times. Frank was determined that this time there would be no interruptions in the operation.

CHAPTER 26 – THE COLD WAR RUSSIAN AIR

The dig sight kept expanding. There were buildings discovered and a few artifacts found here and there. It was less than would be found at a typical dig of this size but every piece was still an adventure. It was northern Russia and it was getting cold. However, the cooling Russian air did not deter Professor Thomas. The air just reminded him how tough the cold war had been the last few years. He was now in the midst of what President Reagan called the "Evil Empire". At this location it did not seem so evil to him. He was a brilliant man though, and he understood that not too many miles away the Kremlin ruled the entire eastern bloc countries and the USSR with an iron fist.

His academic drive kept him focused on the task at hand. He had requested a number of books and papers from colleagues around the world so that he could try to interpret this strange language found on the bronze plate. In waiting however, he did not sit idle. He had busily participated in the dig. He kept hoping more plates would be found.

On an appointed schedule every week Professor Thomas would report to the US State Department on his personal health and general information about his work. This was part of the agreement that had been struck to allow him to participate.

Every word delivered was carefully crafted and messaged so it passed the approval of the People's Party of Russia. Professor Thomas gave the remarks as instructed, in a very monotone voice. It was a very controlled message–enough to show that Professor Thomas was well and was really doing Archeology and simple enough as to not reveal any real facts.

The US State Department protested on the dryness. "You must tell us more or we may need to pull him out."

That, however, was merely a game. Agent Thomas had devised a code that was used in the Contra-Connection operation. He used that code to communicate with the CIA who always sat quietly in the room with the US State Department. Professor Thomas was able to influence the message. Certain key words were used to decode a message from the text. It was a simple algorithm that could be changed every week so as to not make it easily tracked by anyone. There were about a half dozen combinations. His old team helped interpret the message, which within the first few weeks were more to say he was fine, it was an archeological dig and then to provide assistance to his other project.

Influencing the message so that it included his code seemed like a fun distraction. He played the role of an eccentric professor that just had to have his fingers in everything to be kept happy. Keeping the codes straight helped keep his mind keep fresh in the cold weather. Then giving the message was like a kid sneaking a cookie form the jar and avoiding getting caught. He knew he left crumbs every time, but knew that these crumbs would be hard for even the most careful skeptic within the Soviet Union intelligence agency to pick up on.

Professor Thomas was engaged in this project. He felt safe for now.

CHAPTER 27 – THE "CHUNNEL"

Sir Arthur knew that he would either fly from Heathrow or take the train under the channel. He had considered numerous alternatives–Gatwick Airport, boat or any number of the other airports nearby - but each had their disadvantage. He did not take time to pack any clothes or even go back to his house. He took a small brief case that he kept in his office with a few papers, a book and an old college t-shirt from his drawer. Arthur just took as much cash as he could from his local bank and then converted it to Euros. He didn't make a final decision between the airport and the channel until he had finished at the bank.

Sir Arthur opted for the train under the channel. The Chunnel seemed a much safer route for someone who might be followed. Safer or not, he would usually prefer the Eurostar route any day over dealing with the monstrosity of Heathrow. He dreaded the airport and the security. It was much easier to take the 31 mile track and switch trains to go to Paris. The lines were shorter, the people more relaxed and he could avoid the inevitable delays of Heathrow.

He was feeling somewhat confident as the train entered the tunnel under the channel. He was finally reading the morning times when about 8 miles into the tunnel itself the train stopped. There was a power surge issue that caused havoc in the entire tunnel. A nearly 20 minute trip through the tunnel was now slowly turning into what eventually would be about a 6 hour journey.

Every time the engineer felt that they would be allowed to move, it was delayed again. Amidst a train full of angry business people, tourists and several families with young children, Heathrow began to sound like a better option.

Mobile phones did not work here. Arrangements were made to radio in emergencies, but Sir Arthur felt that might be worse for him than just waiting out the ordeal.

He opted to just wait it out.

CHAPTER 28 – AN EVENING IN PARIS

A car had been arranged to pick up Mr. Jim Smith (Conrad) and his companion Jenny. This was not a "company" car so Jim and Jenny would have to stay in character and not be free to talk about just any subject on the ride to the hotel. Jim had fun alluding to business deals without providing any details as they rode through the streets of Paris.

Arrangements were made to accommodate someone with the prestige of Jim Conrad. However, this was Paris and not the states so the charade would have some limitations. Jim Conrad did not have a usual place to stay in Paris or a usual meal that he ordered. Jim Conrad was known to have a château at the ocean so he did not have a need to stay in the city too often. Frank, however, had adjusted things appropriately and had made reservations at a luxurious hotel that overlooked the Eiffel Tower. Again, they were in one of the nicest suites in the hotel. Clothes were delivered shortly after they arrived. Jenny whispered quietly into Jim's ear, "You know, as much as I have traveled around the world–I have never been to Paris, except for a layover at De Gaul."

Jim had been a few times and had seen the tourist sights. It is a wonderful city with the streets architected in a star. It may be one of the largest concentrations of tourist sites anywhere in the world. Jim had only been to Paris a handful of times and ventured out to see a few of these sights on business trips. His wife would always ask him "How was Paris?" Jim always responded, "Conference rooms look about the same everywhere in the world." He exaggerated slightly, but not by much. Every time he had gone to a tourist site he only thought of his wife and how he wished she were with him. One of his regrets was not ever taking his wife to Paris–it had always been a dream of hers to go.

Jim whispered back, "Jenny, let's take a walk in the evening air and see some of the city."

She pulled back a little, looked and frowned a bit. Leaning back to his ear she then whispered back, "Frank would never want to risk us going out. He would never allow it."

"You are a spy, we can sneak out." Jim tempted Jenny.

She did not have to think long. They quietly changed into more casual clothes, grabbed a handful of Euro's and headed out the door. Jenny was careful to avoid the few agents that had been strategically placed around the hotel. There was the couple at the bar. She surmised they were with the company. Then there was the older gentleman in the lobby reading a London Times. He was also a likely company man. The final person, likely on loan from the local office or a French agency was the man hailing taxis in the front and side of the hotel. To most, these all seemed natural, but to Jenny it was clear what their roles were.

They sneaked out the side door behind the front desk that was intended for employees only and made their way onto the city streets of Paris. It was nearing dark and the city lights were coming alive. Jenny sighed a natural sigh of relief and said in a non-whisper, "Where to?"

It was the first time that Jim saw Jenny with what appeared to be her guard down. "How about we go to the Eiffel Tower? It is close and you can't come to Paris without seeing it."

CHAPTER 29 – DRAGOS IN PARIS

Dragos was at a restaurant still stunned at the death of his close friend Bucky. He traveled to France by airplane with the one plate in his possession. Dragos was a little worried he might run into the Russian in the Bucharest airport, but that did not happen. Once in Paris, he checked into a hotel and found a place to eat.

Dragos was not a fan of French cuisine so he made his way to an American style restaurant chain. He ordered a hamburger and American fries. He preferred the more thick tasting German like foods that were more like his native Romanian dishes– something like ground seasoned sausage rolled in a thin layer of cabbage. But in a pinch, a hamburger and chips (fries) would do.

His impatience for the French–long dinners and a delight in the "experience" frustrated his sense of getting the job done and efficiency. This was exasperated by the lack of communication from the English professor. He had not heard from Sir Arthur yet and it was getting late. The distance from England was far shorter than from Romania. He was beginning to worry that his contact would not show. Even worse, he was concerned that the Russian might show up first. He had taken precautions like paying for the flight in cash. He also used an assumed name in the hotel and used cash in all the locations he went. This would buy him anonymity for a while, but he knew that could not last long. He carried the bag with the plate and plenty of cash with him at all times—never leaving it in the hotel just in case he needed a quick getaway.

After his meal, he made his way to the bar to pass the time a little while longer before heading back to the hotel. He had all but given up on the Englishman making it. He was staying in a local hotel, pricy for the location and not as clean as he would have wanted. However, it wasn't the low end and nowhere near the high end. In the middle there were a lot more and that made it a lot harder to trace someone.

As he sat at the bar in the restaurant and watched the French news, he saw the news about the Chunnel being backed up. He couldn't understand the words but could make out the story with the pictures on the screen. He guessed that Sir Arthur was somehow among those caught in the Chunnel. It was a guess, but figured he could give him until morning.

He ignored calls and text messages all day. He did not have a lot. As he glanced back through he saw the one from Ricardo and decided to respond.

CHAPTER 30 – RICARDO IN STYLE

Ricardo arrived in Paris on a personal jet. It stopped in New York to refuel, but then made the rest of the journey all the way to Paris. Ricardo liked living in luxury. That was a legacy from his father that he intended to keep. His father had many connections in South America, Mexico, Cuba and the States. Ricardo had these, but as he shifted his family business to a less violent business he established many more contacts in Europe and Asia. He even did a little business with a few rich Arabs on occasion. His clientele, unlike his father's associates, were often not criminals–just people looking for unique items or skills.

However, many of his contacts that procured these "unique" items were a bit shadier. Some were violent, some just devious and others downright evil.

He intentionally avoided conducting business while traveling. It was his time to relax, reflect and sometimes even fly his personal jet. When he got off the plane he had several text messages and a few voice mails. Several contacts had described what they might be able to get, but only a couple already had something in hand. Three of the texts were of most interest to him.

The first read "RM, one of my clients has something very unique and is looking for bidders. This is a very trusted source—recommend you put your name on list. Steve."

The second was "RM, I might have something unique and want to get rid of. Meeting a contact, if he is not interested let's talk. Dragos."

The final text simple read, "Daddy, your granddaughter took her first step today. Havoc in the house. Lots of Love. Mary."

Mary was his daughter, the oldest of his three children. From an early age she was the apple of his eye. She was raised in the states and she attended a public school in Chicago where his family lived. His father liked living in the town of Al Capone and fancied himself the "Al Capone" of the modern age. His dream was to build a crime syndicate that had the power, influence and ability to avoid the law as the crime families of the early gangster period. Ricardo was one of three brothers that were to inherit this "kingdom".

His brothers were killed before his parents died and he inherited the whole network when his family was still young. He was asked by his daughter to come to a career day at school and talk about his career. He was with a panel of parents and was asked about what he did by one of the children he simply responded "I'm an art dealer".

An inconsequential teacher that was probably just out of college said on his way out with his daughter there "It is so good to have a Hispanic example like you in the community. Helps get rid of those terrible stereotypes."

He started to dismantle his drug empire the next day and decided to go into the art business. He never left the crime business, but certainly changed the nature of his crimes. By the time Mary was a teenager, she had figured out her father's new and old profession. She became "born again" as a Baptist and never let her father forget that she was a proud Hispanic that would not take anything from the crime syndicate.

He found a way to get her a scholarship that she never knew came from him and she married a wonderful man who was an architect. He made a decent living. But Mary loved her father and he loved her. There was no animosity between them, just different lives. At times, he would trade it all in to follow her example. But he lived a lifestyle that would be hard to maintain and had two sons that would want the family business one day. He never felt he could just walk away from this.

He texted her back, "Take some video and give to your mother. I am traveling now and am anxious to see my little pumpkin. Grampie"

He sent a few more text and messages. Then he got to Steve. Ricardo's response was, "Put my name on the list. Can I see a photo? Place picture in the usual place." Ricardo had a bulletin board set up on the internet where he exchanged photos and information. It was cryptic enough that it would be nearly impossible to trace and even if it were traced, no specific information was shared. For example, one time a client wanted a rare sculpture from the early Bronze Age. A source had "procured one from a private collector in Spain". This private collector had his collection displayed on a web page. The bulletin board simply referenced several pieces of fine bronze art work and that this one fine piece had been recently stolen. There was no other reference but it was enough for Ricardo to have a picture to share. The sale netted Ricardo several hundred thousand US dollars in royalties.

Finally, his text to Dragos; "If buyer falls through I am in Europe and can meet. Hey - would be willing to look and maybe bid even if buyer doesn't fall though. RM." It was a soft peddle, but he felt some anxiousness in Dragos' tone in the text and looked for an advantage in bargaining for something on the cheap. He thought, if it were cheap enough maybe he could just throw it into the mix for free for Jim and prepare him for something bigger.

Ricardo turned his phone off and entered an out of the way restaurant where the food was delicious. It would be him and one other gentleman alone in the restaurant. He had some final arrangements to be made before the next day. He slipped into the restaurant and the older man was already waiting at a table with a bottle of wine open and two glasses. Ricardo contemplated winning Jim Conrad's business and more importantly his trust. Things were beginning to be fall into place.

CHAPTER 31 – ANOTHER EVENING IN PARIS

The walk to the Eiffel Tower was short and the conversation was limited to the city and the sights that neither had really experienced. Even late in the evening there was a line to get on the elevator up the tower. It took a little over an hour to reach the top of this 1,063 foot structure. They spent the time going up the elevator trying to name as many movies as they could that featured the Eiffel Tower. Jim won by two or three. They could never quite figure out if Casablanca just referenced Paris or actually showed a scene with the Eiffel Tower.

The view from the Eiffel Tower was breath taking. On a clear day it is said that one can see for nearly 45 miles. Of course at night the vision is somewhat limited. However, even this was breath taking with many of the more popular sights lit in the Paris evening. Easily seen were the Musee de Louvre and the Dome Church. They also were able to spot Notre Dame, Sacre-Coeur and the Arc de'Triomphe.

Jenny looked at Jim, "I want to see them all."

Jim thought for a moment and suggested. "You know that they are closed. Perhaps we can start to see some of them tomorrow–would be good for someone as interested as me in art and ancient manuscripts to visit some of the locations around Paris. We may need to stay a few weeks."

Jenny smiled, "I like the way you think, but you know my skills do not limit us to just the posted hours of these locations."

Jim understood and hoped she was just kidding. On the way down the elevator, Jim pondered his journey over the last year and how hard life had been. He glanced at Jenny as she continued to look out over the city as they descended and the breadth of the city became less visible. Perhaps it was just the dim light, but Jim felt that Jenny was a bit more relaxed and more like a real person– even if just for a moment. Then he realized that he had not felt this real since his wife died. This made him feel a bit guilty, he almost felt as though he should not enjoy life without her.

As they walked off the elevator Jenny observed his solemn postures and said, "Is this whole adventure making you uncomfortable. I mean we are asking a lot of you in this thing."

Jim saw real empathy. He looked past the elusive spy into her real character. "No. This is kind of exciting. It beats accounting anyway."

As they walked to the subway to catch a train to the Arc de-Triomphe, Jenny delved deeper. "Are you thinking of your family?"

Jim didn't say anything for a minute. Then he walked to a bench and sat down. Jenny sat on a bench that set perpendicular to him so she could face him and listen. She wasn't good at listening and caring–it had been about misdirection and cons since she was out of college and into the CIA. But this was not a con–this was a man's life.

"I got a call. I don't know how to say this. I got a call at work on a Tuesday. It is something you never forget–you know, like where you were when the towers came down on 9-11 only a lot more painful. I suppose it is the same pain that was felt by those who had loved ones in the twin towers. I never really thought of it that way until later. I mean I was working a normal day and in a meeting arguing about how IT couldn't get the system up when I got the call."

Jim sat for a few more minutes holding back tears and not really knowing what to say. He started with the appropriate, the truth. "My wife, she was my life. And my two kids, they were my life." He paused to maintain composure. He knew that he couldn't lose it, not as Jim Conrad and he was never quite sure who might be watching. Jim continued. "So when the state police called and said my wife was in an accident and I needed to come to the hospital right away, I thought she might be okay or seriously injured."

Jenny was a little taken back. "I read your file. They had you come to the hospital?"

"I know. The craziest things bother me now. The simple things bother me. All the way to the hospital I am trying to call neighbors to get the older kid, my son, from the bus. The younger one wasn't in school, too young. I am wondering, they didn't say anything about her. Was she hurt also or is that why they were having me come to the hospital, to get her. Then I had the thought that she is hurt and my wife was okay. But then my wife would be calling me and not the police. I am struggling with remembering neighbor's names and don't have any numbers so I finally just call our preacher and ask him to wait for my son. Which he agrees to do . . ."

"But . . ." Jenny starts to jump in and then decides that she just needs to let Jim continue. Her instincts tell her to look around and make sure no one is watching or listening that might blow their cover. She determines that they are not being watched at this time. "I am sorry, Jim, please continue."

Jim started as though he hadn't even taken a breath. "I am making so many calls that I almost wreck. I missed a few incoming ones but decided that they could wait. Well, I get to the hospital that they said and the emergency room has no record of my wife or child being checked in. Then she searches the entire hospital records and finds my wife's appointment and that she had completed it."

"I don't understand, your wife was in the hospital and then checked out." Jenny wasn't clear on the whole story. In her briefing it was simply the facts and this didn't quite fit with all of the facts.

"She had an ultrasound. She was two months pregnant. We hadn't told anyone yet." Jim explained.

"Jenny's face lost expression, "Oh my God."

"I was going to be a father again. And the realization hit me. She had taken my son with her because he wanted to see his little brother. He was convinced it was a boy. She had the whole family. My phone rang again about this time and it was the state police. He must have seen me answer the phone because he was standing near the emergency room entrance and made his way over as I picked up."

"So why the emergency room?" Jenny asked still a little perplexed.

"They had never told me the emergency room. My wife was hit by a truck just a few blocks from the hospital. The state police officer had tried to explain it to me, but I only heard pieces and had not understood. They wanted me at the scene. The van had exploded and killed my wife and children instantly. There were only burnt remains–it was hard to even have a proper funeral."

Jim wiped the tears from his face, "Just what you want on your first night in Paris – a grown man crying."

"Jim, that is terrible. It must have been devastating." Jenny was genuinely concerned.

"I lost everything on that day. The stupid driver of the truck had stolen the truck and he was burned right along with my family. So there was not even anyone to blame. I took about one week off of work and then went back. Nothing has been the same since. I wake up every day not caring if I make it to the end of the day – but somehow I always do." Jim pondered the reality of his situation and how desperate his life really was. The adventure he was on had been a slight distraction, but reality awaited him in a couple of weeks when he returned to his life.

Jenny wondered if that is why he was so willing to take on this assignment. However, she decided that was a question she should not ask him. They ended the evening at a quiet little restaurant near the Arc de'Triomphe and then headed back to the hotel.

They agreed that somehow they would convince Frank that they should stay in the city for a while. Then they could both see some of the sights. In any case, they would see the Louvre in the morning when they met Ricardo.

Jenny decided she wouldn't offer another evening with him, but she would have easily allowed him in the bed if he asked her.

CHAPTER 32 – SIR ARTHUR ARRIVES IN PARIS

Sir Arthur had a lot of time to ponder life and the murder of his wife while trapped in the tunnel. He slept much of the time. He must have talked himself into and out of going to Paris about a hundred times while waiting. By the time he emerged from the tunnel it was still light outside and he had favored seeing where meeting Dragos would lead him. He felt somehow the events of the plates and the death of his wife were connected but he had no idea how. A second motivation for moving forward would be that he could avoid the condolences and concern of others. This alone might have been enough. He did not want to listen to how others had empathy for him. If he couldn't get his wife back, he just wanted to be sad by himself for a while.

The remainder of the trip took longer than necessary but was relatively uneventful.

Dragos was already asleep when the phone rang. Sir Arthur, the professor let him know that he was in Paris and would meet him tomorrow. Dragos felt re-assured that he would somehow be able to live through this and hopefully return back to Transylvania to his normal life.

CHAPTER 33 – EARLY MORNING EGYPT

Amir knocked on Yuri's door. Yuri had anticipated this and she was ready before he got there. Ready for Yuri meant, even though she was expecting Amir, that she was fully dressed, armed with a weapon and in her mind had at least three escape routes if needed. Amir, who may have known Yuri better than anyone, wondered how Yuri always seemed to be ready for anything. It was a gift that had kept her and him alive on many occasions before.

He stepped into her room with a backpack. "Were you followed?" she asked instinctively. She always asked, even after 15 years of working with Amir she still asked.

"No, of course not. The KGB scum is at the hotel down the road. He won't leave until the plate is verified." Amir answered as he shut the door.

"Did you threaten him?" Yuri always liked how Amir was extremely straight forward in his communications. He seldom left anything to guess or wonder about. Yuri could always trust that a mission spearheaded by Amir would not go wrong because someone did not understand what was expected.

"I just told him he wouldn't get the rest of the money until we were sure this was the bronze plate we needed. After about 5 minutes of him rambling about this being the only plate and he followed it all the way from his motherland I just left. He is probably still babbling in Russian or whatever dialect he used to curse me out." Amir concluded.

"I have never liked dealing with the ex-KGB, but they are effective." Yuri pulled the plate out and looked over it. It was plain and incased in some kind of wood backing that had been sealed with wax. Yuri spoke and read many languages but she had never seen anything like the writing on this plate. She thought that is probably why they needed a professor–somebody who could read this darn thing. "Amir, you will take care of this personally tomorrow. I will go with you, but you will take the lead. I want to make sure this goes exactly how we want it to."

Amir was shocked. He had never seen Yuri personally involved before. "Yes, but why not the usual layers? I mean, you are never this close to a sting, usually we add a couple more layers." Amir didn't really expect an answer, Yuri seldom explained herself to anyone. However, he was hardly ever in the middle of the action. He had people who did that and sometimes people who had people to do that. It was harder to trace and effectively shielded Yuri and him from any scrutiny from law or others.

"Amir, this one is personal to me." Amir looked inquisitorially at Yuri. Amir thought that nothing was ever personal for Yuri– not since he had started to work for her. Yuri caught herself, "besides this is my last job and the pay is good. Your cut will be quite handsome. It will be a good start for your retirement or your next adventure."

Amir already knew that Yuri was nearing retirement, so this came as no surprise. He had also amassed enough wealth to keep him and his family comfortable for the rest of their lives. He left the room assuring Yuri he would return in the morning for the plate to take to the professor.

After Amir was gone, Yuri made a call. "Captain, this is Yuri."

"Do you know what time it is?" The scratchy voice on the other end of the phone answered a little annoyed.

"It depends on where in the world you are. Do you want to share that with me?" Yuri was straightforward with her request. She was ready to meet the Captain. The hard part of her task was complete and now it was time to start arranging payment.

"No, not yet. When the time is right we can meet. I assume you have news one way or the other or you would not be calling."

"I have the plate and will have it translated tomorrow, assuming this guy can translate it." Yuri explained.

"I have given him what he needs to translate it." Yuri heard the Captain shuffle through a few papers and then he continued, "Stephanie, you must contact Ricardo Martinez personally to sell the plate after you have the translation. He will have a buyer. I will get the translation directly from you. Is this clear?" The Captain said in a clearer tone.

"I will make sure Ricardo brokerages the sale of the plate."

"No, you must personally sell the plate through him. It is part of the bargain."

Yuri was silent for a moment. "I don't like it. You sound like you are setting me up for something."

"You can assume what you would like. However, I need the translation and you control that. If you sell before we meet, you know you will be able to disappear forever if you would like." The Captain chose his words carefully.

"And payment?" Yuri still felt a trap but would have a little time to prepare for that.

"You will get half when the plate is sold and half when I get the translation. It will be wired to the agreed to account."

Yuri reluctantly agreed and took down Ricardo's number. She knew that she would have no need to talk to the Captain again until the plate was out of her hands.

Yuri's acquaintance Steve had already brought this opportunity to her. She would have to cut him out. She would have to have one of Amir's people text Steve in the morning on the change of plan. But the real complication was that Steve had alluded to the fact that Jim Conrad was the client. He hadn't come out and said that–but the implication and understanding was there that this was the eccentric and elusive billionaire, Jim Conrad. Yuri didn't care about eccentric billionaires, but when she had tortured those responsible for her parent's death so many years ago, one had told Yuri that Jim Conrad had funded the organization responsible for the murder her parents. More importantly though, she was told that Jim could tell her what the key around her neck was for. The terrorist pig that shared this thought the information might save his life. He was wrong. Yuri needed to confront Jim, determine the truth and execute proper judgment if necessary.

For now, she sent Ricardo a text message. "Ricardo, I have an item that might interest your client. Would transact in person with the three of us only. Yuri."

CHAPTER 34 – RICARDO AWOKEN

The text message woke Ricardo up a little after 2:00 AM. It wasn't his daughter, she had a special tone. But he always checked it just in case she was using a different phone. He never wanted to miss a call or text from her.

The text he got was almost not believable. If it were true, he would have the chance to meet another "invisible" person. He was already in the big leagues, but this might help him make the all-star team. Of course, getting Jim to agree to meet might take a little persuasion–but it would be well worth the effort. He knew he was ahead of himself. Somehow he had to verify that this was Yuri and that what she had was worth trying to sell to Jim.

While contemplating what to do next, he texted his daughter. "Hey sweetie, not sleeping over here so thought I would drop you a good morning. Daddy"

He started two or three texts to Yuri and finally settled on "How do I know you are who you say you are?"

Almost as soon as he hit send there was another text. This had the familiar tone from his daughter. "Daddy, breaking into your house sometime today to decorate it for your bday. Surprise. Get some sleep."

That was Mary, feeling guilty for breaking into her own father's house to surprise him. He got a good laugh out of that. "LOL, don't call the police on yourself, have a good night or day I guess."

Then another response, "I will send proof and pictures of item via courier to your hotel in Paris sometime tomorrow. Yuri."

Whoever it was figured out he was in Paris and knew how to find him. Now he would just need to wait and see. He wouldn't sleep the rest of the night. Tomorrow promised to be eventful and he had an early meeting at the Louvre to start the events.

Tuesday
Morning Paris

CHAPTER 35 – MORNING BRIEFING

Frank had already been up for nearly two hours. He was an avid runner and decided that he would jog around the city for an hour before getting ready for the day. When he finished, he contacted everyone he needed to give the appropriate reports and was waiting downstairs in the lobby of the hotel at least 30 minutes before he expected Jim and Jenny. Trevor joined him about 15 minutes later.

Frank yawned as they stood waiting for the car to be pulled around. He was hailing a taxi and pretending to have idle chat with another American–just in case they were being watched. It was a prelude to the day and a brief briefing on expectations.

The CIA had surmised that Ricardo would bring several potential items for Jim and Jenny to consider. Frank was sure that Ricardo would get some piece of furniture but wasn't convinced that would lead them to any real criminals. He wanted "real" terrorist brought out in this scheme. He also made it clear to Jenny that she needed to lead Ricardo in that direction–her future career might just depend on it.

It was all said politely and in a matter of seconds, but the message was clear.

Jim and Jenny were dressed well and stepped into the car like they owned the town. The early morning ride to the Louvre was uneventful.

CHAPTER 36 – THE LOUVRE AND BONAPARTE'S FURNITURE

As they stepped out of the car near the Arc de Triomphe du Carrousel just outside of the Louvre Jim paused for a moment. "Ah, the Musee du Louvre."

Jim gave Jenny a brief history lesson on the Louvre. He explained that in front of them was the court yard of the palace. It was originally built as a fortress by King Philippe-Augustine in 1190 AD to protect the city from the ransacking Vikings. The Louvre had been changed over the following years most notably during the reign of Francois who turned it into more of a palace than a fortress. But this, and the additions by other French kings over four centuries, gave it the charm and beauty it had today.

The modern addition, the glass pyramid provides an astonishing entrance for visitors. It is hailed and loved by some and the "scourge of the museum" by others.

Jim knew the museum history well. His wife had wanted to go to Paris so badly they had completely planned their trip. She wanted to see the Louvre more than anything else.

Jim and Jenny walked to the other side of the arc, built to honor Napoleon's victories in 1805. Jenny pointed out that she saw the arch. "That is similar to the one we saw last night." She was as excited a tourist this morning as she had been last night. It was out of her character. Jim found it charming. "That is the Arc de Triomphe, it celebrated Napoleon's victories." Jim then pointed between the arch and said, "If you look close enough you can see the one we walked by last night."

"Wow, it is amazing." It was early and the museum was just getting ready to open. Jim and Jenny made their way to the main lobby. Ricardo was in the lobby waiting. Jim could see the line already winding around to get into the Louvre. He had never had time to go to this sight, could never squeeze it into the day and really wanted to save it. This was one of the places Jim had wanted to wait to see with his wife. She loved the art museum in Chicago and the one in Milwaukee. They made a yearly trip to at least one of these (and usually both) every year since they had been dating.

Ricardo cheerfully greeted them, "Ah welcome my friends," he said as he reached to shake Jim's hand. "This is a marvelous place, do you have time to walk part of it with me or do you want to get right to business."

Jim did not hesitate, "Let's walk it together—just to see some of the highlights. Can you be our tour guide?"

"Can I?" Ric's smile got even bigger. "This is one of my favorite places to come." He led them to a side entrance where security entered and said "We will go this way, it is good to know people." There was no line and the head of security seemed to know who Ricardo was. He was given a special security pass and two more for his guests. The museum still had not opened and they were now in the halls of the Louvre. "We will go see the lovely lady before the crowds come."

Ricardo walked quickly down the great hall and to a side room where in the center room was the Mona Lisa. "Ah, she is so exquisite.

Leonardo da Vinci was a genius when it came to certain things and this was one of those things. Her expression conveys nothing and yet conveys everything. It is believed that da Vinci started painting her in 1503 and after four years had stopped. He started again 10 years or so later."

Jim jumped in, "Could explain the expression. That is a long time to sit still."

Ricardo turned and looked at Jim. "Ah, the invisible man has a sense of humor. It is not just all business for him." He paused. Ric was good at reading people and wanted to be sure that the well-intended comment hit the mark. He was sure that it did. "She was stolen once from here you know."

Jenny looked at him. "Someone you know?"

"No, it was in 1811. It could not be stolen now." He paused for a moment and then adjusted his story slightly. "It would not be wise to remove this picture. There has been a lot of damage– acid thrown on her, red paint and moisture causing her frame to warp. I think that where they have placed her is good for her and for people to see her."

Ricardo walked through the main hall and explained several other paintings with as much passion and enthusiasm as he had the Mona Lisa. He even pointed to another da Vinci. However, it was clear that his favorite painting was of the lovely lady. Even some of the battle scenes that had been painted and he loved, Ricardo would comment that the artist captured the moment of turning in a most superb fashion, but missed on some of the symmetry that you find in the da Vinci piece.

Jim paused, "Yes, this is one of my favorites."

Jenny looked as though nothing out of the ordinary had happened, but inside she was puzzled. One of the quiet tips given to Jenny and Jim was to not show their ignorance of art. It was expected that in their circles they would have at least a reasonable understanding. So listening and not talking was the best approach, at least Frank felt so. Jenny wholeheartedly agreed and was perplexed at this offer of information.

"Yes, that is a nice one," Ricardo chimed in.

"Gericault's 'Raft of Medusa' captures hope after tragedy. I can nearly imagine the lost destitution of a few survivors from a frigate at sea. No hope in sight and then alas, land. They are not there and tragedy could still befall them. But there is that hope after a disaster that nearly ends their life as they know it." Jim went on to explain a little about 1800 frigates and the desperate time at sea for a ship that went down. He talked a little about Gericault and his life as a painter.

"Yes, it is a great lesson to all." Ricardo's phone then rang. "Excuse me for a moment."

As he stepped away Jenny turned to Jim, "And how do you know about this painting. You are no expert." She spoke firmly but in a very quiet voice.

"I am an expert on tragedy and looking for hope. Not sure I have seen the 'hope' yet, but I at least hope to find hope." Jim concluded.

"Yes, but how did you know about the painting." Jenny retorted.

"I googled Medusa a few months back to do an object lesson at a work function. This was one of the results. The story intrigued me so I studied it a little further. Kind of hit home with me."

Ricardo had started back and Jenny just said, "Well, you just be careful with what you know it could get us in trouble."

Ricardo was still putting his phone back on his belt clip when he said, "French people are so funny about schedules and process. If you let the French rule the world you wouldn't know what rules to follow or even how to break them."

"Trouble?" Jenny asked. "We will need to leave if there is any problem." She was baiting him, but not really wanting to leave.

"No trouble, just a slight change in plans. I need access to a certain part of the museum without any eyes on us. But it will have to wait a little while now." Ricardo paused hoping he had not lost his audience through his honesty. He perceived that he hadn't. "There are still more highlights I can show you. Let's go to the sculptures for a few minutes. Then, if time permits, I will show you my favorite spot."

"Something you like more than the lovely lady?" Jim asked.

"Yes, something more precious than the lovely lady." Ricardo answered.

The museum was quickly starting to fill as Ricardo took them to some of the sculptures. He did not fancy the sculptures with as much enthusiasm but had comments on a few of them. One gentleman was videotaping the Venus de Milo and Ricardo just whispered into Jenny's ear, "I have come for years and the thing has not moved. He may video tape all day and I do not believe it will ever move. A still picture would do."

Jenny laughed. She would explain it later to Jim.

Jenny enjoyed the sculptures much more than the paintings. They seemed more lifelike to her. She would not share this with Ricardo. However, the questions she asked about the sculptures' period and purpose would keep them in this section longer than Ricardo wanted.

CHAPTER 37 – THE TEASER

Yuri's text went to Ricardo. "Bronze plate with what is probably ancient Egyptian writing on it. Courier will be there in 3 hours to prove who I am."

Ricardo received the text while at the Louvre in the sculptures. It hastened his desire to get to the antiquities. He now had two reasons to visit that part of the museum. Neither of these reasons were even the main attraction of taking Jim to the Louvre.

Yuri also informed Steve that she would not have a piece to sell to Ricardo. Steve was disappointed, but it just kept him focused on the other potential items he could sell the eccentric billionaire.

CHAPTER 38 – ARTHUR IN PARIS

Arthur did not know it but he had checked into a hotel just two blocks from Dragos. He also used an assumed name. He wasn't sure why, but was just afraid for his life. He went to the lobby to get a London Times before calling Dragos. It was in smaller print but sure enough, the Times had corrected the story of who had been murdered. Then there was the ominous line "Professor Arthur Borden sought in questioning in attack."

How could he be a suspect? He was there and there were plenty of witnesses that could testify that another man came and did the stabbing. Then he thought that maybe he was reading too much into the story. Perhaps the police are also concerned for his life.

It crossed Sir Arthur's mind that perhaps the bronze plates and the attack were related. But he felt it almost too bizarre to really think there was a connection. However, there were too many coincidences for there not to be a connection. In the end, this could be his distraction for the day and then he would just go back to London and talk to the police. At this point, there was not much more he could do. He made his call.

"Hello, this is Dragos."

"This is Professor Borden. I am in Paris and when you and Professor Bucky get in town I can meet. I assume sometime today?" It was a hope. Arthur knew that they may have made it last evening but was not sure on their time schedule.

"Professor Bucky did not make the trip. But I am ready to meet."

"And you have the plate?" Arthur inquired.

"Yes. Can you meet me at the Café American Pie restaurant in an hour for lunch?" Dragos suggested.

"I do not know where that is but I will find it and meet you there. How will I recognize you?"

Dragos gave an address and then major cross roads to the restaurant. "I will be carrying a green bag with a red bow tied to it." Dragos would need to find a red bow, but figured he could pick one up along the way.

CHAPTER 39 – THE LOUVRE MAIN ATTRACTION

Ricardo would need to rush his guests through the antiquities but would pause at two key locations. He would do this as though it were just part of the plan. "This is my favorite spot in the museum." Ricardo said as they stood near some ancient Egyptian antiquities.

Jim looked with a slight tilt to his head and eyes squinted slightly. "Ric, come on. You like this better than the lovely lady? What makes this such a great place?"

Ric smiled a genuinely big smile. "Jim, this is the sight of another beautiful lady that is not here right now. My daughter was proposed to in this very spot."

"Then this is a special spot," Jim exclaimed.

"Are proposals common in the Louvre?" Jenny asked out of pure curiosity.

Jim knew someone from his church who got engaged at the Louvre so he figured it was probably fairly common.

"Yes. It is quite common for proposals to occur here. It is also common for propositions and the such. But, hopefully unique for my daughter and her husband." He pulled his phone out and took a picture of the spot. Then he sent a quick text to his daughter. "Honey, at that spot again. Thinking of you. Love Daddy."

"A note to your daughter I presume." Jim asked.

"Yes, always when I am here I send her a note." Ricardo started to walk towards an Egyptian exhibit. Jim and Jenny followed. "See those markings?"

Jenny said, "Yes."

"Hieroglyphics are ancient writings whether on clay pots, parchment or stone, yes?" Ricardo was starting to set the bait.

"They are, but they do not seem so unique. Unless of course there is a story that goes with manuscript or pottery." Jenny said. She was getting into negotiation mode just in case. "But surely you did not bring us here to talk about manuscripts."

"Of course not, we are here for something else. But like I said I work lots of angles and may have something unique." Ricardo teased just a little bit more.

Jenny looked at him, "You have a unique Egyptian papyrus for us to look at?"

"Maybe even better than that. Have you ever seen ancient Egyptian writings on bronze plates?" Ricardo dropped it out there.

"Bronze plates are not unheard of but that would be unique. It would need verified. Of course." Jenny was intrigued that Ricardo would have something this unique, this quick.

"I would want to verify myself. I even need to verify the source. But if it is the source he claims to be then I am sure the artifact will be genuine." Ricardo let his subtle victory set in. "But we can talk more of this later, it is time to go to our main attraction in the Louvre today."

Ricardo pointed out a few other antiquities along the way, although his comments were more cultural and historical than about any given piece of art. He commented on the different eras in Egyptian history and how different the cultures really were. It was evident that he was a student of history.

Ricardo also discussed the contrast of warrior and philosopher in ancient Greece (Sparta versus Athens).

"I am not sure they are so different." Jim commented.

Ricardo paused for a moment, "I am not sure what you mean."

"One is a battle with swords and the other is a battle with words. Both seek to shape the culture to one's views."

"Very astute, Jim. Very astute." Ricardo continued towards the only major section they had not yet at least walked by, the vast furniture collection.

As they approached the section of the museum that housed the furniture collection there was a rope with a sign hanging on it written in English and French, "Pardon, Section Closed. Please Come Back Later."

"I think this means that they are ready," Ricardo commented as he stepped around the barricade. Jim and Jenny followed without hesitation.

"You will find pieces of furniture, tapestries and other accents in here from many of the occupants of the Louvre. It is a great collection–more is stored away and not viewable by the public." Ricardo had picked up his step and was checking his watch.

"Are we on a deadline," Jenny asked.

"We have access without cameras for about 20 minutes. I want you to see two pieces." He walked first to unique looking desk that had inlaid steel and bronze. "This was created by Adam Weisweiler in 1784 for Marie-Antoinette. It is a good piece, would show manuscripts nicely and has a great history."

Observant and patient, Jim looked and then spoke, "But this is not your favorite, is it?"

"No. I believe you will like the one around the corner much better."

Ricardo didn't stay with this piece but immediately went around the corner. Jenny and then Jim followed. Jenny caught the piece out of the corner of her eye and then it came into full view. There was a desk with a tall case attached to the back. It was all oak and had a dagger stuck on the left side of the desk near the tall case. The woodwork was intricate and matched well except for an obvious flaw near the opposite side of where the dagger was situated. It was a different pattern that did not match the rest of the furniture piece, yet seemed to still fit in.

"That is gorgeous." Jenny spoke first.

"It was allegedly used by Napoleon but no one is completely sure. Legend has it that he put the dagger into the desk after a military leader reported a set-back in a campaign. He told the leader that the next time the dagger would be used on him. The dagger is still there because he was never let down again by that general."

"Where did the desk come from?" Jenny asked.

"Legend would say that he stole it from a rich family in an early military campaign. But that also is not known." Ricardo walked to the far side of the desk. "And this is different as you see. It was damaged in an attack by Napoleon, so legend goes, and then repaired by one of the craftsmen at Napoleon's request."

"He requested it different?"

"He wanted something that was uniquely his, not a recreation of the old desk."

Jim looked at the piece of furniture as if he were studying a piece of fine art. He bent over looking underneath and then around the sides. His mind, however, was just wondering how Ricardo was going to manage to get the thing out of the Louvre. He would probably never find out, but that was the most fascinating thought to him.

Ricardo stood back with his arms folded; pleased he had found a piece that Jim liked. "I can arrange this in several ways."

Jenny looked at him. "And you can deliver wherever we like?"

"Let's just say this furniture gets rotated out on occasion and can be put in storage for a long period of time. It would be a while before anyone goes to look for it." Ricardo paused for a moment. "Hypothetically, this would give the most of options of where it could be 'stored'."

"And there are other options?" Jenny pressed gently as she ran her fingers across the top of the desk.

"Yes. I could arrange the piece to be on 'permanent loan' to you at your Villa at the ocean. It would be official and could stay almost indefinitely."

Jim's immediate thought was about a villa on the ocean that he enjoyed so much and yet had never really visited and wasn't even sure if it really even existed. He was smart enough not to react to that information though. "So why would the Louvre want to lose such a piece?"

"The story is only legend and it is a good legend. But since it cannot be proven it does not fit with the image of the Louvre. They cannot even verify that Napoleon ever used the desk let alone any of the surrounding stories. Having this off at some rich guy's house 'on loan' lets the truth die or be discovered. Either way, it is not in the authentic Louvre collection." Ricardo explained. "But they would not want it to leave France which is why your villa sounded like a good location."

"How much is it for this option?" Jenny responded.

"The cost of transportation and assurances it would be displayed and not altered."

"And I would want a unique piece to display in it pretty quick." Jim jumped in.

"I would want to get you a few. More profit in the next exchanges for me." Ricardo concluded.

"I think we have a deal Ricardo," Jenny concluded.

"Good. We must move on now. I do not want to cause suspicion." They went back over the guard rails and into the main corridor where the furniture was displayed. Within a few minutes there were other people starting to walk through the gallery. "I will make arrangements to get to your Villa. Will you be in town?"

"For a few days." Jenny responded.

"Good. I will hope to have an item for you to discuss and view. I will call you either tonight or tomorrow."

"Thank you Ricardo." Jim and Jenny responded almost simultaneously.

"No, thank you." Ricardo said as he shook each of their hands.

Ricardo headed for the exit. Jim and Jenny continued to go through the museum to see a little more.

Jim had to ask. "So is there a real Villa that Jim Conrad owns?"

Jenny looked at him. "Yes, it was purchased a few years ago under Jim Conrad's name and is one of his assets. It is right on the ocean."

"That is nice. Perhaps we should stay there for the rest of the week." Jim suggested.

CHAPTER 40 – CAIRO AND THE BRONZE PLATE

Amir held a backpack as he entered the office of Professor Alto. Yuri followed him in as though she were merely a hired hand sent to help out. It was late morning. They had scheduled this time because it provided the largest block of time between classes for Professor Alto. It was his request, but Yuri knew that if all went right it wouldn't matter because he would be dead.

"You can turn off your tape recorder," Amir said before any other conversation began.

Alto reached into his desk drawer and turned off a small tape recorder that he would sometimes use for dictation. "You were captured on video coming into the building and probably several other places on campus. So I may not have a record of what we say but I have a record that you were here."

Amir looked at Alto; "I assure you that there is no record. There are many ways to avoid the simple security measures of most organizations. But why are you worried, you are getting paid handsomely for this work." Amir did not know the arrangements, but knew that there had to be a decent paycheck involved or a Professor like this would simply want the piece in some museum. Most people had their price. Knowing how much Professor Alto made Amir figure that the payoff was about $150,000 US dollars or some equivalent.

"Are you going to kill me like you did Professor Blovaski? Or what you tried and maybe already did with Sir Arthur? I am no idiot. I have seen the reports out of Russia and out of London." Professor Alto seemed nervous and was unsure how he had gotten himself into this mess. But Amir had it right, it was the money. Alto did not know it, but Amir had also guessed the amount right on the button.

"I did not kill any professor. I am getting paid to play a role in this just like you. My role is to have you provide a translation to this plate." Amir pulled the plate out of the backpack and handed it to Alto.

Alto examined it closely, "Amazing." He set it flat on the table and pulled a letter opening knife from the top middle drawer of his desk. "When we are done, what will become of the plate?"

"Some rich collector will buy it. It seems that is how I might get paid for my part of the job." Amir said as he looked on. He didn't know that for sure, but it seemed like a reasonable assumption.

Professor Alto slowly and carefully poked the knife around the edging of the bronze plate. It was encased by a wooden backing, probably added by whoever found this artifact, and then sealed with wax along the edges. It was a fine way to preserve something temporarily. As the seal broke, Professor Alto slowly pulled the plate from the casing and turned it over. He set it down and then examined the casing, the left over wax and every piece of the materials. "I cannot translate this, at least not quickly."

"What do you mean?" Yuri spoke up out of character and looking a bit frustrated.

Amir had never seen Yuri step out of a part or even show emotion unless it was planned. He thought to himself that it is lucky that this is just a simple professor or her cover would be blown.

"I mean I was told there would be a key to translate the engraving on the back of the plate." Alto picked up the plate and turned it around so that Amir and Yuri could see. "Do you see anything?"

Amir responded, "You read ancient languages. You are educated. Can't you translate the text yourself?"

"I am educated enough to know that this is not a known language and figuring out the root languages and interpreting this language could take months or even years. Do you want to wait in the lobby? I mean, this is not what I was told." Professor Alto seemed frustrated with the situation. He wanted this whole affair over with and wanted to get back to his life. Knowing what happened to Professor Blovaski and what was at least attempted on his friend Sir Arthur made the whole ordeal not worth the price he was being paid.

"But is this an authentic ancient plate?" Amir pushed.

"Yes, I would think so. I would need to run some tests but this is likely an authentic plate from some culture long ago. I would guess that Egyptian and/or Hebrew are the root languages for this writing, but it is a guess at this point." Alto set the plate down.

All three stood and looked at the plate and contemplated what should happen next. Professor Alto was thinking through the events and then asked, "Is there a second plate?"

Amir glanced at Yuri just to be sure and then responded "No. Why do you think there might be?"

"Well, the email that Sir Arthur sent me . . . he said look at these pictures. He did not send just one picture. Now it could have been pictures of one plate or it could have been more than one plate–I don't know how many because you deleted the attachments before I got to view them."

Amir looked at the professor. "We did not delete the pictures from your computer."

After a minute of bantering with the professor, Amir excused the professor so that he and Yuri could speak.

Several things did not need to be said, like there was probably somebody physically watching them while they were in Cairo. It was also clear that someone had connections in multiple locations. The thought even crossed her mind that Jim Conrad had orchestrated the whole event. Whoever it was had a breadth of resources that probably at least matched her network of connections. "Find out who." is all that Yuri said. Amir knew that she meant who was watching them in Cairo. Attempts to find out who was behind the whole charade had not been successful, but finding one link would lead to more.

They both left. Yuri's phone call on the street was direct. "Captain, it is not the right plate; there was nothing on the back."

"What do you mean nothing?" The voice on the other end of the line was irritated and short also.

"I think there is more than one plate." Yuri said baiting the question.

"What makes you think that?" The Captain said anxiously.

"Did you save a copy of the emails before you deleted the attachments?" Yuri put it out there with enough ambiguity that it begged an answer.

"It was an unanticipated email. The emails were deleted with haste and there was no copy." The Captain answered regretfully.

Score one piece of information for Yuri. This confirmed that the mystery man was responsible for the emails being deleted, had people in Cairo and London and probably attempted to kill this Professor Arthur. "There was more than one picture which means maybe more than one plate. Since this is not the right one I will sell it for wasting my time while we try to find the other plate or plates."

"Do not sell the plate. Perhaps the error is yours. Perhaps your KGB friend was too hasty in Bucharest and Dragos ran off with another plate."

Score another piece of information. Her team had been followed at least as early as Romania. "Do you know where Dragos is?"

"I traced him to Paris, but have not located him yet."

Yuri continued. "Good. That is where my contact to sell the plate is. I will find this Dragos." Yuri paused for a moment for effect and then continued. "I will either sell the plate I have or hand it to you in person. Let me know what you would like."

There was a moment of silence. "Sell it. We do not meet until you get the plate I want with the translation I want." Then there was a click.

CHAPTER 41 – CAFÉ AMERICAN PIE

Pulling the bronze plate from the bag, Dragos sat it on the table in front of Arthur. "That is the plate? On the phone Bucky said 'plates'. Are there more?" Arthur asked cautiously.

Dragos didn't know who to trust. He had quickly deduced that handing the plate over to this professor would not solve his problem as he had originally hoped it might. The professor was sitting in a near deserted café in Paris. There would be no public handoff as he had hoped. At this point, he was not even sure the professor would be of any help. Not knowing what his angle should be he just decided to tell the truth. It would be easier to keep track of if he did that. "There was another one, but it was taken from me."

The restaurant was mostly empty. It was too early for a French lunch and this was not a breakfast café. The privacy was what Dragos wanted. They had asked for a quiet corner table, ordered coffee and asked not to be disturbed.

"Who took it from you, do you know?" Arthur pushed a little.

"I think maybe we are done here." Dragos started to pack up his things and the bronze plate to leave. The questions were making him more nervous than he wished to be.

"No. Look someone tried to kill me Sunday night. They killed my wife. I got an email from a professor, a colleague from Russia, who is now dead. The email had pictures of this plate and another one. I am desperate to figure out why." Arthur said in a strong, stern, and desperate sounding voice.

It had not occurred to Dragos that there might be another individual as desperate as he was. Still, what if this was an act. Arthur certainly wasn't Russian. He had a clear and distinct British accent—the same voice he had heard the day before when Bucky had called.

Dragos sat down and pulled the bronze plate back out of the bag. Looking at Arthur he said, "My friend, can you read the plate? It would help if we knew what it was."

"It is not a common ancient language, may have some elements of Hebrew and Egyptian. It is a bit odd if you ask me." Arthur continued to look at the text. "It looks authentic but might take months to translate or longer."

Dragos was frustrated. "We do not have that long."

Neither one said a word for several minutes. They were like two lost sheep that were looking for their shepherd together. Neither one of them knew who that shepherd might be. "What do we do?" Arthur finally asked.

Dragos considered the question for a moment. First he was glad he was not alone anymore in this endeavor. His second thought was that everyone he had known that got involved was now dead, would it be him or Arthur next or worse yet both of them? As for what to do, the same conclusion kept coming to mind. He did not want the plate, but as long as he had it then his life and probably this professor's life were in jeopardy. He could draw only one simple plan. "We must sell the plate." Of course, Dragos never minded making a little profit also.

"To who?" Sir Arthur inquired.

"Well, in an open bidding environment so that whoever wants it and us can buy it or will know who did buy it." He wasn't really asking but merely explaining. The only part not clear to him is *why* someone would want this and *why* they would want a professor dead that had seen pictures of the item.

He pulled out his phone and called Ricardo. Ricardo saw the country code and knew who it was. "Yes, this is Ricardo."

"I have that unique item, but I need it openly bid not just sold to an individual. It needs to be seen leaving my hands." Dragos explained.

"Do I get to keep the profit?" Ricardo could tell that this was a desperate move and wanted to take advantage of the situation to some degree. However, doing business with Dragos was advantageous and he didn't want to spoil that relationship.

"I can take 25% and you keep 75%, reverse our typical arrangements." Dragos was giving up a lot, but was really playing to keep his life. He figured that a 25% profit on the sale of the item was a nice bonus whatever that ended up being.

"That seems fair. Can I see the item? Can you get a picture securely to my hotel in Paris quickly?" Ricardo requested.

Dragos was pleased. He did not realize his friend was in the same city as he was. A picture would be good. He could get it in a hurry and could get an answer from Ricardo within a few hours. "I will get it to you shortly. Let's arrange to meet once you have seen the item–I think you will be pleased."

CHAPTER 42 – THE COURIER

Ricardo received a text message just moments before the courier arrived. "Do not mention my name to the courier. Ask yourself two questions. 1) Who could get the first picture? 2) Is the second picture something you would want?"

The courier arrived at the door of Ricardo within a few minutes and had a manila envelope. He only said enough to confirm that the man taking the envelope was Ricardo Martinez. He did not stay but left the envelope with Ricardo. Slowly Ricardo pulled the picture out of the sleeve. It was labeled "picture 1". The dining room table was familiar and the backdrop of the kitchen was a place where he had spent many hours. Only there were streamers along the walls and a few cards just sitting on the table. He cursed and then said to himself "how did he get a picture of my house?" He knew that his security was top notch and that very few people would even attempt to breach it. It was not conclusive proof, but it certainly was compelling proof that it was likely Yuri.

Pulling the second picture out, he saw a bronze plate. Typed at the bottom of the plate was a brief description including dimensions and weight.

Ricardo responded. "1) Believe it is you. 2) Will need to show item to my client."

Ricardo then sent a second text. "Have something you might like. I will meet you at your hotel lobby bar at 6 pm."

Ricardo received a response from Yuri. "I will be in Paris tonight. Let's arrange a meeting with you and the buyer if possible. Tonight."

It was less than thirty minutes later that there was a knock on the door. A different courier stood in the hallway with a sealed manila envelope. Ricardo took the envelope into the room. He opened it and pulled out three pictures and a typed one page description. The page with the description was signed by Dragos. He carefully went to the picture from Yuri. The engravings were different, but the similarity of the two plates was astonishing. His eyes lit up as he realized that this was a sister plate. He knew that he would have Jim hooked on this sale and it would pay well, especially with a 75% commission on one of the items. Ricardo quickly determined that the first plate to sell would be Yuri's. His commission would be greater on Dragos' plate and he was sure it would sell for more.

CHAPTER 43 – CORNER ENCOUNTER

Jenny and Jim decided to walk through the streets of Paris for a little while after finishing at the Louvre. They first went to the Cathedral of Notre Dame. "For a city that has grown somewhat less religious over the years they certainly have some of the most beautiful churches in the world." Jim commented as they went into the spacious chapel area.

On the way out they were handed a pamphlet. Jim motioned for Jenny not to take it–his personal policy on pamphlets. However, Jenny was determined. As they walked away she pointed to an address and time scribbled on the front. "We have a place to go."

It was the side street of a side street, a little restaurant that Jim and Jenny slipped into. There were three tables and a bar area. It was the only restaurant on the block. "Good cover" Jenny thought to herself. "You would have to really know where to go if you are eating here." She also surmised that strangers would be easily spotted on this less than busy road.

The proprietor was French and didn't look like CIA or even French authorities. Usually she was good at spotting the type. One thing she noted, "Don't be too sure of self on who is a spook and who is not." She knew that the real proprietor would have been excused. There is no way Frank would jeopardize the mission by allowing some random French man to talk to the wrong person. She knew this encounter was fully orchestrated, including whatever speech Frank might be giving.

Jenny started to order a bite to eat. Before she could finish Frank sat down with a woman. "I already ordered for you two."

"Well I hope we like it." Jenny said with a crooked smile. Frank's tone already sent a message that he was not pleased.

"I suppose you gallivanting around town like love birds is part of the cover. I mean I let last night slip and then you just wander off today also." Frank leaned back in his chair and waited for Jenny to start talking.

Jenny started with a distracting question, "Who is the..."

Frank leaned forward almost across the table right into Jenny's face and interrupted. "This is Heidi. She is my European contact, part of Interpol. She has worked assignments in the US, South America and Europe. She is very qualified. Trevor is arranging for tonight's encounter. He is on track and Heidi is and I am. Are you?"

Jenny perked up. "I got a text that Ricardo had something, how did you know?"

"We intercepted some communications with him earlier. They were cryptic, but it sounds like the first potential purchase opportunity will be tonight." Frank paused just long enough to let Jenny understand that he was watching the operation. Letting Jenny know that they knew she went out the night before and they knew about the meeting with Ricardo was a clear message to Jenny about who was in charge. Before she had chance to respond Frank continued. "Are you sure you can be professional enough to do this?"

"We are just staying in character. Do you think a man like Jim Conrad is going to sit in a hotel all day?" Jenny didn't back down and was just playing her part. She knew that Frank had rehearsed this conversation in his head and anticipated each of her responses.

"Do you think Jim would take the subway?" Frank responded in a prepared frustrated tone.

Jenny sat back to create a little distance between her and Frank. Then she folded her arms. "He did. And he usually does, it is one of the advantages of keeping a low profile. You don't have too many paparazzi and you can just enjoy the sights."

Frank was about to speak, obviously ready with a response, when Jim jumped in. "We were contemplating spending the weekend at the villa on the ocean. Would you like to join us?"

Jenny laughed her cute little laugh. "Alright, you said your piece Frank. What do you want us to do tonight?"

"I have one more thing to say. You had better stick close to the script. We are getting big players early and may need to do a couple of transactions quickly."

"Do you mean Yuri?" Jenny asked anxiously.

Heidi spoke. She had a distinct German or Swiss accent. However, her English was clear. Not spoken on this day, but she was also fluent in French, Italian, and two Arabic dialects. "Yes, Yuri. In fact, we believe Yuri will want to meet with you in person."

"Is this the artifact that Ricardo will show us later?" Jim asked.

"Already a full-fledged spy I see," Frank responded. "Yes it is. You will want to buy whatever Yuri is selling and ask if there are more items like it. These are the type of things you want— anything to keep Yuri engaged."

"Yes." Heidi continued. "We will pick up this trail through a few phone calls Yuri might make and associates that Yuri hangs out with. With this and a photo, Yuri will be well on the way to becoming an extinct arms dealer to the terrorist."

They discussed several scenarios on how the interactions may occur and several locations where they could be monitored most effectively. It was clear that it would be most important to make the connection and build the relationship and not to worry if they were forced to another location. "Don't blow the cover." was what Frank emphasized.

After eating a quick meal for France, Jim and Jenny left the restaurant. Jenny said, "When we go out tonight we will walk out the front door so you see us go."

Frank just gave a disapproving look.

CHAPTER 44 – A TALE OF TWO PLATES

They met in the hotel bar/restaurant in Ricardo's hotel. The room was clear except for Ricardo, Jim, Jenny and a bartender. It was only 6:00 PM so it was early for anyone to be in the restaurant bar. However, Ricardo made arrangements for the room to be pretty much cleared before Jim and Jenny arrived.

Ricardo sat behind a table large enough for six people but there were only three chairs around it. The bar was a small one lined with various drinks. The main series of alcoholic drinks were in fruit shaped bottles–peach, apple, raspberry, pear and an orange. There were a few others, but these were the obvious center pieces of the bar.

"So can I get you a drink, perhaps a peach brandy? It is a fine drink." He held up his glass and pointed to the bottle on the table.

"Two waters." Jenny responded.

"You like to keep all of your senses about you for business. I like that." Ricardo said as he took another drink. "I like to have a few to clear the mind."

The bartender brought two glasses of bubbly water and left the bottle. Jim had almost forgotten that often if you didn't order "still" water you would get a carbonated water that to him was bitter tasting. He learned to drink it but certainly was not his preference. Ricardo motioned to the bartender and he promptly left the room.

Jim looked at Jenny and Ricardo. Raising his glass slightly he began. "I propose a toast. To a new friend and an enduring business relationship that will please us all. Cheers!"

The glasses all clanged as they hit. "Here Here" Ricardo repeated.

"Are you enjoying Paris my friends?" Ricardo asked after taking a small sip of is drink.

"Yes. It is a beautiful city. I would not want to live in the city but it is a wonderful place to visit." Jenny responded.

"Has he taken you shopping?" Ricardo asked as he lifted his eyebrows a bit and looked at Jim.

"Oh, I will shop whether he takes me or not." Jenny responded.

They spent the next forty five minutes or so talking about the city and the sights that they each enjoyed the most. Finally Ricardo brought out a picture. Before showing them he said, "This we can see tonight. This is a unique item that I think you will like."

"Let's see it." Jim asked reaching his hand out. Ricardo handed him the picture of Yuri's plate. "It's a bronze plate? I like it."

"Yes. It would be a nice addition to the desk at your villa."

"And can we authenticate its origin and that it really is an ancient writing? Do we need to bring in an expert?" Jenny asked as she looked over Jim's shoulder. "And we can see this tonight?"

"Yes, we can meet my contact in a few hours. We can eat dinner and go from here." Ricardo was pleased. He could tell that Jim was enamored by the plate. Jim's response was natural; he was enamored by the whole spy thing. Ricardo continued. "I have arranged for us to meet in the Pantheon. It should be fairly quiet at that time of night and we can have enough privacy."

Jenny could have suggested another venue, but it would look too contrived. "It will just be us three, correct?"

"The person selling the plate will also be there. Will that be a problem?" He knew that Jim preferred to be anonymous, but hoped a find this exciting would draw him in.

"I believe that limited audience will be fine." Jenny concluded. Her real intent was to keep the group small and to include the target of the operation to attend the meeting. She was hoping it would be Yuri.

The restaurant had a superb braised hen with steamed fresh vegetables on the side. Ricardo was a bit surprised that neither ordered a drink with dinner either. The dinner was superb and lasted several hours. Jenny slipped to the restroom part way through dinner. Heidi was waiting in the restroom most of the evening. The location of the meeting was given. It was not one of the agreed upon locations, but there was still likely time to set up a simple surveillance.

As dinner ended, Ricardo added. "My birthday is tomorrow. But I do not expect a gift, I have surprise for you." He pulled another picture out of an envelope and handed it to Jim.

"Another picture?" Jenny asked with a confused look.

Ricardo laughed softly, "No my dear, another plate–a sister plate. We have a 10:00 am meeting to see this plate."

Jenny asked the obvious. "Why doesn't your contact bring both plates tonight?"

"That is the interesting twist. It is two separate contacts. Hence two separate purchases. Less commission for me but a better chance for you to get them individually cheaper than if they were together."

"That is intriguing." Jenny said.

Ricardo would go make arrangements for a car to take them. As Jim and Jenny waited she whispered to Jim "Don't tell Yuri about the second plate tonight."

CHAPTER 45 – DRAGOS' NEAR DEATH

Dragos enjoyed a late dinner and just happened to stop at the desk before going up to his room. "Can I get a wake-up call?" he asked the clerk.

"Of course, what time would you like and for what room? The clerk said in English with a heavy French accent.

"Probably should make it 7:00 AM for room 317." Dragos responded

The clerk repeated the instructions and wrote something in the log book. Just as he was about to turn and head for the elevator the clerk spoke "Oh and monsieur, a Russian sounding man was asking for you. I did not tell him you were here, but I believe he is still in the bar on the other side of the elevator if you would like to meet with him."

Dragos turned right for the door and started out. He could sense that the Russian was not far behind him. He quickly walked towards a busy street. Glancing back he saw the Russian man gaining ground. Dragos saw a church. It had a side door and a front door, he could see both. He slipped into the front door, then quickly out a side door. His hope was that the Russian would take a moment to search the church and he would have time to slip away.

After he exited he could see the Russian entering the front door. He also got lucky and was able to hail a taxi. The taxi took him about six blocks. He got out and hailed another taxi that took him in a different direction about ten blocks away. And then he repeated it one more time before calling Arthur. "Arthur, this is Dragos."

"Yes. It's late you know." Arthur said having just fallen asleep only to have the phone ring.

"I know." Dragos said a little panicked.

"Are we still on for tomorrow or is there a problem?" Arthur certainly was hoping there was no issue. However, the fact that Dragos was calling spoke volumes.

"I had an unwelcome visitor at my hotel. Can I use your room for the rest of the night?" Dragos asked.

Arthur agreed and gave the address. Dragos took another taxi to get there. Realizing how close it was to his old hotel he figured he might actually be safe. There is no way the Russian would ever assume he would be dumb enough to stay that close to where he just was.

CHAPTER 46 – THE INTERESTING DEAL

The Pantheon was not necessarily one of the choices that Frank would have made. Even at night there was frequently someone there for a closed event. It was King Louis XV gift for being healed. King Louis XV pledged to build the edifice to the glory of the patron saint of Paris St-Geneviève. It was Ricardo's choice because it was one of his favorite churches in town. He had called the care taker earlier and asked that he be one of those given evening access and that a section be cordoned off so that he could use it. He heard an emphatic "no" from the caretaker. Ricardo convinced him by promising that the business they would be performing was for charity. That almost clinched the deal. When Ricardo indicated that one of the charities would likely be a large anonymous donation to the church in the next few weeks the deal was clinched. Suddenly it was available and set up per Ricardo's request.

Yuri arrived alone, after Ricardo, Jim and Jenny were already seated. As she walked across the room both parties were stunned. "Can I help you?" Ricardo asked. No one at the table expected a woman. She was stunning. Jim guessed that she was probably the same age as Jenny. He thought to himself that he had met a very beautiful woman that represented good a few days earlier and now was about to meet an equally beautiful woman that embodied evil. Probably an exaggeration but it sure seemed that way to him.

"You are Ricardo but who are these folks." Yuri spoke with directness and continued to scan the room and the area for anything out of the ordinary. Frank had time to install a listening device, but did not have time to get agents in place to have a view. It was probably better that there was not anyone else around, Yuri may have spotted even the most obscure out of the ordinary person or thing.

Jim and Jenny stood, "I am Jim Conrad and this is Jenny, my business associate. You must be Yuri."

Yuri looked puzzled, "You, uh, are too young to be Jim Conrad." She assessed his reaction. There was none.

Frank listened in a van nearby. He said a few choice words to Trevor and Heidi.

"I have a father you know, but he is dead. Did you know him?" Jim was grasping at how to assess the situation. He didn't lie. He had a father and he was dead. Never mind that Jim and the CIA had never discussed who Jim Conrad's father was, if he was named after him or if someone else had played this role before. The gamble paid off.

"Sorry to hear about your father." Yuri shook hands and then sat down at the table. She pulled the backpack out and placed it onto the table. Then slowly pulled out the casing and set it on the table. Then she pulled the plate out and placed it onto the table. "I am sure you need to validate that it is an authentic plate." Yuri concluded trying to read the reaction of each person, especially Jim.

Jenny observed Yuri since she first saw her. She knew the budget. They had discussed it earlier in the day at the restaurant. She had been allocated a specific amount and she had not decided her negotiation tactic yet. "We could authenticate the plate or we could make a deal without the authentication."

"You would do that?" She looked directly at Jim. "You, or should I say you and your girlfriend, are not as savvy as I would have thought."

Jenny looked at Yuri, "I am Jim's business manager, not his girlfriend."

Yuri kept her eyes on Jim. She hesitated before she spoke in order to ensure that her message was clear – she wanted to deal with him. "Well, are you savvy?"

Trevor had to physically stop Frank from heading out the door of the van as Jim spoke up. "I suppose that you have a reputation to maintain and I am someone that could ruin that if you gave me a forgery."

"Okay, I can see that. But it could be an expensive lesson." Yuri responded.

"I don't think so," Jim continued. "You see with what I am planning to pay for an item that has not been authenticated would not be a huge loss." Jim remained expressionless.

Yuri studied him then spoke, "Let's take a walk." She was clearly talking to only Jim and no one else.

Jim stood and started to take a walk. Jenny thought, "Frank will not be happy." She was correct. The voices were out of range and there was a civilian having a conversation with one of the biggest criminals in the world. Things were not going as Frank had intended. Frank wanted to go put an end to it immediately but knew that he just needed to let it play out a little.

Yuri left the plate behind with Ricardo and Jenny. She walked out the door with Jim and started down the street. She was quiet until they were down the street. Then she turned to face him. She spoke softly. "Do you see that van about 100 feet down the road?"

"Yes." Jim didn't say anything else, but he also knew that Frank was inside that van.

"There is someone in there that is probably monitoring our conversation, at least the one we were having inside." Yuri looked for a reaction.

Jim responded quickly. "I always assume someone is monitoring me. I try to be careful, but it is inevitable."

Yuri looked at him closely. She still did not have a good read on him. The van could just be a van and it could be a van full of French police. It could also be the Captain. She was not sure and she did not like being unsure of her surroundings. "Did you know your father funded terrorists?"

Jim took a line from Ricardo. "I am not my father. I am not looking to buy guns from you. This is a simple hobby for a businessman."

Yuri felt comfortable, at least a bit. She was now ready to do business which was more about using Jim to find out about her past than it was about making any money from him. She began. "So this plate has a high value, it may be worth nearly $20 million US I am told. It is unique. It was found some place in the northern part of the old USSR, in Russia I believe. It has never been translated but is supposed to be a dead language that has its roots in Hebrew and Egyptian. "

"If it were translated and had a good story it might be worth $5 million. I would speculate it would fetch closer to $1 million as is. I will pay you $250 thousand." Jim kept his eyes on her. He knew that he was in trouble with Jenny and with Frank, but was having a lot of fun negotiating with dollars he didn't have. Jenny and he were told not to spend over $2.5 million. He figured that if this one cost less than a million they might be able to get the second one also. At some point they would need to break away and tell Frank about the second meeting. Then he might actually be thrilled the tax payers saved money on this deal.

"So why do you collect such artifacts? Why not collect paintings?" Yuri asked, avoiding the talk of money for a minute. She also started to walk further down the street.

"I am just starting. I am fascinated with history. History is best told in the written form and not by a famous painter." Jim walked next to her.

"Your father, did he treat you well?" Yuri continued in a casual conversation hoping to get just a few tidbits of information to help on her ultimate quest.

"I would rather not talk about my father. But I have a question for you." Jim carefully changed the subject so as to not tell a story that could be contradicted at some point.

"Okay. I will answer your question then you answer one of mine. And it won't be about your father." Yuri almost felt like she was a teenager playing a game. Only she knew that Jim was not as innocent as a teenager–very few rich people have not stepped on others along the way.

"Sounds fair. What is your real name?" Jim asked.

Yuri stopped for a moment and looked at Jim. They had rounded the corner and the van was not in sight. "Alright, but if you repeat it then I will kill you. My real name is Stephanie Baker."

"Stephanie Baker. Okay, so what . . ."

"I think it is my turn." Yuri interrupted. She hadn't really thought of a question. However, she decided to take the conversation to a new level. "If I take your embarrassing low offer, will you go on a date with me–just two people on a date?"

Jim looked uncomfortable for the first time in the evening. "When?"

"You used your next question rather quickly. Anytime in the next few weeks. We could go anywhere really. Any ideas?" Yuri spoke before she realized she had asked her next question.

"Now that we are even on questions–let's call that game done." Jim raced through his mind all of the possibilities. This could help in her capture and could lead to new criminals. This could also have Frank send him home right away. But as the single man, Jim Conrad, he would probably say yes. "All right. It's a deal. I will choose a place and check my calendar."

Yuri pulled out a card with a telephone number on it. "You should know that when I get the second plate, and there is another one that I will secure, it may cost you more." Yuri liked sentences that could be interpreted in multiple ways and she appreciated people who could see that. She was sure Jim was one of those men. However, she was not sure if she liked him or if she would kill him in proxy of his father for the death of her parents.

As they walked back, she pulled out her necklace. "One more thing - I have a necklace. Your father knew what it went to. Do you know?"

Jim examined it as though he would even have any idea. "I don't think I know. I will ask Jenny if she knows anything about it."

"No, let's keep it between the two of us. Just check through your father's things and see if there is anything that might give me a clue what it is to."

Jenny stood as Jim and Yuri approached the table. Yuri looked at her to observe her reaction "The plate is yours. We made a deal. Ricardo, you can keep the cash. Jim will call me later for a date." Jenny's eye twitched slightly.

Yuri left out the back without saying another word.

Ricardo spoke up, "Well how much did you buy it for?"

Jim looked very proud of himself and knowing full well that Jenny would not be as happy. "$250 thousand US and a date sometime in the next few weeks."

The ride back in Ricardo's car was quiet. The tension between Jim and Jenny could have been cut with a knife. Ricardo was not sure if it was because Jenny liked him and didn't like the date or because she was blocked out of the negotiation. He only hoped this would not interfere with their business tomorrow. To be sure he asked, "I will see you tomorrow morning? Yes?"

"Ricardo, you did well tonight. I think this arrangement has a lot of potential. We will see you tomorrow morning." Jenny ended. Then she and Jim got out of the car and started into the hotel.

CHAPTER 47 – ONE WAY DEBRIEF

On the way to their room Jenny said quietly, "You know you might have just ended this whole thing. Agreeing to a date is just asinine."

The backpack with the plate was wearing on Jim a little, but it was Jim's guilt that was beginning to get the best of him. Maybe he had played the cards incorrectly and jeopardized the mission. In the middle of this thought a hotel door opened. Jim and Jenny were dragged into a room. Frank was standing there with Trevor next to him. Frank had his gun in his hand. "If I reported this to headquarters they would pull the plug in a second. I oughtta just shoot you - it would be easier on my sanity. Do you know how far overboard you went Jim and you let him Jenny. Incompetent. Wouldn't you agree?"

Jenny started to explain. "But…"

"The question was purely rhetorical. Do you need that defined for you? I don't need to hear a word from you. I don't want to hear from you. The only bright side is we now know who Yuri is and that Yuri is a woman. That's one thing. And you are going to have the chance to see her again. That means we will also."

Jenny tried again wanting to explain that they were going to see another plate in the morning. "We . . ." Jenny did not have any guilt. She was focused on the mission.

"Don't talk. I meant that. In fact, go see your Paris tomorrow. Pick out a nice restaurant to take Yuri to while you are out. I don't want to see or hear from you until dinner." He looked at Trevor, "Now get them out of my sight."

Trevor escorted them to the door.

Jenny was half undressed before Jim was even all the way in the door. "Shouldn't we talk or are you going to be mad all night?" She was down to a bra and underwear pretty quickly.

Jenny tossed her blouse onto a chair and came around to Jim's face so they could talk close enough in a whisper so that no one could hear even if they had a device in the room. "What do you want to talk about?"

Jim had trouble looking her in the eyes, not because he felt guilty but because she looked very nice wearing next to nothing and her controlled anger was a little sexy to him. He decided to play on that a little. "We could talk about the brilliant deal I made."

"Which part was brilliant, the money or the date? Was the date your idea or hers?" Jenny asked.

"Look, she doesn't like my dad. Heck I barely remember if he was a good guy or not—but she blames me. Her asking me on a date could just be to kill me."

Jenny laughed her little laugh. "I don't remember your father that well either. And it could be a deadly date. Sorry, you did make a good deal."

Jim reached over and kissed her. It was a nice passionate kiss. Jenny continued after the short embrace ended. "You more or less guaranteed at least one additional meeting."

"And she told me she is after another plate. She called it the 'other' plate." Jim continued.

"Interesting. We may have it by tomorrow if there are only two."

Jim looked at Jenny, "Don't we need to tell Frank about the meeting tomorrow?"

"Not a chance." She said as she gave Jim a playful kiss. "He asked us to go see the city ourselves. We will have fun with this one. And just so you are clear, it is still an open offer for you to join me for the night."

Jim gave her another nice kiss. "Not tonight." Those were his words and he painfully stuck to them.

Wednesday
Paris

CHAPTER 48 – DRAGOS' PLATE

Jenny and Jim took a nice leisurely walk to the Metro underground. Jim was carrying a new backpack with the bronze plate in it. Jenny suggested that there might be a benefit in comparing the two items. They spent the next 2 hours switching trains, taxis and a bit of walking to elude anyone that might be following them. By the end of the first hour, Jenny eliminated any of the subjects she thought might be following them. They kept the evasive tactics for a while longer just to be sure. Jim referred to it as the "tour of Paris under the ground–a place all tourists should see."

The end destination would be a small conference room in a hotel just a few blocks from the Opera de Paris Garnier. Jim and Jenny had both determined that this would be their stop after the meeting. It was another great site in the city that they both wanted to see.

Ricardo was in the lobby for them. He greeted them with his normal enthusiasm and explained that his contact was looking for a public auction, but not to be concerned. He felt that they could arrange something if the other plate was suitable.

Entering the conference room, there was a single table with two gentlemen sitting at the table. Jenny observed that they had just entered the only way in or out of the room. She did not like that. There was a bag sitting on a chair that was left of one of the gentleman. Jenny surmised that this gentleman was from a Slovak country. The other gentleman appeared to be a well-educated American. Both seemed a little surprised when Ricardo walked in the room.

Dragos spoke, "Your colleagues, I assume Ric?"

"Dragos, you always assume too much. These are potential buyers. But I understand your request. We will accommodate what you need if we get to a sale." Ricardo clarified.

Dragos was trapped, with only one exit. He was more than a little angry with Ricardo but was left with little choice. "All right then, let's at least have some introductions. I am Dragos and this is my friend Professor Arthur Borden."

"Pleased to meet you." Arthur said with his deep British accent. Jenny was surprised, she expected an American accent.

"I assume you have brought him to authenticate the plate?" Ricardo asked.

"Uh yes, that is the reason." No other explanation should be given as far as Dragos was concerned.

"I am Jenny and this is Mr. Jim Conrad. And we assume that the conversation will be kept confidential. Jim likes to keep a low profile." Jenny and Jim shook hands with Arthur and Dragos. Then they all sat down around the table.

Dragos' eyebrows raised, "The Mr. Jim Conrad. I do say it is good to finally meet you."

Arthur was quiet. He had no idea who Mr. Conrad was and didn't really care just so he could help this problem go away. He was anxious to call his children and let them know that he hadn't fallen

1

off the end of the world since his wife died. Then again, he felt as though he had fallen of the edge of the world.

Ricardo introduced himself, primarily for the professor. He knew everyone else in the room. A waiter came into the room and took an early morning food order of coffees. They also ordered a fruit and cheese tray.

After a very short conversation Dragos got right to business. He reached down for his bag and set it on the table. Then he slowly started to pull something from the bag. Instinctively Jenny put her hand on her gun ready to use it in an instance if necessary. As the contents came out it was a plate very similar to the one they had just purchased the night before from Yuri. It even had the same casing. Jim blurted out, much to Jenny's dismay. "How come this plate's casing is attached."

Ricardo's first thought was that his commission just went way up. His second thought was that this might quickly explode into an out of control situation. His second reaction nearly proved to be true. He saw Dragos reaching back into the bag for what was likely a gun. Gently grabbing Dragos' hand he said. "We did not have a chance to tell you, but we purchased a similar plate last night from someone else. It was purchased at a greatly reduced rate because it had not been verified as authentic. Perhaps Professor Borden can look at it now."

Jim realized he had just said the completely incorrect thing. Ricardo was surprised; he had never seen Jim misstep yet. Perhaps he was human after all. Jim pulled his backpack onto the desk. He pulled out the backing and then the bronze plate and laid them on the table. Dragos immediately knew that his is the one the Russian had taken from his friend Bucky.

Jim was a little hesitant but was really curious. "Arthur, what is the casing for? Why would one be out of the casing?"

Arthur picked up and looked at the second plate as he answered, "It's just a protective cover. It serves no purpose but to keep the item protected from the elements. It is not ancient, put on by some archeologist until it can be properly preserved in a lab. You would take it off to put some new covering on it – but there is no real other reason unless…" He paused and turned the plate over. Then he picked up the second plate.

"Unless what?" Dragos asked.

He started to chip away at the wax seal on the other plate. "You wouldn't open it unless you expected to find something on the other side." He popped the plate out. Two pieces of paper fell from the back. There was also something carved on the back of the plate. "Interesting." Professor Arthur Borden was intrigued by this new find.

Jim and Jenny and Ricardo were puzzled. Dragos was worried. They were all startled by the knock on the door. "Room Service."

They quickly covered the plates on the table and invited the waiter into the room. He pushed in an open tray with a selection of meats, cheeses and fruit. There were also five cups of coffee. Dragos' face went white and said as he reached for the gun in his bag, "The Russian."

Jenny noticed the change in Dragos' demeanor and instinctively reached for the closest thing she could find which was the casing of one of the plates. In a single motion she flung it across the small room towards the waiter. Then with her other hand simultaneously pulled her gun. Jim and Arthur both headed right for the floor. Ricardo was also reaching for a gun. The plate's casing hit the Russian quickly enough to divert his first shot slightly. Dragos was hit in the chest.

The Russian had recovered quickly and now had two guns in his hands. Jenny got a shot off that hit him directly in his forehead before he had completely recovered. Two shots were fired before he fell. The first grazed Ricardo's shooting arm. The second went into the ceiling.

Jenny quickly moved to make sure the Russian was dead. Grabbing his phone she looked at the recent text. The last sent text listed the hotel they were sitting in and a note that indicated that he was going in to get the thing. A response was from the unknown sender was, "Be there in less than 10 minutes."

Jenny said, "Grab the plates and the notes, we have to go."

Ricardo was quickly on the phone texting. He looked at Jim, "Take the professor and the plates. I will get Dragos and me out of here. We can settle on price later." He was insistent and direct.

Jenny looked quickly at Ricardo, "We can't leave you."

Ricardo just responded, "We will just slow you down. I can get us out of here and can answer the questions that will likely be asked. Call me later when you are someplace safe."

Sirens could be heard in the distance. Jim and Arthur had managed to put the plates, the one casing on the table and the notes in the backpack and were out the door with Jenny in less than two minutes.

CHAPTER 49 – THE EVEN COLDER RUSSIAN AIR

The cold Russian air made it difficult to think and difficult to work. After eight weeks of attempting to translate and continuing to excavate a site, he was no closer to finding additional plates or even discovering the meaning behind the one they had found.

Professor Thomas also realized that his communications with the states were getting more scrutiny. There was a greater distrust of what he might be saying. The code made for a few awkward sentences which made the senior USSR military officer suspicious that there were innuendos that were being communicated that were not understood by the Russian interpreters. He was right about the messages but looking in the wrong place.

Professor Thomas knew that it was only a matter of time until it was discovered that he was passing messages onto his team across the sea. He started staying later to translate and to leave what he was sure would be his final message. It was vital information that only he knew.

It took a couple of weeks to complete the task, carefully removing the wax seal in a way that it could be sealed back as he finished. He slowly and lightly etched a code on the back of the plate–not the message, but a code to decipher the message. Cleverly, he used the front of the plate's existing text to communicate the message. It would require a few minor changes to the original plate facing but only the keenest observer would notice. The archeologists in him dreaded this part of the code. He would save it for last because of that and because there were likely a couple of keen observers right in camp that would notice the differences.

Even if the changes in the front were noticed, and he was sure they would be, no one might ever consider taking the plate from the sealed case. Then, even if they did, there were only a dozen people or so that could translate the codes. Finally, if they were translated and the front of the plate was decoded for his message, it was so cryptic that one would have to know what they were looking for in order for it to make any sense.

Nothing is fool proof, but Professor Thomas felt that there were enough safeguards in place that only his intended audience would be able to get the message. Coming from behind the Iron Curtain, he was uncertain when they might get it. The only certainty in his mind was that his next message to his team in the states would be his last.

He would communicate where he had hidden the key information that his team would need. The next night he would make the necessary minor changes to the front of the plate. Then, he knew, it was just a matter of time before he was discovered and would befall a tragic death.

As he sealed the plate for the last time he tucked two pieces of paper into the back of the plate. The first contained the original manuscript/hieroglyphics from the other side. He knew that they had already been photographed, copied and catalogued – but he needed to preserve one more copy. Then he added the second note to his new friend that would likely never forgive him. It was written in Russian, "Sorry Sven. My most sincere apologies. Sam."

CHAPTER 50 – THE FRENCH POLICE

Detective Pierre finished getting statements from Ricardo as Dragos was being attended to by paramedics. There were no cameras to record the events or even who entered and left. The best witness, the real waiter was found dead in a broom closet. The whole story just didn't add up, a random Russian guy having a grudge against a Romanian who had used an assumed name. It just didn't seem to fit. It was a good thing that Detective Pierre knew Ricardo. The official report would not even mention that Mr. Martinez was in the building. Ricardo's detective friend encouraged him to leave town, but kept his name out of the formal investigation.

As he finished jotting down his notes he was heading out when a Major Luan flashed her badge. "I am from the Ministry of Intelligence. We have been tracking this Russian. What can you tell me about what happened detective?"

Detective Pierre saw a beautiful blonde haired woman in front of him. She seemed confident and spoke perfect French. Yuri watched Ricardo and Dragos out of the corner of her eye as she listened to Detective Pierre explain the situation. "He had brought some things into the country with him."

Pierre motioned for one of the other officers. He looked at Yuri. "We just found this wood frame. It looks like it has wax along the edges. It looks a little like a picture frame but who can be sure. I guess it might even be a small tray from the hotel but I doubt it. We are sending it to the lab to be analyzed just in case it means something." He took it from the officer's hand and handed it to Yuri.

Yuri looked at it closely, "It is probably nothing. But let me take your number in case I need something further."

Detective Pierre handed her a card and then turned to say something to another officer. When he turned back he could see Major Luan already out the door on her way down the street.

As Yuri walked out the door she mumbled. "Impatient stupid Russian." Yuri was already on the phone calling and texting several French connections. She insisted that Amir get to France as soon as possible with the professor. She knew that it would not be long until she had the second plate.

CHAPTER 51 - ON THE RUN

Jenny was about three steps ahead of Arthur and Jim all the way back to the hotel. About the only thing that Arthur could ask was' "Where are we going? What just happened?"

Jenny slowed down just long enough to discuss with Jim, "It has to be Yuri."

"Do you think?" Jim blurted out sarcastically.

They walked right into their hotel, right past Trevor who was reading a French paper – only he didn't speak any French. Jenny found this amusing. She couldn't very well pass any signals onto Trevor or the other few agents around the hotel with Arthur around. It might blow their cover.

Jenny packed several fake IDs and enough spending cash for a while. She jotted a quick note and was ready to head out the door in less than five minutes. On the way out the front door she dropped the note next to Trevor's feet. Trevor would pick it up after they were by and out of sight, "will call." It was simply enough to indicate trouble but not panic. Jenny wasn't sure Trevor would get it but he did.

They walked a few blocks and then hailed a taxi. Jenny would take them on a nearly hour tour between subway trains, taxi's and walking to be sure their trail would be hard to follow should someone be on their way. They made their way out of the city to a hotel outside of the city where they paid cash for two adjoining rooms. Little was said until they got into the room. They opened the suite door but congregated in one room.

Jenny sat on the edge of the bed. Jim was in the desk chair and Arthur was on the small sofa. "So how do you know you can trust us?" Jenny asked, looking at Arthur.

"Well, I am not dead. That is different than the people that are around me." Arthur said as he was clearly trembling. The gravity of the situation was starting to sink in and he had nothing left to give to maintain composure.

Jenny pressed anyway. "How do we know that we can trust you?"

"I don't really care. I lost my wife . . ." Arthur paused so that he could clarify. "No, my wife was killed with an old friend of mine in London a couple of days ago. Then I find out that a professor who I only knew by reputation was murdered in Russia. And he had sent me an email. The attachments that were part of the email were removed. Surprisingly I got scared and ran to Paris to meet this guy I had never met named Dragos. Now Dragos gets shot. Is he dead also?"

"I think he will live. But why meet Dragos?" Jenny continued.

"I am an expert in my field, ancient languages especially Mediterranean area languages. Dragos had a plate and thought I might be able translate quickly. He was wrong though, I looked at it and it was clear it might take months or even years."

Jim pulled the plates and set them on the bed. Then he took the pieces of paper and handed it to Arthur. "Can you translate that paper?"

"The first is a near duplicate of the front of the plate. See?" Arthur laid the paper right next to the plate. Then he pointed to some similarities and to some of the few differences. "There are some differences but I am not sure why."

Jim continued. "Can you translate the second piece of paper? It looks different."

"Yes. Well, no. But I can tell you that it looks like modern day Russian. I don't speak it but surely someone does." Arthur spoke confidently.

Jenny pulled her phone out and typed a few words into the phone. Then she thought for a moment. "Sorry Sven. My most sincere apologies. Sam." She paused and looked at Arthur and Jim. "That is the translation. The real questions are who is Sven and who is Sam?"

They all thought for a moment on this new information. Jim spoke first, "I think what we really want to know is what Sam is sorry about."

Jenny had her phone busy searching several websites for Sven and Sam and plates. She was fairly certain that someone was out there looking for a search on these items but she was just as certain that her phone was secured from being traced.

Arthur focused on the front of the plates, occasionally turning over the plate to look at the markings on the back of the one plate.

Jim lay across the bed and watched the news. He didn't understand a word but it was clear that there had been a shooting at a hotel. He gathered that there was one fatality and another injury or two. His mind kept wondering back to the original conversation about danger. He knew that he had clearly passed that threshold now.

Jenny stopped her search abruptly so much so that Jim noticed. "What is wrong?"

"Uh, my phone was being traced." Jenny said nervously.

"I didn't think that was possible." Jim responded.

"It is possible. It is just not probable. They didn't lock in on our location, but they will know the right side of Paris. We probably have less than two hours before we should move on." Jenny said a little frustrated. "We should leave in 30 minutes to be safe."

The level of uncertainty concerned Jim. However, Arthur was in a different world. He was oblivious to the entire conversation. He spoke as though everyone were just watching him. "I know why?"

"Why what? Jim asked.

"Why Sam was sorry? That was your question, right?" Arthur said with a slightly confused look on his face wondering how Jim hadn't followed the conversation.

"Yes. Sorry. Why was Sam sorry?" Jim pressed further.

"Sam altered the plate that has the writing on the back. The other paper is probably the original contents of the plate." Arthur said satisfied that he had a good hypothesis.

"Well, that is a good guess. I mean it doesn't look quite like the front of the plate. There are some similarities but it is clear even to a layman . . ." Jenny was interrupted.

"No. I mean the front of the plate was altered. This was an authentic ancient record that Sam altered. Sam was a brilliant archeologist and professor, why would he alter a record like this?" Arthur was talking out loud to Jim and Jenny but seemed to almost be talking to himself.

"You know who Sam is?" Jenny asked.

"Yes. And I think I understand where the plates were found." Arthur explained that as a young professor with a young family he had been given the opportunity to go to the USSR to participate in an archeological dig. He and his wife had opted not to take a long assignment in the USSR. Arthur enjoyed his assignment in the UK and had no interest in tracking across the USSR for who knows how long. He had heard that his friend, Professor Samuel Thomas, had a tragic accident while on this expedition. Arthur's wife just reminded him how unsafe it would have been if he had been the one to go.

"That explains a lot, but why would someone want you dead. Just because you saw the plates that you can't translate? That does not make sense." Jenny explained.

Jim looked at Arthur. He could see the glistening in his eyes. It is one that every parent sees as their child realizes how to do something for the first time. Jim had seen it in his children many times. "He can't translate the plates but he can translate the message on the back of the plate."

Jenny looked questioningly at Arthur.

Arthur looked at the back of the plate. "I believe that I can." He continued to study the back of the plate for a moment and then continued. "Me and perhaps ten other people."

"Why ten?" Jim asked as he started to get the same glistening in his eyes.

"We had a retreat while I was in college with Sam and nine others. It was a mixture of professors and students. We spent most of the summer devising our own 'ancient language'. It was Sam's exercise in teaching how languages are created and how to look at interpreting them. In the end we learned a lot about creating languages and a lot about interpreting them—exactly what Sam had intended. But we also had a unique written language that only the ten of us knew."

"And you and Sam were two of them." Jenny pushed now.

"Yes. Most have died over the years. I keep in contact with Professor Alto in Cairo occasionally. Even sent him a copy of the email I got with the picture of the plates. However, he never got the attachment. I think Timothy Rugsby or something like that went to work for some computer company in Silicon Valley. I saw his picture on a dotcom startup once. The only girl was Terri somebody. I lost track of her but she was a student—probably still living someplace. Everyone else died somewhere along the way starting with Sam."

Jim continued. "Well, get translating."

Jenny reminded that they should move to another location and then translate. They packed up what little they had and went down the stairs. As Jim stepped out of the stairs, he saw Yuri at the desk. He stepped back into the stairwell and let Jenny know.

Jenny pulled her gun and waited. She watched the slight reflection off of the light fixture on the ceiling to see if Yuri would take the stairs or the elevator. She could only make out shadows but there was not a lot of activity in the hotel. It was lucky for them that she chose the elevator.

Stopping at the front desk, Jenny asked the hotel clerk for a recommendation on a good restaurant just inside the city. She got one and said 'Merci' before the clerk could explain that she had company. That was Jenny's intent as she made her way out to the side of the parking lot where she selected a car and hotwired it.

CHAPTER 52 – THE NEAR DEAD END

Yuri was resourceful in finding people. She would simply track them using a conversation with a taxi driver, cameras from the Metro and a little luck. This time it wouldn't be so easy to track Jim and Jenny. It wasn't likely that they found a taxi. She knew that they had either obtained a ride with a local resident or stolen an automobile. Both of these would be hard to trace quickly.

She knew that the restaurant was a dead end but made her way there anyways. It was her only clue at this point. If the Captain found Jim had the plate, she might not meet the Captain and find out what he knows about her parents. There was not time to wait for the date with Jim either, that might be too late.

She was sure that by this point Jim had figured it was her chasing him, but she was not sure if they had discovered that there was something on the back of the other plate. Her next stop might be the hospital to see if Dragos could shed some light on the situation or perhaps a call to Ricardo. First she would need to check-in with the Captain–an unpleasant but necessary step.

Yuri called the secured number, "I don't have it yet."

"Are you having trouble fulfilling your end of the bargain?" The Captain said in his rough and now clearly disappointed sounding voice.

"You didn't say anything about a second plate. That has caused some complications. You need to be more specific with your information." Yuri explained. She did not like excuses but was forced into having one at this point instead of having the plate in her hand.

"Who does have it?" The Captain asked.

"There was somebody with Dragos that took the plate when Dragos was shot." She paused and then suggested the improbable. "I think we should meet and discuss the situation."

"Find me and the plate. Then we will meet." The Captain said firmly. It was what Yuri expected but had hoped that the Captain might relent based on the developments.

"We will meet tomorrow at 4:00. I will have the plate." She proceeded to give the Captain directions on where they would meet and told him to come alone. She would have the plate and the translation from Professor Alto.

Yuri made two more phone calls. The first call was to Ricardo. Ricardo's phone was out of service. She requested that he call her at his earliest convenience. If she could reach Ricardo she might be able to arrange a hasty date with Jim. The second phone call was to Amir giving him instructions to get the professor to Paris as quickly as possible. Amir knew that meant a chartered flight in the air within an hour.

CHAPTER 53 – REPORTING IN

Jim directed Jenny to an area of the city he had some familiarity with near his company's office. They checked into one hotel room under assumed names. Once settled into the hotel Arthur proceeded with translating the back of the plate. He started by making a few notes and trying to remember what he could about the language they had invented so many years before. He hadn't used it for many years but it was such an impactful experience he was surprised how much came naturally. But he insisted that he write down what he could remember before he actually started translate. He did not want to be biased by the words on the plate and misinterpret something.

Jenny was impatient and decided to take the opportunity to call and check-in with Frank. She stepped out of the hotel and found a nearby park where there were very few people. Frank answered quickly. "Where are you? I tried tracing your phone."

"That was you? I thought I was being tracked by Yuri." Jenny was frustrated. She knew that Yuri had found them without the trace. This meant that she was very good. She also knew that Frank had to know something was up.

"Trevor got your note and the fact that you were with someone. We traced that someone. He is Professor Arthur Borden." Frank explained to Jenny.

"Yes, I know who he is." Jenny responded not wanting to share too much information.

"Did you also know that he is wanted by the London police for questioning in the death of his wife?" Frank continued.

Jenny thought for a moment and considered her next words carefully. She looked across the park at a statue and pondered what she knew about the professor. He was not a killer that was clear. He didn't have a weapon in the hotel earlier and ducked under the table with Jim. "I don't really know the man." Jenny said.

"What were you doing with him? Did you know Ricardo was involved in a shooting in Paris? Were you? Did you also know that Ricardo is on a flight back to the states?" Frank was very direct. He could be, it was a secured line.

Jenny was playing out the scenario. She knew that the bullet in the Russians head was hers and if anyone explored the ballistics that it would prove to be hers. Her gun, however, could not be traced to the CIA. She was undercover and her gun was not traceable unless it was taken from her hands. "We were there. Ricardo had another artifact for us to consider."

"And you didn't tell me." Frank said furiously. His cursing rant continued for over a few minutes but the sentiment was the same "you didn't tell me."

"Uh Sir, last night you asked that I not say another word." It was blatant disrespect and she knew it. But she was not going to be bullied by her boss.

"You insubordinate . . ." He stopped himself. "Just so you know, according to the official police report Ricardo was not there. You and Jim were not there and neither was the professor. There was also no artifact that was mentioned in the report. What happened to the deal?"

Jenny had been vague to this point, now came time to commit to a story. "The deal was never finished. But Dragos is someone that might need to be added to the list of criminals we are working with. He is from Romania."

"Alright, we can add him. Where is the professor? We probably need to get him to the authorities on this other thing. What is the artifact and where is it?"

Jenny responded. "When we left our hotel, Arthur went his way and we went our way. He took the artifact. It is a plate similar to the one we purchased last night." Then she considered how much to tell Frank and opted for the lie. "Both plates seem to be from Russia and I think this guy that came in shooting up the meeting was just trying to get them back to his country." Jenny had to lie about Arthur. She wanted the translation and suspected that the Russian was after the translation more so than the plate. She knew that if Frank knew that Arthur was with them he would insist that she bring in a known fugitive and that she would never get that translation.

"Seems reasonable." Frank responded. "But why did you let the professor take the plate?"

Jenny now had to back up her lie with reasoned logic. "The plate didn't belong to us because we hadn't purchased it. To just take it would have tarnished Jim Conrad's reputation."

"Good call. If you get a chance to buy this artifact again, make the deal. I think you are right, it is what Jim Conrad would do."

Jenny hung up amazed that Frank actually had a compliment for her. That would be one she would have to remember and remind him about at the evaluations that would be done on performance when the operation was complete.

CHAPTER 54 – THE TRANSLATION

Jim and Arthur were just sitting in chairs talking when Jenny walked in. Arthur was explaining what had happened in the tube in London. Jenny was a bit taken back. "Why aren't you working?"

Jim looked at Jenny with a grin on his face, "You work for me, remember." It was sharp, it was witty and Jenny laughed a real laugh, not just her cute little cynical laugh.

After a few moments Arthur jumped in. "Well, in reality, we are done."

"Really?" Jenny commented. Jim and Arthur both had a smug look on their face. They knew that it was killing Jenny to find out what they knew but neither of them was readily offering any information. Jenny knew the game and was trying to decide her next move.

Arthur could not wait any longer. He stood up and went to the small desk in the room. Jim and Jenny both followed him to the desk. Jenny and Arthur stood next to each other with Jim looking over their shoulders. Arthur picked up a small hotel note pad with a series of numbers and a few letters on it. "Here." He handed Jenny

CONVERGENCE 169

the sheet of paper. "It is in essence three pieces of information and that is it."

Jenny pointed to the last one. "That is a longitude-latitude number."

Jim looked frustrated. "How did you get that so quickly? I mean it took us a few minutes on that one. Do you know where?"

Jenny looked at the numbers. "I would guess somewhere near Iowa or Kansas. Where is it exactly?"

Arthur looked at Jim. "I said the states and he thought Switzerland." Arthur was pleased with himself. "But obviously you have a better sense than even I do."

"Geo-caching with friends on long weekends." Jenny quipped without even thinking it might jeopardize her cover. "What about the first two numbers. I have no clue what those might be."

Jim was happy to jump in. "The first one is an old bank routing number. Based on the number I am fairly certain it is a Swiss Bank number. But it does not use the new IBAN format so it is not easy to determine the bank."

"And the second number?" Jenny asked.

"It is the right size to be an account number. I am guessing the two go together. That is why I assumed the coordinates were Switzerland." Jim concluded smugly.

"Perhaps the routing number is for a Swiss Bank that has an office in Iowa?" Jenny surmised.

"No. Swiss banks in the US have a different routing number than their parent companies. They must be two different pieces to the same puzzle." Jim explained.

Jenny thought for a moment. Jim and Arthur went back to their seats and picked up their conversation where they had left off. Jenny was talking to herself, mumbling as she tried to determine the next step. She knew it could not be a completely open conversation because she and Jim had to consider how this might jeopardize the mission and if they could just pass it on to Frank. Finally she said,

"Arthur, there is a business office down near the lobby. Go see if you can get the exact location of these coordinates and anything about what is there."

Arthur looked a little unsure about the situation until Jim indicated he could take the plates with him. They had no intention of leaving without him. Arthur was still slightly reluctant but left anyway to go find the computer.

Jenny looked at Jim. "All right boss, you are no help here. Any suggestions?"

"I already had a plan. I was just waiting for you to ask." Jim said eagerly.

Jenny sighed and laughed together. "It better be good, but not too good."

Jim walked to the desk where the phone was. "We will just call the bank and ask about it."

Jenny looked at Jim. "We don't know the bank."

Jim continued. "Yes, but Jim Conrad has a Swiss Account and a bank in Switzerland. You told me this. Also, I am Jim Conrad, a well-respected businessman around the world. Surely my banker would be willing to call in a favor on an old account number we found. Remember I am an accountant. I know a little about what to ask and how to say it."

Jenny knew the account number and the security information. She had conducted business with USB on Jim Conrad's behalf for a little while. It was one of the three accounts that were used as a cover for the formally fictitious Jim Conrad. Maintaining three accounts allowed money to be transferred so it appeared to be a much larger sum that what was really there. An agreement with the NSA kept the large transfers unnoticed by homeland security.

"We better go in person." Jenny concluded. After Jim's brief objection she took a minute to explain that several people had been killed trying to get this plate. The fewer people that knew they had the information the better. Then she concluded, "Maybe you should have that date tonight with Yuri."

"Why?"

"If we can convince Arthur, and I think we will be able to. Then we will all be safer without it. The only thing I can't figure is why she is chasing us to get the plate and then wants to turn around and sell it to us. That seems odd. Maybe you can find out on your hot date tonight."

Jim had a little uneasiness about the situation, but didn't express it. He pulled the card out that Yuri had given him and started to punch the number in his phone. Jenny stopped him. "Use mine. Yours will be tracked automatically by Frank. I don't want him knowing we are going out of town until we are gone. Even if he is tracing my phone, he will need more time to find me than you will give him and I will know he's tracing it. Arthur is likely still a target and we need to keep him safe until we figure this out."

"Until we figure this out?" Jim didn't like the sound of that.

"Then he goes to the authorities in London." She handed Jim the phone. "It's ringing."

CHAPTER 55 – ARRANGEMENTS

"Hello. Who is this?" Yuri did not see a return number. Not many people had her phone number and she only rarely got calls. She made them, but received only a few. She hoped it was Ricardo. But she was even more pleased when she heard who was actually calling.

"Yuri, this is Jim." Jim kept it short and intended to say very little. He almost stumbled and called her Stephanie, but managed to get out the right name.

"Are you calling to arrange the second installment of your purchase?" Yuri said trying to be a little playful. It also might help her situation.

"We had a near encounter at the hotel earlier today. I am not sure if you were still looking for payment or if you had something else in mind. I mean is it safe?" Jim asked realizing that any answer he might get could be a complete fabrication.

"I'm a pussycat. It's safe. I may be in the market for something you have though. I just may need a loan, perhaps. We could discuss over dinner if you are willing too."

Jim arranged a dinner for an Italian restaurant near the Eiffel Tower. It would be an early dinner with lots of witnesses. Jenny and he walked by it the other night and commented "who would ever eat Italian while in Paris". That is how he knew the restaurant. He now knew the restaurant must be frequented by world spies who are pulling a 'sting' operation and have stumbled into a bigger plot that they are not sure what it is about. Must be a common thing, the restaurant was busy the other night, he thought to himself. Yuri and Jim finished the arrangements and both expressed they were looking forward to seeing each other again.

Shortly after Jim hung up the phone, Arthur walked in the door with a couple of sheets of paper in his hand "I have it. I have it." His whole distrust of Jim and Jenny seemed to be gone and he was excited about what he had found.

"Okay, what did you find out?" Jim asked as he shut the door that Arthur had left open.

Arthur laid out four sheets of paper on the bed. One had typing and three were pictures. "This" he said pointing to the first picture "is the original bank, or rather Des Moines Workers Savings and Loan, in Des Moines Iowa. No it is not a Swiss bank and no it never was. It did go under during the whole Savings and Loan problem years ago but its assets were purchased by Des Moines Savings Corp and it survived until the fire of 1998." Arthur pointed to another picture. "The safe survived, you can see it here. It was rebuilt around the same safe, no changes to the safe–made national news for probably 30 seconds. It has been bought and sold several times and is now owned by Bank of America." He pointed to the final picture. The paper had a brief history on it and the address and telephone number of the bank.

"Seems like a lot of info that doesn't seem to tell us anything." Jenny remarked.

"Yet," the professor chimed in, "every piece of data is just a piece of the puzzle. It all means something–just not yet."

"Well let me add to how we are going to try to solve another piece." Jenny continued. She explained to Arthur that they would get rid of the one plate. Arthur was not keen on this, he didn't want to lose the historical value that he hadn't deciphered yet. Jenny assured him that they were keeping the one plate and conceded to keep the paper that had the original markings copied down for the second. She also explained that Jim would likely purchase it back once whoever had the codes on the back gotten what they needed.

Arthur thought for a minute. "And they will try to stop killing me?"

"I can't promise that, but if they have the plate they are going to need you or one of the others who understand the code." Jenny paused for effect. "That is why we are taking you out of the country with us to Switzerland."

They talked for a little while longer while Jim freshened up. Arthur carefully put the one piece of paper into the casing and placed the plate into it. They carefully melted the edging to reseal the wax to the edge. It was a bit rudimentary but would fool anyone who hadn't examined it closely. Their hope was that whoever unsealed it would not notice or would just assume poor workmanship.

"If they get the code, aren't they just going to end up where we go in Switzerland?" Arthur expressed his concern. He was a little worried, but really anything to get rid of the plate seemed like a good idea to him.

"And I hope by then we will know what we can and are long gone." Jenny concluded.

CHAPTER 56 – THE DATE

The Italian restaurant was dimly lit. The décor was authentic and obviously created an ambiance that would attract tourist that were near the Eiffel Tower. The restaurant did not have as many patrons as Jim had hoped. However, there were enough for Jim to have a little comfort. As Jim entered the restaurant he was greeted and asked how many were in his party. Jim responded, "Reservation for Jim Smith. I am expecting to meet someone."

"Oh yes, the lovely lady has already been seated." Jim was led to a corner table that had no visible exits and only one clear site line to anywhere else in the restaurant. A perfect place for a murder, he thought.

Yuri stood, almost eye to eye. She looked striking, "You look great. I am impressed." Jim said to her as he was dazzled by how well she looked.

"It is a date." Yuri explained.

"Please sit." Jim pulled the chair out slightly and tried to be as gentleman-like as he could.

"I took the liberty of ordering a light before dinner wine and an appetizer. I hope you do not mind." Yuri told Jim as she took her seat.

"Thank you, that is thoughtful of you." Jim sat the bag he had onto the table. He had put it into a non-descript laundry bag from the hotel they were in earlier. "It is customary to bring a lady a gift on their first date. Sorry for the poor wrapping."

Yuri glanced inside the bag to see if the contents were what she had anticipated. "A loan, I suppose you mean."

"I collect rare books and writings, letters and things like that. One of my favorites is a great original by Ben Franklin. I am not sure I want this one. It seems to bring a lot of murder with it. I would also appreciate it if you kept the giver to yourself."

Yuri looked suspiciously at him. "Did you take it out of its casing?"

"Why? The professor said the casing was to protect it. He couldn't imagine why the first plate I purchased was out of the casing unless the previous owner was going to reseal it more professionally. Perhaps you know since you were the previous owner."

"That is how I got it. I can't speak to those before me." Yuri considered how much of what Jim was telling her was true and how much was a lie. She couldn't tell.

"I would like you to find me something unique sometime— it would keep Ricardo happy to get a commission." Jim said to hopefully entice an additional meeting with Yuri just in case the CIA needed it.

"I assure you that I will have something for you, perhaps I will even sell this back to you. I am curious though, how did you convince the professor to sell it?" Yuri had learned from a young age to ask questions to get little nuggets of information to build a profile to get what she wanted. Once, when she was in her early twenties, she kept asking an older gentleman who was about 40 years old questions that eventually revealed where the three million dollars' worth of jewelry was kept that belonged to his wife. In a drunken stupor, he even revealed the combination to the safe. Of course, Yuri's beauty and seductive charm also helped.

Jim didn't really want to say that the poor professor was just scared to death for his life and just gave the thing away so he told a plausible lie. "Well, $250,000 goes a long way for a professor who thinks his life is in jeopardy. He gladly took the money and I didn't have to promise him a date."

"And Dragos?" Yuri asked just to see how far she could push Jim.

"Dragos, we will settle with him later when he recovers a little."

Yuri looked at Jim. "Thanks for the gift. I do not know if I have ever had a date bring me something quite so nice and unique." She placed the bag next to her at the table and hit a few buttons on her phone. Then she said, "Let's order."

It was only a few minutes later when a waiter, not Yuri and Jim's, brought out breadsticks. He was a darker skinned individual, probably middle-eastern Jim surmised. After setting the bread down, he picked up the bag and left the restaurant. Yuri gestured assuring Jim that this was okay. Amir, without introductions, was off to a hotel to have Professor Alto look at the plate. Jim was sure he would be there until Yuri received confirmation that the plate was what was expected. Yuri responded in French and then turned to Jim, "What would you like Jim."

"I will have the lasagna with meat sauce and some 'still water'." The waiter had clearly understood because he had already written the order down but Yuri repeated the order in French for him.

Once the waiter was away Yuri asked. "How many languages do you speak?"

Jim responded, "As far as you know just one."

Yuri looked back into Jim's face, "You are truly an interesting character. You are not at all what I expected."

About halfway through the meal Yuri got a text that Jim surmised was a confirmation that the bronze plate was what was expected. He was right. However, she simply responded back to the text and didn't say a word. They enjoyed a meal that, for Paris, was extremely short. They were out of the restaurant in about an hour. Yuri suggested a short walk before they call it a night. Jim was surprised, he anticipated that she had what she came for and dinner would be it.

Walking towards the Eiffel tower, Jim assumed that he would get his second date to the Eiffel tower that week. He was surprised when Yuri instead took him to a side entrance of the Musee de l' Armee and was met by a security guard who let them in.

Yuri walked Jim through some of her favorite exhibits. She explained how warfare had changed through the years. She particularly liked some of the advances in espionage and how that had been around since the beginning of time. Once the highlights had been seen, they left through the same side door with the same security guard present.

Yuri came close to Jim and was near his face. "In my line of work it is sometimes difficult to date—always having to pretend like you are someone you are not. It sounds funny I know, I mean my job is pretending to be someone I am not. But tonight with you, I mean you know who I really am and what I really do." Her face was a little red and she almost seemed like a young girl on one of her first dates ever. "Well, I had a good time. Can we do it again sometime, not as payment but just as fun?" She leaned over and gave him a very short kiss, almost just a peck on his cheek.

Jim looked at her considering the irony. He normally lived a very mundane everyday normal life and was now pretending who he was. Who he was may have been false, but his words were sincere, "Stephanie, I have had a lot of fun. I would like another date sometime."

He gave her small kiss on the cheek and they each went their separate directions.

CHAPTER 57 – TRAIN TO ZURICH

The ride was smooth and the click-clack of the train cars gliding on the track was minimized. Jim thought how different this was than the Chicago Metro train that he would take downtown sometimes. Of course, the train downtown was a stop and go commuter train that traveled on a twisting and turning series of tracks. He wondered if Amtrak would be closer to this experience or his Chicago train experience. Trains were so much more utilized in Europe he surmised that this had to be better than anything he might find in the states on a track.

The sun was going down and the Alps could be seen on the horizon. Jenny intentionally waited to call Frank. She wanted to make sure they were well on their way so that Frank could not stop the trip. She would also avoid telling him where she was going just to keep the professor safe. Jenny slipped away from Jim and Arthur to find a private sleeping car to make the call.

Frank was pacing the floor by the time he got the call from Jenny. "Where have you been?" He didn't even wait for Jenny to say hello.

"Now Frank, I am on assignment and you don't get the luxury of regular check-ins. You have done this before and you know the drill. It is my call when it is good to check in and even what I tell you." Jenny explained.

Frank had never been an undercover agent himself, but he had been on the other side of the operation enough that he knew the protocol. "This is different and you know it. You have a civilian with you. I do not want Jim Conrad hurt and I don't want to jeopardize this mission."

Jenny believed both but wasn't even sure if Frank remembered Jim's real name. "Jim is fine. We are heading to Belgium to look at an old parchment written by Martin Luther–an individual collector has the piece. He is looking to sell it."

"Did Ricardo give you this contact?" Frank asked suspiciously. He knew Ricardo was on a plane or just barely off of the plane and it seemed unlikely they would have had time to communicate.

"I gave him a secure text number that he has given to a few of his colleagues so that he can have them contact us directly. So we are not sure who this is, but the person was recommended by Ricardo. I don't believe he is a criminal, just a private collector."

"Seems like a dead end for what we are trying to accomplish." Frank said impatiently.

Jenny just responded. We need to do a few meetings like this to keep up our appearance. If we only consider stuff from criminals then someone is going to get wise to what we are doing."

Frank seemed satisfied, "I suppose so. But if you have a chance to meet with additional people let's talk, especially if it is Yuri."

Jenny hoped she knew the answer but had to ask, "You lost the trail on Yuri?"

"She is elusive, but I am sure she will not pass up the opportunity to do business with Jim again. She seemed to take a liking to him." Frank thought for a moment. "So, do you want a team in Belgium just in case?"

Jenny considered just telling him the truth, but then she would have to explain why they were still with the professor. "That would be great. We will be just outside of Namur. Text me the contact info and I will know how to reach them if we get in a bind. We should be back in Paris by tomorrow evening."

CHAPTER 58 – RICARDO GOES HOME

Ricardo was not thrilled that his friend in the Paris Police Department had insisted that he leave the city for a few days until things settled down. He knew that he would need to be in the area for Jim. He did not relish spending a few days in the states and then getting back on a plane to go to Europe. It was a long flight. But it would be good to go to dinner with his wife and children to celebrate his birthday. It was one of the few times they would all get together and he did not like to miss those opportunities.

He dreaded customs in the US and especially in Chicago. It wasn't like he couldn't figure out a way to get something into the country. He could get just about anything he wanted into the country. It was just that it always took forever to get through customs. If he could figure out a way to influence that with his money and power, he would. However, he knew that if he tried it would probably draw undo attention to him. That would not be acceptable.

He waited to respond to his text and phone messages until he got into his limo taxi that would take him to his near north side home. There were a number of messages on various topics. Of note, the following messages were among them.

The first note was from Yuri, "Can you connect me with Jim?"

Next was a message from his daughter. "Glad to hear you are coming home. If you are not too tired, let's do breakfast at Walker Brother's."

Then there was a message from Steve, "Does your buyer like famous historical documents?"

The next message was from Jenny. "Surprised you left town. Is everything okay?"

The final message he received was from Yuri. "Connected with Jim for last part of the payment. We will do business again soon I am sure."

Ricardo was satisfied. Things were turning out just as he had hoped, taking out the shooting incident that left Dragos in the hospital. He called the hospital and they reported that he was stable and would likely have a full recovery. He knew that he would have to arrange for a change in name and a move to a new room so that Dragos could just disappear and not have to answer any questions. Then he could eventually leave the country unnoticed. He had already set the stage for these changes and made a quick call to confirm that they were underway.

Next he sent a text to his daughter. "I will be fine. In pretty early. Tomorrow at 9:00 AM will be great."

Ricardo called Jenny next. It was late in Europe but he felt that they needed an explanation. Jenny got the call almost as soon as she got back from talking to Frank. "Ric, everything go okay after we left you earlier today?"

"But of course. I just needed to leave town for a little while until things blow over. You are not involved in any way I assure you." Ricardo paused for a moment to hear a reaction. There was none. "In fact," he continued, "I have a present for you."

"Really, for me or Jim?" Jenny asked.

"It is for you. It is a bullet that I found that had no place where I found it." Ricardo explained.

"You are resourceful." Jenny exclaimed.

"In my line of work it is useful. I am lining up additional items. Ask Jim if he likes historical documents. I might be able to get one."

"I will do that." Jenny agreed.

"Let me know his thoughts. I will call tomorrow and if it makes sense can be back in Paris by the end of the week." Ricardo concluded.

Ricardo opted to call Yuri the next day because of the hour. He made several other calls including a quick note to Steve. He didn't like dealing with Steve, but this situation seemed to dictate a potential deal. Steve was shady, even for Ricardo. He was a left over contact from his father's time. But Steve was resourceful and was almost always a player.

It was not a mansion; it was a home that just fit well with the north side elite in Chicago. It was surrounded by similar houses, most of which were occupied by business and community leaders in the area. None of these homes were as secure and well watched as Ricardo's was.

He nodded at one of the guards as he made his way into the house. He couldn't help but wonder how Yuri had been so resourceful. He was sure that none of his staff or guards would have accepted a bribe and there was virtually no way someone could get on the grounds without being noticed. Now that he was home, this bothered him. He did not like to feel vulnerable.

As he walked in the house one of the servants indicated that his wife had gone to dinner with the two boys. He was thrilled to see the kitchen decorated with streamers and cards. There were two cards, one each from Ricky and Victor's families. He read each of them in turn. There was a big one from his daughter Mary's family. Finally, there was a card from his wife, Juanita. He carefully read it. At the bottom his wife's card it read. "Open the freezer, from all of us."

Ricardo had a full size freezer and a full size refrigerator in his spacious kitchen. Opening the door, the only thing in the freezer was container after container after container of Butter Pecan Ice Cream, his favorite. A small note was taped to one of the containers; "Happy Birthday." It was signed by his wife and each of the children.

Each year they had done something unique to celebrate his birthday; this was one of the more creative things they had done. He knew that he would not eat all of it, but got out a container and dished himself a bowl of ice cream.

Walking to the other room, around and through the streamers, he noticed a note next to his electronic digital photo frame. He had hundreds of pictures on this thing and it took forever to cycle through. Of course his wife and daughter would add new ones at their whim. He had one of the servants just choose some from the computer and keep it up to date—that way the servant could make sure that he didn't inadvertently delete a picture that his wife or daughter had added.

Ricardo picked up the note next to the electronic picture frame.

"Daddy,

I added a few pictures for you. Guess which ones. Also, I didn't know you knew Jacob and who is that woman with him? I haven't seen him with another woman since his wife died. Anyway, I also have a video of your granddaughter taking a few steps that I left on your computer. Go watch it sometime.

Love, Mary"

Ricardo was not sure what she was talking about. He didn't know a Jacob. For now, he was tired from the trip and ready to relax. So he skipped looking for his daughter's pictures, what she meant by Jacob, and looking at the PC to see his granddaughter walk. He could do all this later. Instead, he sat in his favorite brown leather chair and turned on ESPN. There was a re-run of a Cubs game on TV that he started to watch as he ate his ice cream. He fell asleep before he finished the game or the ice cream.

Thursday
Europe

CHAPTER 59 – EARLY MORNING IN PARIS

By the next morning in Paris, Inspector Pierre was well past the events in the hotel from the day before. He had a homicide in an alley way to deal with. It appeared as though one of the local youth gangs must have killed and robbed a professor from Cairo. He had seen similar murders in the past. It was rare, but usually occurred when the victim resisted just giving the money to the hoodlums. This was all speculation because there was no real evidence left at the scene. He couldn't help but wonder about the irony of two murders in his city and both murders were of visitors to the city.

Yuri slept well once she got to sleep the night before. It was a late night waiting for a final translation and now that she had it, she was ready for what was anticipated being a very eventful day. Her first call was to the Captain, "I have it."

"You have the plate?" The Captain asked anticipating the news.

"I have the plate and the translation." Yuri said emphasizing the word "translation". She knew that the Captain would want to avoid meeting her until the business was complete. But she would not allow that to happen. As soon as she gave up the plate and the translation then her leverage was over. She would carry both with her until her curiosity was satisfied.

"Good, you can sell the plate as we discussed and get the translation to me. I will call you later to tell you where to drop off the translation so I can pick it up." The Captain instructed.

"You know that is not how it will happen." Yuri corrected. "I have a room reserved at the Palace of Versailles. I booked the room under Captain Hook. Ask at the front desk. I will be there at 10 this morning and come alone." She hung up not waiting for an answer.

CHAPTER 60 – USB IN DOWNTOWN SWITZERLAND

Downtown Zurich is a bustling clean city that has a beautiful lake at its edge. The pictures of the Alps and the city at the base do not do justice for the beauty that is the city itself. The stereotypes about cleanliness and punctuality are very well founded in the reality of the city. Jim and Jenny walked right along the lake to get to the bank. They were not in a hurry, decided to just enjoy a leisurely walk.

Jim and Jenny went to the bank without the professor. If things got complicated, they wanted to be able to escape with just the two of them. It was a risk, but they had to take it. Arriving at the bank at nearly 10:00 AM, Jenny asked for Fritz Kohler. Fritz was the banker that Jenny had worked with in the past. He was the banker assigned to Jim Conrad and handled all of his affairs at this bank, his personal banking advisor. He had a number of other accounts, but his primary responsibility was to keep Mr. Conrad satisfied.

"He will be in later today but I can have one of our other bankers help you." The person at the desk said. He brought up Gretchen who introduced herself and offered assistance. "I am

Jenny and usually do the business on behalf of Jim Conrad. This is Jim."

Gretchen verified the account information and realized who she was talking to, "Mr. Conrad, I am so sorry, come with me." She led him to a private room. As she walked she also motioned for someone to come over. Quietly she whispered that Fritz needed to be contacted at once. He should be told to come in at once because his account member was here in person, Mr. Jim Conrad. Once in the room she asked, "How can I help you Mr. Conrad or would you like to wait for Herr Fritz Kohler?"

"You can call me Jim and I am fine with your help. Fritz does fine work, but in this matter I believe you can probably assist me." Jim said it with confidence and poise.

"I will do what I can Herr, I mean Jim." Gretchen responded respectfully.

"I have found an old routing number and account number among my family's personal items. I would just like to determine if it belongs to me or someone else." Jim asked.

"Can I have the routing number?" Gretchen asked anxious to provide whatever help she could.

Jim wrote the routing number on a piece of paper and handed it to Gretchen. She stepped to a computer terminal and typed a few things on the computer. She seemed a little frustrated. She stepped out to go see if she could find someone who might know the answer. It took a few minutes but Gretchen came back into the room and had the name of a small private Swiss bank that was located on the edge of Zurich. It had one location and had been in business for nearly 250 years. Gretchen offered to connect him by phone but Jim and Jenny indicated that they would go visit the bank directly. "Just tell him to call Fritz or myself at USB if they have any questions or you have any issues. I will post Fritz on our conversation."

"I appreciate your help." Jim answered politely taking Gretchen's business card.

Gretchen walked them to the door. They caught Fritz as he was on the way in. Gretchen had to introduce them. He had dealt with Jenny but never met her. He had never even talked to Jim before. Fritz looked at Jenny. "Good to meet you in person, how are you Jenny?"

"Good to finally meet the person I speak to so often also. I am doing well. How are you?" Jenny responded.

"Oh, just fine. The grandchildren are sick but hopefully they will be over that soon." Fritz indicated.

"Including Harriet, the baby?" Jenny asked.

"She was spared. We are glad of that. What can I help you with?"

"Gretchen helped us, but I am glad to have finally met you in person and that you were able to meet Jim." Jenny assured Fritz.

"All right. Come back when you can and we can talk further." Fritz offered.

Jenny agreed. They shook hands and thanked Gretchen. Jim expressed his appreciation for the work that Fritz put in on his behalf. "Well, it is my job and I enjoy it very much." Fritz said with a sense of pride.

Jim and Jenny were then on their way to the next bank.

After getting the basic information from Gretchen, he once again left the bank. Instead of going back to his previous engagement he stopped at a park bench and made a phone call reporting the visit of Jim and Jenny to the bank to his contact at the CIA. It was very early in the AM in Maryland, so Frank's boss thanked Fritz for the information. He decided that Frank might already know this and if he didn't, it could wait until the morning, morning in Maryland that is.

CHAPTER 61 – PALACE OF VERSAILLES

The majestic Palace of Versailles is visited by millions every year. King Louis XIV turned it into a royal palace in the 1860's. It is a cultural center piece on the edge of Paris. The rich history includes being a home to royalty and the place where dignitaries meet to discuss world events including surrender conditions of superpowers. However, before Louis XIV, it started as a small château used for hunting.

Yuri was once again using this extravagant château to hunt. This time it was primarily a hunt for more information on her past. For this she intended to use the Captain. She disguised herself with a new hair color and clothes that she would not normally wear. She knew that by the end of the conversation, if she was not satisfied with the information provided the Captain would be dead.

Yuri positioned herself at the end of a long table. There were only two chairs. A glass of water was placed at each end of the table. She faced the main door, one of two exits from the room. She ensured that the one behind her was secured from the inside. She would see the Captain as he walked in. The bronze plate was placed at the opposite end of the table from her. The translation was on top of the plate. These were really insignificant items in her mind. She figured out that the numbers were likely tied to a bank account and the other numbers were coordinates. What they meant was more important to the Captain than to her. All these years she was pretty sure she knew who killed her parents and how they were killed. However, she never knew the "why". It might not bring her satisfaction but it would complete the picture. The Captain might provide insight into this.

Yuri sat for almost 45 minutes, then at precisely 10:00 AM the door opened and a tall slender man walked into the door. He looked like he was in his late forties or perhaps even fifty. He did not make his way around the table. It was clear by the set-up that there was no expectation of a formal handshake. But he introduced himself in a clear and distinguished voice. "Hello, I am the Captain."

Yuri had intently listened every time she spoke to the Captain and listened to each inflection in his voice. He was clearly American. This voice was clearly American but it was not as raspy as the man she had spoken to. Both voices were experienced, maybe sounding a little "used" or "old" but there was a difference. She was convinced this was not the man on the phone. "You are not the Captain. My agreement was to talk to the Captain, not some carbon knockoff.

The man sat down. "I am not the man you have been talking to, he works for me. But I am the Captain and I am the one you want to talk to."

Yuri was not convinced. However, she sat down anyway. She had mounted a gun under the table and put her finger on the trigger just in case she didn't like what she heard. "All right, you have my payment in front of you. What do you know about my parents?"

The man picked up the bronze plate and examined it. Then he picked up the paper. Yuri pulled a second gun and pointed it across the table. "Set the paper down, upside down. You owe me some information first."

The man placed the paper upside down and looked across the table. Yuri placed her gun on the table and looked at the man. He spoke. "Stephanie, the first thing you may not know is that the man you knew as your father is not your real father. He married your mother shortly before you were four."

"You are lying. I have seen the records." Yuri said emphatically.

"It is easy to forge a birth record and the parent's name. The marriage record you have seen is a duplicate online record. If you go to the actual courthouse you can see the real marriage date." The Captain replied.

Gaining her composure, she continued. "Okay, but he was my father. Why was he killed and did Jim Conrad the senior have anything to do with my parent's death?"

"Your parents were both spies." The man explained.

"I know that." Yuri said a little impatiently.

"Yes, but what you do not know." The man pulled a gun and aimed it at her before she could grab her gun from the table. "What you do not know is that the man you knew as your father was Jim Conrad."

As his sentence was finishing a quick and quiet whistling sound could be heard from under the table. The silencer insured that the visitors outside of the room would not be disturbed. And the shot caught the man off guard. He was not able to get off a shot himself. Yuri quickly gathered the plate and the translation. She knew that the man probably would have someone in momentarily. She grabbed her two guns and made her way out the back door.

Inspector Pierre would now have another random non-Frenchman homicide to investigate.

CHAPTER 62 – AMIR

Yuri made her way to a nearby church where she could just clear her mind. Her internal debate was whether she should pursue the information that was on the plate or should go figure out if her parents were married when she was four and if so who was her real father. Might she have a parent she never knew about? As she used her phone to do a little research, she realized where the coordinates that had been translated would lead. It was in the same town where her parents had been married. As she researched the history of the bank at those coordinates she found that it was once the "Des Moines Workers Savings and Loan" or "DMW S&L" for short. The connection between the three letters on her necklace (DMW) and the bank seemed strong. What she would do next was becoming clearer to her. It was not long after this realization that her phone rang. "This is the Captain. You still have something I want."

"I gave your other Captain a chance to get it until he pulled a gun on me." Yuri said with disgust.

"That was not authorized. He had a personal issue with your step-father." The Captain explained.

Yuri knew that this was too well orchestrated. This was the Captain executing his contingency plan in case something went wrong with her execution. She continued. "Maybe so, but the price has increased. I want ten million Euro in cash and additional information. And as a show of good faith I want the answer to one question now."

"I can agree to that. But what assurance do I have that you will keep your part of the bargain?" The Captain asked.

"You don't have any. But if your information is useful, then I will want to talk to you again." Yuri teased the Captain.

"Deal. What is your question?" The Captain asked.

"Who is my biological father?" Yuri asked.

"I know the answer to that. But that is an important piece of information that will get you to come back and talk to me. I will tell you this though, he is already dead."

"All right. I will call with arrangements later today. And I better get you and not another knockoff. I won't talk at all this time unless it is you."

Yuri called Amir. "Amir. I am going to the states. I need you to wait here and help track down the Captain for me."

Amir listened intently as she explained her plan to set an appointment with the Captain. He may or may not be the one to attend but when she didn't show, Amir could follow him and figure out who he really was. Amir could use their entire network of connections in Paris if necessary to track the Captain. She hoped to be back to Paris to deal with the Captain within a couple of days. Amir assured Yuri that he would not let her down.

Yuri changed her appearance once again and changed her identity. Then she left immediately for the airport.

Amir picked up the phone. "Hello, do you know who this is?"

The Captain answered, "Do you have information for me?" Amir explained to the Captain the extent of Yuri's plan. "Amir, I will need the copy of the translation you made."

"She will know that it was from me. You will protect my family?" Amir asked.

"I am surprised your family is even a concern for you. But yes, we will keep them safe." The Captain continued. "This is the time. I do not cherish losing the direct connection with Stephanie, but this information is more vital now. It will complicate things a little."

Amir understood and made arrangements to get the information to the Captain.

CHAPTER 63 – A SMALL SWISS BANK

After a brisk walk, Jim and Jenny agreed that they would take a taxi to the bank instead of walking. They did not mind the walk, but the distance was a little unclear and they were anxious to understand this mystery. It only took a few moments to hail a taxi.

The taxi dropped them in front of what appeared to be a medium size house. Jim and Jenny felt they might just be walking into someone's front door and not a bank. The driver insisted this was the appropriate address and then finally gave his personal cell phone number in case he had to come back to get them. The yard was nicely manicured and the walkway very picturesque. There were businesses around and a few other structures that looked like houses. This was not downtown Zurich, but it was not residential either. As they reached the front door there was a small brass plate that indicated it was the bank they were looking for. Jim and Jenny were relieved to see that.

Walking in the door, there was a foyer with a desk in the middle. A staircase led to the next floor. The edge of a kitchen could be seen behind the foyer. There were two private rooms that could be used for consultation and another two that were offices. An older lady behind the desk asked in German, then French, then Italian and finally English if she could help them. She managed to ask in all four languages before she received an answer.

Jim explained in English, "I have an account I would like to access."

She answered in only English. "Let me take you to one of the bankers to assist you."

She stood up and led them to one of the offices. A younger gentleman stood from behind a desk and greeted Jim and Jenny. "I am Hans."

Jim explained again, "I have an account I would like to access. I am not sure it is mine, but the number was with my family papers and I just want to make sure the rightful owner has the information."

Hans assured Jim that the security features would only allow the appropriate person to access the account and that he might not be able to provide information on the account if it did not belong to him. He then asked for the name and account number. Jim provided his own name, not knowing what other name he should give, and the account number. Hans perked up immediately. "James Conrad, it is my privilege to meet you. I will need to verify who you are first. I hope you understand."

Jenny asked first. "The account belongs to Jim?"

"The account is Jim Conrad's account and that is the appropriate number. As I said, we will need to verify that you are the Jim Conrad that owns this account." Hans explained.

Jim and Jenny were both surprised the account was in his name but just decided to play along. Jim said as he started to reach for his passport. "Sure, I have my passport. What else do you need?"

"Per our policy, I will need to check you DNA." Hans interjected.

Jim looked confused and was a little worried. "You can validate who I am by calling my banker over at USB. I am sure he would come over here if needed."

"It will not take long. I already have sent a message to have a nurse come over. She will be here shortly. Do not worry; this is standard practice for the first time you come into the bank in person and subject to spot checking after that. We have been doing this since the early 1980's." Hans tried to be reassuring but even he could tell Jim was nervous. "It is a simple needle prick, perfectly safe. We used very advanced techniques that provide quick results."

Jenny looked at the banker, "I am his business manager and I do not recall Jim ever giving a DNA sample."

"I can look it up while we wait. We keep pretty good records." Hans typed on the computer and turned the monitor so that Jim and Jenny could also see. "We even have a video of getting the DNA from you. I remember hearing about this. Perhaps you do not like needles so they took the DNA while you were already out? If we need a more extensive medical team I can arrange that."

Jim stood dumbfounded as he watched a nurse take several DNA samples from his hair, mouth, skin and blood as he lay unconscious. Jenny asked Hans to step out for a moment so she could talk to Jim. Hans agreed. They needed to wait for the nurse anyway.

"Jim, what is this? I don't recall this ever happening and I was in on the planning of this for over a year. Your name didn't come up until just about two weeks ago as playing this role."

"Jenny, this is footage from when I had my appendix out over five years ago. This is several years before my wife and kids died. My second child was not even born when I had my appendix out. I don't understand."

Jenny continued. "It means that the DNA will match. But it also means that this was the operation all along and I did not know it."

They motioned for Hans to come back into the room. Jim started, "I was a little queasy but am fine now." Hans was not sure what "queasy" meant but understood "fine now".

While waiting for the nurse, Jenny continued to ask questions– a little surer they would pass the DNA test but a lot less sure of why they would pass. "So, when do you take the DNA sample? I mean how did you make sure Jim was Jim when you took the sample?"

"I cannot answer that directly for Jim until we have completed the validation. I hope you understand, we try to protect our clients in every way." Hans explained.

"I understand, but in general how do you do it." Jenny asked.

"It is the beauty of the DNA test now. We give one when the account is opened and then we have a true lineage of the owner. If someone gets an account number through fraud or deceit, the account integrity is protected by matching the DNA to the account. If an owner forgets his or her account number then the DNA is the best proof of ownership. It also helps on survivorship of an account. Of course, legal documents can trump this sometimes, but according to the account when opened there is a clear line of succession. If it is by 'bloodline' which is almost always the case after a spouse then this ensures no fraud." Hans seemed pleased with the measures as he explained them.

"Okay, but what about accounts opened before the 1980's." Jenny pressed.

"We had to do extensive work to collect everyone's DNA at the time. The science was still new and there were skeptics at first. But getting the DNA that early provided the integrity we needed. We still have a few accounts not converted to the DNA standard, but that is a very low percentage even with the few clientele we maintain."

It was enough information for now, but there still was not a connection that could be made. Jim certainly had not opened an account and it seemed unlikely that Jim could have been part of a plan 5 years earlier. Yet, somehow he was. Jenny kept it to small talk until the nurse arrived.

It took less than 15 minutes to validate that the Jim Conrad standing in the room was indeed the authentic account holder. He was present in person, had a valid passport, knew the account number and passed the DNA test. Hans had now met the account holder of one of the most prestige's accounts at the bank.

Hans invited them into one of the conference rooms. There were a few computers and a large flat screen TV that could display information on the screen from the computer. "Per the account instructions, we have managed your account and sent updates to the prescribed email account. You understand that you have one primary account with us, but we manage an entire portfolio that includes other accounts around the world."

"That makes sense." Jim interjected not really knowing what to say or even what to expect.

"Would you like to review your assets, Jim?" Hans continued.

Jim was a little excited, even though he knew the money wasn't really his. He had always dreamed of being a multi-millionaire. He kind of got that when he took on the persona of Jim Conrad, but this bank believed that was who he really was and would probably write him a check if he asked for it. "Yes, let's see the summary."

The screen filled with an historical chart that went back to the mid 1980's. It trended up considerably over the years. There was a small ledger that listed cash assets, business assets, assets held at other institutions and liabilities on the left side of the screen. Jim looked, "That is a lot of dollars." Jim exclaimed.

Hans looked at Jim. "You have my sincere apologies sir. Those are not US dollars, those were in British pounds." He hit a button and the amounts were instantly changed to US dollars. "Of course this does not include the items in the vault or the safety deposit box."

The amount was updated real time based on interest and changing stock prices. Jim read an amount, once liabilities were removed. The account value was somewhere near $92 billion US dollars.

CHAPTER 64 – THE AFTERSHOCK

It took a few minutes for the shock to wear off. "You have done a fine job of managing my portfolio." Jim said almost indifferent to what he had just seen.

"I can show you some trends. There were a few years where we did not do so well. I apologize for that. Overall, though, I believe we outperformed just about any measure." Hans was pleased he was the one at the bank to meet and share the information in person with Jim.

"So, what is the account history?" Jenny asked.

"It looks like the account has been out there since the late 1970's. It was opened by your father, James Conrad, with a considerable amount of money. Let's see." Hans was going through different computer screens that meant almost nothing to Jim or Jenny. It was nomenclature in German and was abbreviated. Hans continued. "You inherited the account from your father. A few years after his death a woman came claiming to be his wife. She had all of the correct paperwork showing that his entire estate should go to her. She even knew about the email account. She did not know the account number. However, there was an even bigger issue for her, your father wanted the account given only to his child – you."

"So he died just a few years ago?" Jenny asked.

"No, he died in the late 1980's. He had arranged an email account before they were wide spread. We eventually got a response back from the email that stated where to send account status. It indicated where and when we could get your blood. We took your blood and validated that you were indeed his son. Then we documented you as the account owner. You became the sole heir to his fortune. I guess it is fortunate for you that you found the account information. Perhaps your mother or stepmother can explain–whoever gets the email."

"Do you have a picture of the woman, she came in didn't she?" Jenny asked hoping for additional clues.

Hans looked at some info on the tape and then switched to a different system where he proceeded to go through a serious of picture until he pulled up one. "According to when she came in and our security system at the time, this would be her."

Jenny didn't say a word, nor did Jim. But they drew the conclusion at the same time–it was Heidi that had assisted them from Interpol on the sting operation. Jenny knew that it meant Frank might be in trouble and this whole operation may be a farce for an even larger agenda. She knew that Frank volunteered for this assignment; the real question was who decided this was the operation to have in the first place.

"Where are the vault and the safety deposit box?" Jim asked while Jenny continued to contemplate their predicament.

"The vault has been with a bank in the UK for many years. It is small like this one. We keep track of it as one of your assets. It is at a very specialized bank that secures interesting items. It was donated to your father by a James Timmons shortly after your father opened his account here. The safety deposit box is in the back. He came in about a month before his death and opened that box. It looks like he also transferred nearly $25 billion dollars into the asset pool of this account. That is when he added you to his account as the sole heir also."

"I do not have a key, can you access the box?" Jim asked.

"Oh they are not locked. They are in a vault and it is locked, but the boxes are basic. I assure you the contents are confidential. I can bring yours out." Hans offered.

"Please." Jim responded. Hans left the room. Jim was just waiting to say something. "Jenny, I guess I really am rich."

Jenny looked at him. "I would think you could walk out of here with the money and nobody would even know—except the ones who are really after it right now."

"Who is that?" Jim was almost scared to ask. This little adventure had all of the sudden become personal. He thought he knew his father. He grew up with the man who claimed to be his father. The man he called father had married his mother when she was pregnant with him. Now to find out that his father was someone else.

Jenny looked at him. "This whole mission was a set-up. I just don't know by whom." This was a lot of money and whoever was orchestrating the effort would soon be coming after them. "We will have to find a way to shake some trees to find out who is behind this. They will come after us."

Jim looked a little disturbed by what he was about to suggest. "Okay, you're my financial manager, but the best way to find out who it is would be to move the money they want further out of their reach."

"I think you may be right." Jenny said just as the banker walked back into the door.

"As you say in America, the customer is always right." Hans commented realizing that perhaps it might have come across as listening in on the conversation.

Hans handed the closed box to Jim and started to turn for the door. Jenny stopped him. "Hans, you do not need to leave. We would like to make a few changes to the account."

Hans turned, his face turning a bit pale. He looked a little worried. Often changes meant that the account would move someplace else. Jenny continued. "We would like to move all of our assets and account history to a new primary account at this bank. I am concerned that we have compromised the account ourselves. It would also provide a way for us to potentially figure out who has been monitoring the account without informing Jim. We can leave the old account open with only, say $100 in it."

"That is an unacceptably low amount for one of our accounts, but in your instance I believe we can make it work." Hans said. "Should I have the occasional deposits transferred out as well?"

"Who is making deposits?" Jenny asked instinctively.

"The only influx of money, besides the growth in the portfolio, comes from an anonymous deposit into one of your Cayman Island accounts. It is then transferred here until we decide how to reinvest."

"Yes, let's move that to the new account also." Jenny asked.

Jim called Arthur at the hotel just to let him know they would be back soon.

Hans set up the new account, explained how it would work and provided Jim and Jenny with a password they could use for limited transactions over the phone. He agreed to send an update to the email address indicating the new balance. Jenny took a few minutes to create a new g-mail account and asked that the updates for the new account be sent to jimconrad2@gmail.com as well as any pictures of anyone who came to the bank inquiring about the old account. Jenny also withdrew enough cash to keep them going for a while.

Jim found time to gather the contents of the safety deposit box. It was a single item. He wouldn't tell Jenny until they left the bank even though she kept trying to get an indication of what it was. As they walked out the bank towards the taxi Jim pulled out a key with distinct markings on it "DMW" and a hand written piece of paper with the same coordinates as were found on the back of the plate. He then said. "I think I know where we are going next."

Jenny looked at him. "Where?"

"What do you think of Iowa?"

CHAPTER 65 – THE LIE

"What are you doing in Switzerland? I have a team in Belgium in case you need help and you are in Switzerland." Frank was furious with Jenny and called just moments after he had received a call from Tom, his boss at Langley, letting him know that one of their operatives at USB had been in contact with Jenny and Jim directly.

Jenny and Jim were in the taxi and she couldn't be as direct as she wanted. "I felt it was a good idea for Jim to meet his banker in person so we changed our travel plans." Jenny was not at all happy with the phone call, Frank was not supposed to call her number unless it was an extreme emergency – too much of a chance that their cover might be blown.

"When you are done, do you plan to come back to Paris?"

"We are going to have dinner and then head to the train station to go to Paris." Jenny knew that it would not be the case and she wanted to warn Frank about Heidi but this was not the time or the place. She would call from the airport–either Zurich or across the pond.

CHAPTER 66 – NEW ARRANGEMENTS

Professor Arthur Borden was not given a complete explanation. He knew it and it bothered him. He was told the account belonged to some criminals and that their best approach was to just leave it alone. Jenny assured the professor that they would find him a safe home in the area and would contact him when they were sure he was safe. His only consolation was he could keep the plate and paper while he waited. He was warned to not try researching anything online or contacting others until this thing blew over. It was a warning that they did not need to give. Jenny arranged a quick call to his children so they knew he was safe.

Jenny called Ricardo who was very pleased to hear from his new friends. She called for a favor, "Of course, what can I help you with?"

Jenny explained that they wanted out of the country and needed a "different" identity so that they would not be tracked. They also needed a safe place for Arthur to hide out. Ricardo was happy to oblige and within the hour had someone at the hotel assisting with proper documentation. It was expensive, but at this moment money was not an object. Professor Borden was given new credentials just in case he needed them. The forger would also become Arthur's new friend and his place to hide out for a while.

Jenny and Jim, with their new identities, made their way to the Zurich airport.

CHAPTER 67 – THE GATHERING

Amir was greeted at the hotel room door by Heidi. "The Captain is inside."

Amir walked into a spacious hotel room, larger than most for a downtown Paris room. There was the Captain sitting in a wing backed chair with an oxygen tank next to him. He did not have to use it, but it certainly made breathing easier, especially after a cigarette. The ash tray was full but the Captain did not have a cigarette lit at this moment.

"Sit down Amir, let's chat." The Captain said.

Amir made his way to the couch that was near the chair. He pulled a piece of paper out and handed it to the Captain.

Heidi asked Amir as she sat down next to him "Are you sure it is correct, Professor Alto was able to translate it."

"I am sure. Now where can we move my family?" Amir said almost demanding.

"Do you think she will even be a factor anymore? She has served her purpose." The Captain responded afterwards taking a gulp of oxygen.

"She will find out and she will come after you and she will come after me. She is very resourceful."

"I can imagine she would be more interested in you than in us. It was, after all, you that arranged the death of her parents." The Captain said directly.

"Yes, at their request." Amir pleaded almost to himself for a crime he committed and had never forgiven himself for. He never knew why, but when the Captain approached him those many years ago and told him that he knew everything that happened Amir panicked and agreed to watch over Yuri and then to eventually betray her to save his own skin and that of his family.

The conversation was interrupted by the vibrating of the Captain's phone and at almost the same time Heidi's phone. It had a distinctive beep that caused each of them to immediately reach for their phone.

It was an email message that might have just saved Amir's life but he would not know that or the contents of the message. The Captain looked at Amir and told him to get out. They would contact him later.

He didn't question the Captain's word. He had seen that look on Yuri before and knew that it was time just to do what he was told. After the door shut behind Amir, The Captain looked up at Heidi reciting the email from memory. He spoke the words slowly to Heidi to emphasize each syllable.

"Dear Mr. James Conrad,

We appreciate your continued business with us. Your recent withdrawal brings your new portfolio balance to $100. We will provide our typical asset summary at the end of the month."

The Captain's phone rang as did Heidi's. After each having a brief conversation, The Captain said, "It has to be Jim. No one else could access the account. You need to get to the bank and pull their security tapes. I don't care how much protection they have. You must confirm who accessed the account."

Heidi responded, "I can do better than that. I work for Interpol and my American friends have told me that Jim and Jenny were seen with a wanted man, Professor Arthur Borden. I can put out an all-points bulletin to bring them in. Every law enforcement agency in Europe will be looking for them."

"Brilliant. That should get them in much quicker." The Captain said anxiously.

"I will still make a trip by the bank to confirm it was Jim and to see if Yuri is also involved. I am not sure where he would have acquired the account number otherwise."

"Yuri and Jim working together, wouldn't that be ironic?" The Captain concluded.

CHAPTER 68 – FRANK TALKS TO JENNY

Finding a quiet place within an airport to make a call without it being evident that you are standing in an airport is not an easy task. Jim and Jenny finally paid an enormous fee to get into a first class business lounge for one of the airlines. Inside the lounge were several small and nearly soundproof rooms. Sophisticated equipment might pick up the background noises but she was just calling Frank. He wouldn't feel the need to monitor and evaluate the call to that level of detail.

Frank did not waste any time. "Are you someplace you can talk?"

"Yes, it is fairly secure." That was the best way for her to assure Frank that the location was random enough that someone wouldn't be recording her conversation but had not been checked for bugs or other listening devices.

"Are you on your way to Paris like we agreed?" Frank sounded like he was angry and firm all at the same time.

"Frank, things have changed." Jenny started to explain.

Frank would not let her finish. "Yes, Interpol has decided to put you on a watch list and as someone wanted in questioning."

"For what?" Jenny asked in disbelief. But she realized the reason and figured out who had likely put them on the list even before Frank answered.

"For harboring a fugitive, you were seen with Professor Arthur Borden." Frank continued.

"He is hardly a fugitive. That aside, I would bet it was Heidi who issued the bulletin." Jenny continued.

"Why would you say that?" Frank asked.

"She is a crook, a thief or something. She is part of this whole thing." Jenny said.

"What whole thing are you talking about?" Frank pushed.

"This whole operation is a front for a petty theft or rather a large theft." Jenny threw it out now. Frank would have to delve into that comment.

"You mean our operation is a farce. I don't think so. We have a legitimate plan to track and capture the arms dealers to terrorist. We have already connected with one of the biggest and most elusive, Yuri." Frank explained.

Jenny now had to give more information than she wanted to, but she needed Frank's help. It would put him in jeopardy also. "Jeez Frank. Jim Conrad had a real bank account with billions. Our Jim is the only one that could access it because he is the real Jim Conrad's son—they know that because of DNA testing. Jim was a real person and we have been played into thinking he is a fictitious character."

"Are you saying this whole operation is a front for a robbery?" Frank concluded and asked in the same breath. And thinking about Jenny's words, specifically 'had an account' he continued. "And you said he had an account, does that mean it no longer exists?"

"I am not only saying this is major theft, but that there has to be a mole in the agency, someone who helped orchestrate this entire event." Jenny said.

"I get it. You really should come in. We can figure this out when we get you and Jim safe. Putting him at risk is not fair. Besides, if there is a mole and you are a wanted criminal. It might look like you were guilty."

Jenny had considered her options and was fairly certain that it was more dangerous coming in not knowing who the mole was than staying on the run. Besides, Interpol could look all they wanted, in less than an hour she would be out of their jurisdiction on the way to the states. "I can't come in. With the mole, it isn't safe. But you can help."

Frank concluded in his mind that her logic was sound. He didn't like it, but in a similar situation he would do the same. He knew that it was fruitless to argue with her about it. "How can I help?"

"You can find out what you can about Jim's family or shall I say Jacob's family. Really both. You can create a short list of potential moles in the agency." Jenny explained.

"Your name and my name will be on that list, you understand." Frank knew that he had to approach it analytically and consider all possibilities even if it some were absurd. "What will you do?"

Jenny responded. "There is a vault in the UK that belongs to Jim Conrad. There might be answers there. Also, Professor Borden is knee high in this thing. Perhaps we can find more about his connection in the UK. But pretty much we will keep a low profile, incognito you know."

"Incognito huh, that is pretty much how Jim Conrad has been his whole life." Frank concluded.

Then Jenny added, "Frank, Heidi is in on it. I know that for a fact and have proof. She is a connection. Find out who she might know at the agency. And watch yourself."

Frank's simple response, "Take care of Jim. He is your responsibility. Be careful and check in frequently."

Jenny hung up feeling that her options were limited within the agency. She had spent so much time in the field she did not know or understand the politics at Langley or even many of the players. Frank would have to push that end. Jim and she would have to move forward with the Iowa connection and hope that led to some answers.

CHAPTER 69 – HEIDI

Heidi paced the floor vigorously as she tried to convince the banker at the small Swiss bank that there was a warrant out for the arrest of three fugitives. She wanted to pound her phone against the desk but then she figured she would lose the connection. She explained that at least one, a male, was seen entering their bank and she just needed confirmation. The banker refused to share any information without an order from a Swiss court. This, of course, would never happen.

Heidi knew that she could strong arm him, if not through pressure with her title but by literally putting a gun to his head, if she were there in person. But there was no way she would make it to Zurich before the bank closed. Tomorrow the trail would be cold.

The Captain sat on the couch sending text messages and looking at his laptop on occasion. He sent one to Heidi. When Heidi finally resolved that she would not get anywhere with the banker she just hung up.

The Captain said, "Get people to the Bank of America in Des Moines as soon as possible and send plenty. We better go also."

Heidi looked at him and asked. "Iowa?"

"Yes." The Captain said with certainty.

"Which branch? Why?" Heidi continued.

"You have the address. I sent you a text with it. Part of the message had coordinates on it. This bank is at these coordinates. I am sure Jim and maybe Yuri will be heading there now."

"You don't think the vault in London?" Heidi asked.

"I already have tickets booked for three to Chicago. Let's go to Iowa." The Captain responded quickly.

"Who is the third person?" Heidi inquired.

"Our Yuri insurance policy." The Captain said. Heidi knew exactly what he meant.

CHAPTER 70 - INSURANCE

Amir sat in the hotel bar taking a drink. His religion did not allow such a thing, but he had given up that tenant long ago. However, while he was home with his wife, his living child and his grandchildren he observed abstinence from alcohol. He also observed some of the most adherent Islamic customs and pretty much all other moderate Islamic customs.

He had not even returned to his own hotel for the drink. He was still in the lobby of the Captain's hotel when Heidi called to meet with him. "It is an easy walk, I am downstairs." Amir responded.

After hanging up Amir quickly came to his senses. He called his wife while he went out the front door. The abrupt ending to his meeting and the quick call back meant nothing but trouble. He quickly told his wife to execute their emergency plan. She was frantic but they had discussed that in his line of work the family needed a safe house and emergency plan. In Lebanon, it was fairly easy to find a place to not be found. Amir was fairly certain that she would be safe.

He was not as convinced about himself. Hailing a taxi seemed to be too slow, so he headed for the nearby Metro station. He had a pass and was certain he could hop one of the trains before Heidi figured out where he was at.

Heidi observed the bar and did not see Amir any place. She immediately asked the front desk attendant if she had seen a Middle Eastern man recently. She pointed out the front of the hotel. Heidi immediately exited the hotel and saw Amir heading down the stairs of the Metro.

She pursued vigorously after him. She did not have a ticket handy but just jumped the gate flashing her Interpol badge to the attendant. Amir caught a glimpse of Heidi out of the corner of his eyes and knew that he would not make a train in time so he headed immediately for the exit.

Exiting from the top of the stairs he got lucky and caught a taxi. Heidi was just behind him and stepped in front of a car. She pulled the driver out and drove after the taxi. Amir coaxed the driver into staying ahead of the car behind them by placing a stack of money on the front seat and promising more. Then he made a quick phone call to one of his associates. In essence his message was, "bringing company and need your help. Where do you want me to go?" Once he had an address he instructed the cab driver to a specific address.

Heidi knew that if she could just get next to the taxi then she could flash her badge and it would all be over, the taxi driver would just pull over. Traffic was tight and that seemed impossible. The traffic did not slow down enough to just get out of the car, although she started to several times just to have the traffic clear and move before she could get around the cars and up to the taxi. It was frustrating but also crowded enough that the taxi could not just speed away either.

When they finally got to a little open road and to the less crowded area of Paris, the taxi pulled into an alley way. Amir dropped additional money on the taxi driver's front seat and hopped out heading down the alley.

Heidi pulled into the alley blocking the taxi car in. She hopped out and started after Amir. "Amir, you do not want to do this."

Amir said, "I feel I am dead no matter what I do. But I must at least try for my family." He continued down the alley a little way.

Heidi un-holstered her gun and proceeded cautiously deeper into the alley. Spotting one gunman, it was what she had anticipated, a quick trap. She did not know how many. She continued to scan as she walked cautiously into the alley avoiding the first shooters direct line of sight. Then Amir turned and said. "Can't you just let me be?"

His location was a decent giveaway as to where other potential shooters might be. "Amir, I do not intend to hurt you. I merely need you to travel with me." She really hoped he would just walk out of the alley and no one would need to be shot.

"I have done enough for you. It is time I go home." Amir was determined that he wanted out of this situation immediately.

Heidi had a second shooter in her sights and decided to take a chance. She could likely take out both of them before either could get a shot off. If there were more, then it might be a different outcome than she wanted. She took the one out that she saw second. Then anticipating how the first shooter would need to position himself to get a shot at her, she was ready and shot him.

A third shooter behind Amir poked his head up and got a shot off completely missing Heidi. It came even closer to hitting Amir than it did hitting Heidi. She was able to quickly dispatch of him also. Amir walked with her back to the car. The taxi driver said, "That was amazing" just before Heidi shot him in the head.

Heidi took the car to the airport and left it in the tow zone. Amir and she went to meet the Captain and wait to catch their plane to the states.

Thursday Morning
Chicago

CHAPTER 71 - RICARDO AT BREAKFAST

Walker Brother's Pancake House has several locations in the Chicago area, several closer to Ricardo's house than the Lincolnshire Walker Brother's. But Ricardo only ate at the one in Lincolnshire. The food was just as good at any of the establishments, but the atmosphere at this one was wonderful. The entry way has ornate stain glassed windows with some of the most famous composers as the centerpiece. The restaurant is elegant and simple. The food is magnificent from the fresh squeezed orange juice to the flavorful crepes and of course the Dutch Baby.

Ricardo would often go across the street to play a round of golf after breakfast. Today, however, after enjoying his favorite-the banana crepes, he would head back to the house and relax.

Mary had already reserved the large party room in the back. Ricardo preferred privacy even if it were just Mary, him, his wife and the grandkids.

They each ordered the fresh squeezed orange juice and talked about Paris. His wife went with him on many trips and expressed disappointment, teasingly, that he had not taken her this time. It was her favorite city in the world besides Chicago.

Mary finally asked in the conversation. "It is tragic that Jacob is in a coma, isn't it?"

Her father looked perplexed and asked. "I do not remember a Jacob that I would have a picture of. It must be someone else's picture and one of the servants or you just loaded it onto the electronic picture frame by accident."

"But daddy, you were in the picture with him." Mary pressed.

Ricardo was still confused, "How do you know him then?"

"I don't know him that well. We go to the same church but it is a big one and he goes at a different time. We have met and even had dinner at their house before his wife was killed in an auto accident." Mary continued.

"I think I would remember that Mary, maybe you should just show me the picture later." Ricardo suggested.

Mary responded. "Yes, I will show you tonight when I come over." Then she just continued on to another subject.

Before breakfast was over, Inspector Pierre had called Ricardo personally to warn him that his friends had shown up on an Interpol watch list. Ricardo figured this might be why they needed the fake passports and decided he would call them sometime after breakfast.

Breakfast was every bit as good as expected.

CHAPTER 72 – JENNY/JIM ON PLANE

Jim and Jenny had selected to travel by coach by design. The plane was only about half full, so they were able to move near the back of the plane and have complete privacy. They could stretch, sleep and talk. It was as much room as first class without paying for it. Jim would have thought that was a bargain before he became so rich.

Once the plane was off, Jenny did not waste time. "Tell me about your family, your parents and growing up." She was in an all business analytical mode ready to solve the mystery.

Jim considered the question and said, "I told you about my wife and kids. Tell me a little about your family, your parents, do you have any siblings? Have you ever been married? You know, the whole nine yards."

Jenny was taken back a little. Her intent was purely to profile the situation and see if there were any clues that might help shed light on the current predicament. Perhaps something his mother had told him. It wasn't that she didn't want to get to know him, but she was focused on solving the problem that was in front of them. "Jim, I have never been married, my family is very unique–it is one reason

I am really estranged from them now. But I do love them. I have a boat load of siblings and I want to hear about your growing up to see if there are any clues to your biological father."

Jim looked a little embarrassed. "Okay, but my growing up is boring. Promise me though, you will tell me all about you growing up when this thing is over." Jim wasn't sure this would end well. But, it only mattered a little to him either way.

Jenny continued. "If you still want to, I will personally take you to meet my family when we are done and you can ask my father yourself." It was a promise that she hoped she would not need to keep. "For now, tell me a little bit about your family. I will ask specific questions if I think there is something to explore."

"OK, I was born in mid-size town in downstate Illinois called Peoria but grew up in nearby Pekin. But I might have been conceived in Colorado. My mom was an army brat and they were stationed at the air force academy the last year my mom went to high school. But she was from Illinois, at least they lived there almost ten years while she was growing up. My grandfather worked in the armed forces recruiting office. My mother and father were high school sweethearts."

Jenny jumped in. "But we now know he was not your real father." Jenny said it judiciously so she wouldn't offend Jim in any way.

"We could call my mother. She lives in Asheville, North Carolina now. I know her number." Jim explained. He was now purely analytical in his evaluation of his life also. He would not be offended by Jenny's questions.

"We might need to but it might only put her in jeopardy. I think we should wait. Besides, calling from a plane is too easily traceable and you can bet someone is monitoring your mom's line."

Jim continued. "I grew up a pretty normal life. I have a younger sister and a younger brother."

"So someone, maybe Jim Conrad, got involved with your mother in Colorado." Jenny was thinking through the possibilities.

"I don't think so." Jim interjected.

"I know it is hard to accept, your father not being your father, but we had pretty . . ."

Jim interrupted. "No, I mean to go to the academy you need to be a top student. I suspect that a lot of the CIA comes from the various military institutions. Perhaps my father came from the Air Force Academy and joined the CIA. Then he started the first Jim Conrad and plotted to take money."

Jenny looked at him. "It's plausible." She thought for a moment more. "Then Frank should be able to look at who joined the CIA that attended the academy around those years."

"I still think calling my mother is a better idea." Jim concluded.

"Frank can access the data and find out pretty quickly and we can keep your mother out of it." Jenny argued.

"Yes, but if there is a mole in the CIA and if we lose Frank as an ally, we are in trouble. Besides, if I go to my home town then I can visit with my great uncle. He can call my mother and ask on our behalf." Jim said. "Of course, after you meet my uncle you may have a completely different view of me."

Jenny figured that Frank was probably already getting himself in trouble and she did not want to jeopardize his life. "I suppose you have a way to ensure your uncle's phone call is not recorded."

"My great uncle, not my uncle and yes I know how he can have a private conversation." Jim concluded.

CHAPTER 73 — INTERPOL

The message came through from Interpol while the Captain and Heidi were in the airport waiting to board a plane for Chicago. Officers in the Zurich airport had seen the two suspects getting on a flight for Chicago under assumed names. The message also indicated the plane had already landed and customs had been cleared. There was an APB on the rental car and the American authorities had been alerted.

Frank had already heard the message from his superiors at Langley and was in the process of getting an American military plane to get him and his team back to the states. He had a lot of explaining to do to his boss, Tom, but that would have to wait. His first priority was to get Jenny and to make sure Jim stayed safe.

Inspector Pierre called Ricardo and let him know of the change in status of the situation. Not only were his friends being pursued, they had been spotted and traced to Chicago.

Ricardo sent a polite text to Jenny. "They are onto you. Change ID's and cars immediately. RM."

Jim and Jenny had barely left the parking lot of the rental car company at O'Hare airport when they received the text. An alias for Jenny would be easy. She always carried a couple with her. In her line of work it became a necessity. They were ID's that no one else knew about. However, all of the alternative identities for Jim had been created and vetted by the CIA. If there were a mole in the agency, they could trace all the identities for Jim. Jenny knew that they could probably get by without an alternate ID for Jim in the states, but she had an idea of where to get one just in case it was needed.

Jenny suggested dumping the automobile first. And Jim suggested leaving it in the long term parking lot of the airport. They could take public transportation or a taxi from there to find something else. They parked in the remote parking, took the train to the international terminal and hailed a cab.

Jenny had an alternative identification for Jim but had to decide how to get into the bank after hours. With a little bit of convincing to the night guard and the fact that there was a banker that happened to be working late, they were able to get into the bank. After opening the safety deposit box, she looked at Jim and said. "Your new alias is Jacob Caldwell. Remember the identity well."

"That might be a stretch." Jim said jokingly. Then he continued in a more serious tone. "You don't think they will be tracking my real name also?"

"As for all concerned, Jacob is in a coma. Sometimes the best disguises are the most obvious." Then she indicated that they should hurry. They needed to find a car dealer that was open late. Jim was about to buy an automobile. First they stopped at a drug store where they each transformed their look slightly by adding highlights to their hair and a few cheap accessories.

The auto dealer was delighted to get a late evening sale. He was sorry they wouldn't finance, the dealer knew his profit was much more when someone decided to defer payment. However, the dealer would not turn down an all cash deal. Jim added the last touch, "Can you wait to process the plates for about a week."

"Well I can but the state doesn't appreciate us waiting too long. You might not get them until after the temporary tag expires." He said.

Jim continued. "Yes, but our daughter is turning sixteen this week and this is her birthday gift. Her mother," he said as he looked half annoyed at Jenny, "thinks she might want a vanity plate."

"I understand. We can hold off on sending anything to the state. Just let us know pretty quickly." The auto dealer concluded.

As they drove off Jenny turned to Jim and said, "Nice touch. That should keep the state from being alerted to us if someone is tracking your real name."

Jim and Jenny drove a couple of hours south. They could have made it all of the way to Pekin, but didn't want to show up too late to Jim's uncle's house. They found a hotel about 20 miles off of the interstate to stay the night.

CHAPTER 74 – YURI IN IOWA

Yuri arrived in Chicago. She rented a nice sports car to drive to Des Moines, Iowa. A sports car might be less conspicuous but the ride to Des Moines was a nice open ride in the car, not like the cities in Europe. She found that each part of the world had its own flavor of uniqueness. Some were positives and some were negatives in her mind. The freedom of the open road was one of the positives for Yuri for the states. The state trooper behind her was one of the negatives.

"Ms. Terri Flanders, you were driving a little fast." She apologized but didn't really care if she got a ticket. That is another advantage of a fake identity. The police officer wrote her a warning and was on his way.

She slowed for a while but was anxious to get to the bank. She would not make it before it closed, but could scout the area and then go in the next day. She assumed there was some significance to this bank and what she might find in the safe deposit box. She hoped that she would finally know why her parents gave her a key.

A few hours later she arrived. The first thing she noticed was the non-descript automobile parked near the bank. Someone else was casing the bank or watching for someone to come to the bank. She was certain that it was likely trouble.

Yuri, under the alias Terri Flanders checked into a local hotel. There she spent the better part of two hours devising her plan to enter the bank unnoticed.

CHAPTER 75 – ANDREW'S AIR FORCE BASE

The four engine cargo plane skidded to a stop at the end of the runway and made its way to its prescribed unloading zone. Frank, Trevor and four other agents were off the plane before any cargo or any other people were unloaded. They had work to do and had made arrangements for the minute they hit the ground. Within the hour they would be in a company gulfstream on their way to Chicago. Frank requested the jet be ready at Andrew's Air Force Base for his team when they arrived.

He had hoped to avoid a long stay in Washington DC and hoped to completely avoid checking in. At this point he did not want the distraction. He figured having the Gulfstream on location and a quick turnaround on the flight time would enable him to avoid these things. However, the first face he saw walking off of the plane was that of Sr. Director Tom Sportsman. Without missing a beat Frank said, "Tom, good to see you but you know we have to move equipment and get on our flight. I need to get the team to Chicago."

Tom was a slightly overweight man, too many years behind a desk, but was still in shape. His stern look was as lethal a weapon as any gun in the field of combat. He was also known for his slick political maneuvering when necessary. "Frank, we will talk now. Your team can move any equipment. You can catch the plane running on the runway if you need to." Frank did not need to give his team any instructions. They got the look from Tom and were off to do any work that needed done. Tom called as they left, "Trevor you stay behind. As second in command of this operation I want you to get the same message. I don't want any excuses later because of a misunderstanding".

Trevor turned and returned to the side of Frank right in front of Tom. "Yes sir."

Tom didn't say a word for about five minutes. The CIA is not the military and Frank did not have to stand at attention, but he pretty nearly did the entire time. He knew that Tom was just trying to make him feel uncomfortable. He did. His fear was Tom would pull the plug right then and there on the whole operation. As Sr. Director, Tom knew that he probably should.

Tom got right in the face of Frank, looking up slightly since Frank was a bit taller. "Frank, if you allow one hair on the head of Jim Conrad to be harmed I will get your pension, I will get you fired and will somehow figure out how to get you tried for treason – somehow." Tom paused for a moment. "Frank, it is a civilian out there in your operation. You must keep Jim Conrad safe."

Trevor relished the conversation. He was young and ambitious. He would gladly step in and take charge if Frank screwed things up. He didn't dislike Frank, he was just opportunistic and was ready to take advantage of any situation he could.

Tom continued. "Trevor, if he lets anything happen to Jim Conrad you can shoot him on the spot."

Frank just looked at Tom. He knew that Tom could probably back up any of the claims if he wanted. But Frank was not easily intimidated. "Yes sir, now if you would let me do my job and get my team in place, I can get this operation back on track."

"There won't be an operation if Jim dies, we will all be crucified." Tom said unforgiving.

"Sir, get out of my way so that won't happen." Frank said as he gave a stern look back at Tom.

Trevor broke the tension when he spoke up. "Tom, I can shoot him now if you would like."

Tom then broke from his character and laughed. "Frank, just go get the job done and we will all be okay." Tom turned and got into the back seat of an SUV. The SUV pulled away.

Frank turned to Trevor, "You were ready to shoot me?"

Trevor smile, "I would have only shot you in the leg."

They walked towards where the Gulfstream was parked in a hanger. Frank continued, "Let's go find Jim and Jenny."

Friday Morning
Chicago Time

CHAPTER 76 – GREAT UNCLE ROY

It was a simple ranch house in a neighborhood on the outskirts of Pekin Illinois. There was no reason to be paranoid, but Jenny was cautious just the same. She parked on the side street, noted the side garage door entrance and that the back yard was fenced in with a tall white wooden fence. She assessed possible intrusion and exit routes should there be any issues. Jim was assessing different concerns.

Jim was concerned that he hadn't seen his uncle in so many years that he might not recognize who he was. Jim thought that ironic, he had changed identities and was worried his uncle might not know who he was – Jim was only half sure who he was after the last few days. It was still fairly early, so the second worry was that his great uncle would not be awake. He was in his seventies now and that usually meant more sleep, Jim thought. He remembered that his Uncle Roy's wife had passed away about five years ago or so. His Uncle Roy not only sent flowers, but called when Carol and the children were killed in the accident.

Jim knocked.

It was a couple of knocks later that his Uncle Roy opened the door. He was about 300 lbs, bald and had a t-shirt on that barely covered his belly. It was evident that he had just gotten out of bed. Jim was just glad he had pants on. "Well Jacob, good to see you. Come on in and bring the lovely woman with you. She is a darling looking thing."

"Hey Uncle Roy." Jim gave him a half hug. "This is Jenny."

"Well Jenny, do you have a much older sister." This is the Uncle Roy that Jim remembered. Then Roy continued. "I am just kidding you. I shouldn't embarrass little Jake like that. Hey, I hadn't heard that you came out of your coma so quickly. Those doctors can do amazing things nowa days."

Jim looked at his uncle. "Well, I am not really out of the coma yet."

"Yea, I would be dazed around a woman like that too." They had walked into the kitchen and Roy already had a beer in his hand. With the refrigerator still half opened he looked at Jim and said. "Can I get you one?"

Jim responded. "I don't drink anymore, remember."

"Oh yea, I almost forgot. How about missy, I mean Jenny?" He took a drink then held the open beer out towards Jenny with questioning eyes.

Jenny looked at him with a big smile. "I couldn't possibly. I really don't start drinking until after ten in the morning."

"She's a clever one boy, I will give you that." He sat at the table facing Jim and sat his beer down. "I know that I am no success story, but I can spot trouble a mile away. What's eaten ya boy?"

"I can't tell you. But once we are out of here you will have to pretend we were never here." Jim said in a serious tone.

"I haven't seen Jacob in years. Talk to his mom on occasion. Maybe you oughta call her and ask. Heard he was still in a coma or something like that." Roy took a swig of beer and sat it down. "Now you all came here for something. You know if I can help I will."

"Can you call mom?" Jim asked.

"Sure. She will be at the mall on her walk at this time but she has a cell phone. You want me to tell her you are alright."

"I don't want you to mention that I am here." Jim explained that Roy should say how hard it is to talk, can't understand her on the cell phone, perhaps there is something wrong with it. "Have her call you from a land line – not her home phone though. That is why now would be a good time to call her." He continued.

"I can do that, but what I am supposed to ask her." Roy insisted.

"I want to know who my real father is. I need to know who he is." Jim pleaded.

"Boy, you know who your real father was. You grew up with him, loved him and buried him." Roy looked a little hurt. "Do you need more than that?"

"I know who my real father is, but I need to know who my biological father was." Jim took a bag that had most of the money they had left and dumped it on the table. "My biological father's money and there is more. Someone wants it and is after us. I need to know to help figure out why."

"Boy, I can't think of a better reason to call your mother. Give me a few minutes." Roy said as he made his way to the hall bathroom.

Roy left the door to the bathroom open half way as he went. Jenny found it more humorous than anything. She could see the door and hear him urinating, but could not see anything else. She was glad about that. After a loud belch he went into the living room to make his call.

Jim helped himself to the refrigerator for some orange juice and got a glass for Jenny. They could hear parts of the conversation, especially when Roy raised his voice.

"I can't hear you woman. Go call me from another phone." After a short delay they heard. "I don't care if you aren't home I want to talk to you now."

The phone rang. "Where are you calling from?" Roy paused. "Yes, that is nice of the Chic-fil-A to let you use their phone."

Jenny and Jim chatted quietly and only a little. They really tried to listen more than anything else. "Look, I know you came back pregnant from Colorado. I am not dumb." Jenny walked to the door to see Roy sitting in the recliner with his legs up. He gave a quick wink and thumbs up.

"I need to know now because I want to. And if you don't tell me I am going to tell Jacob's siblings that he is only their half-brother."

Jenny heard Jim's mom through the phone. "You wouldn't dare."

"Yes I would and you know it. And if you tell me I won't say a word to them." Jenny considered how that sometimes it paid to be viewed a little crazy. She just couldn't decide if it was an act or if that was just who Roy was.

She couldn't hear what Jim's mom said, but she heard the phone slam down. Then Roy said, "And goodbye to you also."

Jenny went back to the table and sat down. Roy made his way in. "Jacob, I love your mom to death and I just hurt her terribly. You have to fix this when you get all done figuring out what you need to."

"I will. Did she tell you?" Jim asked.

"Tim Baker, he was a fourth year cadet at the academy in Colorado" Roy finished. "Now let's go to breakfast."

Jenny hoped he would get dressed first. He did.

CHAPTER 77 – THE GREAT BANK HEIST

When you suspect you are the target of surveillance and you need to gain access to the place under surveillance then a simple disguise is not sufficient. What you need is a diversion big enough to take someone off the trail and then not realize that they are off of the trail. It is better to make them think that you were never there or that you had a reason to go somewhere else or that you already have what you came for.

Yuri was going for the latter. She called the Captain. "Yuri, you have decided to come back?"

"Were those your boys I slipped by at the bank earlier today?" Yuri said searching for information but also sending a not so subtle message.

"What bank are we talking about? Why would I need men at a bank?" The Captain responded.

"The men that are at the bank that is in Des Moines Iowa. My parents were kind enough to leave a key with me to a safe deposit box at the bank. Even as the bank has changed owners, they have kept the safe deposit boxes." Yuri explained.

"I thought we were going to meet in Paris." The Captain countered.

"I figured if your boys are here, then you are not far behind. But they are not too good." She paused for a moment. "Do you even know what was in the box?"

This was good information for the Captain. He did not even know there was a safe deposit box at the bank. He had a hunch that Yuri's parents were married in Des Moines and that the geo-coordinates in the translated text were centered on a bank in Des Moines it was likely that Yuri and/or Jim would end up there soon. "Are you planning to share that information?" The Captain responded from his hotel room on the outskirts of Des Moines. Heidi was in the room with him.

"I now know something you do not know. But I will share the contents with you in good faith." Yuri offered.

The Captain knew that 'good faith' meant it would not be enough information to satisfy him and she would need to see him in person to share the rest. "I am listening."

"There were three items in the box. The first was some cash. Big deal I know. The second was a translation table for the back of the bronze plate. Useless to me now that I have the translation and it is probably useless to you also. And finally, a key with the name of a Swiss bank on it. That is the most interesting piece to me."

Yuri had already called a friend in the states that was forging an older looking key with the name of a Swiss bank on it just so she would have something to give the Captain when they met.

The Captain continued. "And if I want the key?" The Captain didn't want the key. He just wanted Yuri out of the way. However, he had one more play for her and that was to use her to get to Jim Conrad, in case they could not get to him in any other way.

"We will need to meet face to face of course. Shall we say at the Museum of Science and Industry in Chicago tomorrow at noon? Of course, I will expect you to come alone."

"I will be there." The Captain gave instructions to leave one car in front of the bank just in case Yuri was lying and also to keep an eye out for Jim and Jenny.

Yuri waited until after lunch and made her way into the bank with a family she had convinced to go in with her. She told the father that her husband was abusive and had hired thugs to make sure she didn't get into the bank and take out their money. She told him she didn't want the money, only her family heirlooms from the safe deposit box. She came in arm and arm with her new instant family of two kids and a husband. The father and two kids waited outside the vault area while Yuri went into the vault to get her safe deposit box. She opened it and there were a couple of things in the box. The first was an old ring. The note said, "This was your grandma's wedding ring and is now yours." There was also a few thousand dollars in cash.

There were two letters. One was sealed. The other had been opened. Both had her name on it. The open envelope also had a little note in parenthesis "(read last)". Yuri opened the first envelope.

Stephanie,

If you are reading this letter it means that I have died and your mother is ready for you to know the truth. Of course she was always willing to tell you, it was me that was the prude and did not want you to know.

I, Professor Samuel Thomas, am your real father. It is not that I did not want any children but I was just a man that had, shall we say, many women in my day. I would not have been a good father. Your mother, a wonderful woman, almost became my second wife and we dated only a few months. She can tell you what happened. Her version of the story would be better and more accurate than mine.

I started a trust at this bank and it should be plenty of money for a good education by the time you get to college or as a home down payment if you don't get it until later in life.

I know that sorry will mean very little by the time you get this. So I will just say that I will watch you from a distance and will love you.

I really expect nothing in return, because I really gave nothing.

Sincerely,
Professor Samuel Thomas

Yuri now knew who her father was and decided to open the second envelope. She expected this one was likely a note from her mother. She was partially correct.

Stephanie sweetie,

We don't know how long it will take you to get this. Your biological father said that he would make sure you got to the safe deposit box if it was the last thing he did. There is no easy way to say this; we are dead because we chose to have ourselves murdered. I can't tell you exactly why. You may be mad at us but there was no other way.

We will tell you a little. We found out that we were involved in something bad and that bad people were using us to get rich.

We both signed up to serve our country because we love our country. Once we found out what they were doing they had only one thing over us and that was threatening your life.

If we told you more, it would put you in danger. We only hope that you are able to have a normal life.

It is hard to understand and it was a very hard decision to make. We could not do the wrong thing and we could not put your life in danger.

You do not have to, but we would like justice served on those that tried to steal from the American people. We have always believed in justice. Find Jacob Caldwell from Pekin, Ill. Give him the routing and account number from the back of this letter. Tell him that he will need to use the name Jim Conrad, even if he does not have a passport that states that name. Tell him to be careful as he tracks down the account and then to be wise how he uses what he finds. Only he can use the information.

We both hope that somehow you understand that we did this because we love you.

With all our love,
Mom and Dad

The number on the back of the letter matched what Yuri found on the bronze plate. There was a little nominal cash in the box. Yuri memorized the name of her father and returned all of the items to the box except a handful of cash. She walked back out with her new family and drove to the shopping center to return her borrowed family to the real mother and wife. Yuri slyly slid $2000 cash in between the seat and the center console before getting out.

She now had about a day to get to Chicago and plan her encounter with the Captain. It was a stark realization that she had killed the wrong people all those years ago. Now, however, she felt that the Captain might be one of the people that deserved to die. But she was going to be sure this time and she was going to find out who else was involved.

CHAPTER 78 – MY HOMETOWN

Jim waited to tell Jenny the likely connection between Yuri (aka Stephanie Baker) and his real father until after breakfast and after they dropped Roy back at the house. So Yuri and Jim (Jacob) shared the same father. This man was more than likely a CIA agent who played the role of Jim Conrad.

The scheme was becoming clearer to Jenny and Jim. Whoever was doing this was trying to get Jim Conrad's money which was likely seed money from an earlier CIA operation that had grown. Although the growth in funds was unprecedented and there were still deposits into the account on occasion. Regardless of how the money got there, the current Jim Conrad was needed to access it because his name and identity were associated with the account. So why not use Yuri, if she was Agent Baker's daughter (aka Jim Conrad senior)?

They knew that Heidi was part of the plot and so was someone from within the CIA. And the CIA agent had to have influence on Jenny's current operation. On top of that, the bank account information was on the back of an ancient bronze plate that came out of Russia. And for some reason there was a reference to Iowa. The answer was with Iowa, Heidi, and Yuri. They would need Frank to come through with information on the mole and Jenny was sure that they could solve this thing.

They decided to take the day to think through a clear action plan. They had hoped the bank would send an email of someone tracking them. Other than an email note that indicated someone called from Interpol asking about their visit, there had been no correspondence. Jenny figured it was Heidi and there might be no other correspondence from the bank. She figured a day break from the whirlwind they had been on would be great.

It might not be the safest place. Jim had assured her that he had no direct relatives living in the town except his great uncle and a few very distant cousins. Sure, there were lots of old high school friends that he had not talked to in years or even taken the time to connect with on any social sites on the internet.

Jim took her on a brief tour of his small town. He showed her the former site of the Pekin mall, one of the first indoor malls in Illinois. It was long gone, but he had hung out there a lot as a youth. He took her downtown and they walked around pointing out where he used to ride his bike as a little kid and where some of the stores that were once there were now something different or just vacant. It was still a quaint little town.

Jim tried to explain the Marigold festival, but Jenny could not get the concept of a festival centered on a flower. "You will just have to come sometime." Jim finally told her.

They also walked the trails at the Mineral Springs Park and went into the pavilion. They topped it off by going to dinner at a local bar. It was a place that Jim had frequented often when in town after high school until he quit drinking. "However," he told Jenny, "they have the best wings I have ever tasted."

CHAPTER 79 – THE BEST WINGS

They were seated just off of the edge of the bar at a table near the pay phone and hall to the restrooms. There was an old juke box on the other side of the hall. The table was in the way of anyone who had to come out from behind the bar to the seating area. Jim and Jenny didn't mind. They ordered and waited for the wings to arrive. The waitress was visibly a little annoyed that each only ordered water to drink. Jim knew that they would tip well enough that she would forget that by the end of the night.

Jim's back was to the door so he didn't see her walk in the door with three of her friends. He didn't even notice her until she came to the juke box. But even with her side view as she selected a song on the juke box he knew it was Tammy. Jenny noticed his change in demeanor and sudden speaking quietly. "Who is she, an old girl friend?"

Jim pointed at Jenny and quietly said. "Bingo."

Only a moment later, Tammy turned to see Jim sitting at a chair. Jim could tell that she had not lost much of her beauty over the years. Her figure was pretty much like it was when they dated in high school. Her face was a little worn, but still very attractive.

"Oh My," she stated clearly loud enough for the others to hear in the bar. "Jacob has returned to our small little town."

"Hello Tammy, how have you been?" Jim said trying to be polite and short.

"Let me buy you a drink." Tammy said waiving the waitress over.

Jim looked at Tammy and said. "Thanks, but I don't drink anymore."

"And who is this prissy little thing you are with, some hooker. Is your wife not giving you enough?" Tammy said, again in a loud voice intended to provoke a response from Jim.

Jim responded calmly. "This is Jenny. My wife died in a car accident over a year ago."

"Well I am sorry about that, but you are still a prick." Tammy said and then returned back to her table with her friends.

"You dated her?" Jenny asked. "I hope your tastes have improved over the years."

"My wife was wonderful. Then I have been out with a secret agent and a world renowned arms dealer. So you can judge if my judgment has improved. Tammy was a long time ago in high school. Then it kind of just ended when we went to different colleges." Jim explained.

"Why is she so bitter then?" Jenny asked.

Jim smiled. "I guess it is me and women in hotel rooms. It must be my charm."

"What do you mean?" Jenny pressed.

"When I got engaged I came back so everyone could meet Carol. I came about a week before Carol. She couldn't get out of work so she had to come later than me. I came here for wings and drinks with some friends. Tammy was here the first night and we talked. On the second night we drank a lot and talked. Then we headed for a hotel room. She had brought a slinky nightgown and went into the bathroom to change. I had enough sense about me to leave, even though I was pretty sloshed."

"You left her there?" Jenny laughed.

"Go figure. Best decision I ever made. It was one of the things that convinced me not to drink. I left her there with no ride and with the bill. I got a few nasty letters from her for the next year or so. Carol got a few also. It is one of the reasons we didn't come to visit my home town too often. It was good when my parents finally moved." Jim concluded.

Jenny agreed that the wings were absolutely fabulous. They were nearly half way through their meal when Tammy came back to the table. This time her three friends were standing near her. "Jacob, I just thought I would let you know that I married Bobby Swenson."

Jenny looked at Tammy. "So who is Bobby Swenson?" Jim knew that the Swenson's were a very well to do family with numerous businesses in town. They were also known as the local bullies.

"Bobby was the star quarterback when we were in high school and may be the richest man in town." Tammy continued, "I called him and told him how you came on to me tonight. I told him you were with some bimbo and still came on to me. My friends all saw it too."

"Tammy, you are a treat." Jim said. "Come on Jenny, let's go."

"That is great advice. I am sure his brother and a few friends will be here any minute. If you are still here it will not be pretty." Tammy said laughing. Then she flashed a gun from inside her purse. "And just in case he doesn't show up I might need to do something."

Jim had left his gun at Uncle Roy's house but was sure that Jenny had hers. She didn't go many places without at least one. Jenny picked up a wing. "These are delicious. I think we should order more." Jim knew the look. It was the same type of rebellious look she gave Frank when she was about to disobey what he said.

Tammy looked at Jenny. "I don't think you understand. Do you think he won't hit some two bit tramp?"

The response would have been too easy, something about how Tammy might have experience in that department. But Jenny held her tongue. Instead she said. "You should call him and tell him the truth."

Tammy looked at him. "Honey, you will get what is coming to you and so will Jacob."

Jenny motioned to the waitress and then ordered another set of wings. Tammy went back to her table cursing the entire way back and then she sat down. The bar tensed up pretty quickly anticipating a fight. The waitress warned that there would be no police intervention on account of Bobby owning the bar now. She suggested it was best if Jim and Jenny just left.

Even though Bobby was a year ahead of him in school he remembered that Bobby was taller and built fairly big. As he walked through the door he noticed that Bobby was indeed about a half foot taller than he was and had improved in stature since high school. Three more people walked in behind him. Each had a shot gun in his hand. Bobby had a hand gun shoved in the front of his pants. Jim and Jenny were now standing facing the entourage that had just entered.

After a brief quiet interaction between Bobby and Tammy, Bobby and Tammy both walked up to Jim. Bobby spoke. "You mess with my wife you mess with me. This is going to be very painful."

Jim looked at him and said, "Do you think I would be interested in your wife when I am with this lovely woman. Sure Tammy looks good, but there is really no comparison." Jenny was smiling at the accolades. "Besides, I assure you that Jenny handles a gun far better than Tammy."

"I know you used to date Tammy. You must have some twisted fantasy for an old girlfriend. She wouldn't lie to me." Bobby said while his hand was nervously on his gun. He was deciding whether to pull it or just beat the crap out of Jim.

Jim didn't like either prospect.

Jenny had already assessed the situation. Two of the three men holding shotguns had shots at Jenny or Jim. The third was largely obstructed by Tammy. She moved slightly to position herself where she wanted. In a single motion Jenny pulled her gun and shot one of the men in the knee cap and the hit the other's gun knocking it out of his hand. Before Bobby could react she had her gun pointing at the forehead of Tammy. Strategically it would have been better to be pointing at Bobby's head but logistically Tammy was closer. It also gave Jenny more satisfaction to have the gun at her head.

Jenny said. "I would suggest that you dispose of your gun carefully and your friend do the same." Jenny physically reached into Tammy's purse and got the gun out.

She looked at Jim and then at Bobby. Jenny then said. "Bobby, from when I say 'go' you have three minutes and not a second more to have a fair fight with Jim, if you still want to defend your wife's lies."

Bobby did not wait for go, he threw a punch at Jim that caught him in the jaw, nearly knocking him to the ground. It hurt but Jim remembered one of the moves that Jenny had taught him a few days earlier and was able to turn the next punch into a defensive move that twisted Bobby's arm into a very painful position.

Bobby recovered and tried to lunge at Jim. Jim went low sending Bobby to the ground. Bobby grabbed Jim's ankle and pulled Jim halfway to the ground. Jim grabbed the gun from the table and put it to Bobby's head. Bobby said, "I thought this was going to be a fair fight?"

Jim looked and said. "As I see it the gun was about equal distance from each of us. I just got to it first. He paused a moment and said. "Jenny, let me know when the three minutes is up."

Jim gave Bobby a final kick and told him to "take your cronies and that fine example of a lady you call your wife out of the bar and get lost". As he gathered himself and his friends, Bobby explained how he would personally use his vast wealth to sue and then destroy Jim.

CHAPTER 80 – FRANK

Frank continued to have his frustration with Jenny. She hadn't checked in all day. He knew her phone was off and that worried him. He was thrilled when late in the evening she finally called her on the phone. Jenny had stepped out from the house once they had gotten back to Uncle Roy's house.

"Are you okay?" Frank asked.

"I am fine. We have just been laying low. Have you been able to find anything out about the mole?" Jenny explained. Jenny thought that perhaps if laying low was defined as a bar room fight that involved guns, she was telling the truth.

"No luck so far. Tom seems anxious that we find you. But you know Tom; I wouldn't think he would be involved. I am still looking." Frank said.

Jenny continued, "You have to work that angle and keep track of Heidi. We are going to try to meet with Yuri, get her to come to the states. Yuri and Heidi are both involved in this in some way."

"Yuri is in the states, we have tracked her to Chicago." Frank said. "But wait to contact her. Heidi has also come to the states and is involved. I want to make sure it is safe for you. I will call tomorrow when I know more." Frank continued. "So keep your phone on," he emphasized. Then he concluded by asking them to "make your way to Chicago. I think we are close to solving this thing. Frank told Jenny that they had removed the APB on them and that they were not wanted fugitives in the states at least. It had frustrated Heidi but she understood the politics of having an agent getting that kind of scrutiny in the states when there was no evidence they had any extended contact with the fugitive Professor Borden. This was reassuring to Jenny.

Jenny agreed to move towards Chicago and that they were close to solving this thing. What she didn't tell him is that they were only about three hours from the city and that the next morning they would be going to a bank in Des Moines Iowa as a detour before going to Chicago.

CHAPTER 81 – YURI ON THE INTERNET

Yuri purchased a new laptop and two walking GPS devices to prepare for her encounter on the next day. She also met up with a contact in the states that provided the fake key to a fake Swiss safe deposit box and a few other supplies she might need.

She spent the next few hours preparing and then she spent some time researching a "Jacob Caldwell". According to recent newspaper reports he had just been in an accident and was in a coma. Yuri figured that this was not a coincidence. She found out about his families accident about a year ago and about his workplace, through LinkedIn. She also found a recent photograph online that looked an awful lot like Jim Conrad.

Jim's involvement became clearer. Although, she was not sure how much he understood yet. Perhaps he understood everything and was just playing her. After her meeting, she would call Jim and see if they could meet again.

CHAPTER 82 – A SURPRISE VISITOR

Jenny walked back into the house while Jim and Roy were watching an Illinois game. "You could have called from here; I wouldn't have known what you were sayin anyhow." Roy said without getting up.

Jim looked over his shoulder. "Did we find out anything new?"

Jenny looked disappointed. "No. I think we are set though with what we should do. Who is winning?"

Roy continued to look at the TV. "Illinois is up by 4. It is just after half time."

Jenny looked at the TV. "I will take that beer now."

"It's in the fridge." Roy responded.

Jenny went and grabbed a cold one and sat on the couch next to Jim. The game was close and exciting. When there was about 3 minutes left there was a knock on the door. Roy just ignored it. Jim asked if he wanted him to get it. "Don't matter to me much. At least until the game is over."

Jim got up and walked to the door. He opened it. Standing in front of him was Ricardo and his two sons Ricky and Victor. "You want to have us in?" Ricardo asked.

Jenny instinctively pulled her gun but kept it hidden next to the chair. Walking into the room, Ricardo looked at Roy. "Why don't you find someplace else to go for a while?"

Roy looked at the three men and then at Jenny and Jim. Jim said, "These are friends and we probably have some business to discuss."

"Can we wait for the end of the game?" Roy asked, still not moving from his chair. His eyes had returned to the game.

Ricardo looked at the game and the time left that was displayed. "As long as it doesn't go into overtime." Jim got Victor and Ricky a beer. Ricardo declined. Illinois won on a last second shot.

Once the game had finished, Ricky lifted his jacket revealing his gun to Roy. "Now it is time to go for a walk."

Roy just said, "I guess I will just go for a walk. It's not that I need the exercise or anything." He continued to talk to himself as he walked out the door.

Ricardo didn't say anything. It was clear that he was waiting for an explanation from Jim. Jim spoke, "So how did you find me."

"My daughter." Ricardo responded.

"Your daughter? How did she know where I was?" Jim was perplexed.

"I always snap a picture when I meet someone new. It inadvertently ended up on an electronic photo album in my house. My daughter, Mary Frazer saw the picture." Ricardo said.

"Oh," Jim said with a surprise look on his face. "Your daughter is Mary. What are the odds?"

"It is, as they say, a small world." Ricardo responded.

Jenny asked, "You know Mary?"

"She goes to church with me." Jim explained.

Ricardo looked at Jenny and said, "So you see, that is the dilemma, Mary says what a great guy Jacob is and I was starting to like Jim Conrad. Only they appear to be the same person. And if Mary didn't know you for so long I would say you were a fed. And if Mary didn't speak so nicely of you, you would be dead."

"Thank goodness for Mary. I always liked her." Jim started. Jim tried to think how he could explain it and decided that the truth, at least most of it might be the best course of action. "It is not a dilemma. Until a short time ago I was Jacob Caldwell. Then I found out that my father was really just my step-father." Jim then said. "My biological father was Jim Conrad senior."

"And the warrants for your arrest and the running?" Ricardo challenged.

Jenny jumped in to help cover. "Someone pretended to be Jim Conrad for years and used his money. Jim is wealthy and when I finally found Jim senior's real son there were some very unhappy people. The intruder has some powerful friends and they are after us." She then told him they were no longer considered fugitives.

"Who confirmed his identity?" Ricardo asked.

"Well I did of course." Jenny explained. "His real father asked me to hunt him down and make sure he got his inheritance. "But a small Swiss bank that holds the majority of his holdings had to confirm his DNA before they would release those funds. We did that while we were in Europe this week."

"That is why you were in Switzerland." Ricardo concluded.

Jim added. "Precisely. And if I am going to jump into the high world of the rich and famous I will need to look like I have money–a good collection of fine manuscripts would help. I also need connections. Hence, I needed to meet someone like you who had connections."

Ricardo seemed to accept the explanation as plausible. He had checked Jim's background (as Jacob) and concluded that however he got involved in this scheme; he was always just an accountant making an average living before. "These powerful people, do you know who they are?"

Jenny looked at Ricardo. "We are trying to figure that out, but until we do we are trying to keep a low profile. We have friends helping."

Ricardo said. "I was beginning to look at you as a good friend. Now that I know that you know my daughter, I consider you a very trusted friend. You are welcome at my house and to my protection whenever you like. What can I do to help?"

Jenny looked at Jim as if to say that she would answer on their behalf. Jim kept quiet. "We appreciate the offer and will probably need your help soon, but we need to work some of the angles we have first."

"Very well. But I must warn you that if I found you I am sure the others trying to find you are not far behind. I would suggest leaving tonight. Roy seems to be a good fellow and he is an Illinois fan so I would hate to see anything happen to him." Ricardo concluded. Then Ricardo and his two sons left.

Jim and Jenny were packed and half way through writing a thank you note when Roy walked back into the house. "You two don't have to leave so fast. I got room for you."

Jim expressed his gratitude and told him not to lie if anyone asked, just tell them "Jacob and his girlfriend came by to see you and then moved on."

Jim and Jenny began their drive to Des Moines. They would find a hotel along the way.

Saturday Morning
US Central Standard Time

CHAPTER 83 – THE BANK ENCOUNTER

Jim and Jenny were at the bank first thing in the morning, about an hour after they opened. It was Saturday and they wanted to be sure that they were able to get to the safe deposit box before the bank closed. It was early and there was already a small crowd within the bank.

Jim was led back to the vault where he could look at the contents of the safe deposit box. He had to wait a few minutes for one of the banking managers to free up. It was a two key system that required his key and one from the bank. Once unlocked, Jim would be given his privacy.

Jenny had gone to the restroom while they waited. As she walked out of the door, she saw Frank standing in the lobby. Frank saw her and immediately made his way over to her. Jenny smiled, "Hey Frank. Why did you come this way?"

Frank looked at her sternly. "I should ask you the same question. You said you were heading for Chicago."

"Jim is on his way to Chicago. I will meet him later today at a hotel." Jenny responded, knowing that Jim could come out at any moment and spoil her misdirection.

"You are supposed to be keeping him safe." Frank responded.

"Whoever is tracking us is looking for two people and not one. He is probably safer this way." Jenny paused for moment but not long enough to give Frank a chance to ask anything else. "So what are you doing here?"

Frank simply responded. "We tracked Yuri here. We are sure she has moved on to Chicago but just had to serve a warrant to get the information from her safe deposit box."

In the vault, Jim opened the safety deposit box with the banker. The banker took him to an adjacent room where he could examine the contents in private.

"Did you find anything of interest?" Jenny asked wondering if somehow it was the same safe deposit box.

"Just an old ring, a little money and a couple of insignificant letters." Frank indicated. Then he asked, "Why are you here?"

Jim pulled a sealed letter out of the box and carefully opened it.

Jenny responded to Frank. "Ricardo told us that he had heard that Yuri was coming this way. I just thought it would be good to do a quick reconnaissance before heading to Chicago."

Jim read the letter.

Jacob,

Your mother and I had a short fling while I was a senior at the Air Force Academy in Colorado. We thought we loved each other. However, if we stayed together it would have ruined my career and embarrassed her father so we mutually agreed to move on.

By getting this letter it means that Stephanie started you on a path to a Swiss bank account that eventually led you back to this small bank. I can't tell you what to do with the money; it is all in your name. I do not even know where it all came from. I know some was swindled from criminals and some from the US government.

Please help Stephanie if she needs it. There were corrupt CIA agents that were conspiring to get the money from Jim Conrad's account. If they find out you exist then your life will be in danger. You will have to choose whether to expose them or just let them be.

The conspiracy was led by Agent James Corso and included an agent named Heidi ???, Samuel Thomas, Leland ???, and Frank Warner. They were known as the Fabulous Five for some of their intelligence work at the agency. There may be more, but this is what I know.

With love and caring,
Tim Baker

There was nothing else in the box. Jim put the letter in his pocket and headed out to meet Jenny. He didn't make it around the corner and he saw Jenny talking to Frank. He could not hear what they were saying.

"Well, you and I can ride to Chicago together." Frank said.

Jenny did not have a real reason not to head back with him. She saw Jim over Frank's shoulder and was glad that he had paused. Jim raised his cell phone for Jenny to see and then started to dial. Jenny started to answer, but her phone rang before she got a word out.

"Jenny." Jim began.

Jenny held one figure up to Frank and jumped into her cell phone conversation. "How is your drive to Chicago?"

Jim had slipped into an open office and closed the door and blinds. He was looking through the blinds as he spoke. "Jenny, I know who the mole in the CIA is or rather who they are. The letter was quite clear."

"Okay, traffic should not be bad on a Saturday." Jenny was just trying to make sure the conversation looked normal.

"Frank's name is on the list." Jim said excitedly.

"That is disappointing. It was smart of you to call ahead. Just find another hotel when you get there and call me with the information later." Jenny continued.

They said bye and Jenny resumed her conversation with Frank. "I can get to Chicago on my own. I do not want to blow our cover."

Frank looked at her and said. "No, this is an order. We can work out the details later of how you connect with Jim later. Where is your car? We can get your stuff and head up to Chicago now."

Jenny simply said. "Jim dropped me off in town and then headed to Chicago. He has all of my stuff. I was just going to rent a car later."

As they walked out the door, Jim observed Jenny discretely drop something in a planter at the doorway. After they left, Jim went to the planter and found the car keys. The game had now changed.

CHAPTER 84 – THE BITTER RUSSIAN AIR

Sven Choski could not believe it. He immediately went to the artifact cleaning room to find Professor Thomas. He was not there. He sent a guard to go fetch him and Commander Blootov out of bed if they had to.

He took the bronze plate from the containment area and set it down on the table. Then he took the field casing supplies and started to clean and then enclose the second plate that had been found overnight. Months and months of frustration had finally turned up a second plate. Having both, more words and characters might make the translation go smoother. It also proved the first plate was more than just an anomaly.

Commander Blootov arrived first. He was excited but did not care about these things too much. His biggest excitement was the accolades he might receive if this were successful. Professor Thomas walked up just as the second casing was being completed. It was done in a rudimentary way and eventually would be professionally sealed and cared for. But this was a working sight.

"My friend, my friend." Sven exclaimed. "I have exciting news. We have found a second plate." Sven excitedly handed the plate to Professor Thomas.

Professor Thomas took it in his hand and started to study it. Again, the spy in him was gone. "Marvelous." He said first in English and then repeated in Russian. Professor Thomas studied it for nearly five minutes. Sven looked over his shoulder intently.

Commander Blootov sat in a chair nearly nodding to sleep. He knew that the honor of reporting it would be his and after the two scientists were done drooling on it; he would take a picture and dispatch a courier. He would also call the Minister of Knowledge's office when it opened in a few hours.

Samuel Thomas set it on the table. Sven set the other plate right next to it. It was too late by the time Samuel realized that the scientist in him had momentarily forgotten what he had done to the first plate. He knew that Sven would know momentarily.

He underestimated the time it took Sven to notice. "What is this? What is this? What have you done Sam?" As Commander Brotoov sat up to see what the commotion was, Sven realized that he had just sentenced his friend to death. Sven just did not understand why.

After a moments insisting, Sven pointed out some of the differences in what the plate had originally looked like and what it looked like now. Commander Brotoov understood that this American had defaced Russian artifacts, probably in an attempt to make the USSR look bad to the world. He knew that he now had his personal victory – exposing such a conspiracy would be triumphant. He immediately had Samuel Thomas watched around the clock.

After talking to his superiors his instructions were clear. At about 2:00 AM the next morning Professor Samuel Thomas was taken to an area of the dig sight that was the deepest, only about 20 feet. Most people would survive a fall of that distance, but it is plausible that someone could snap their neck and die in a fall of that distance. Even on the way to the location Samuel knew that his neck would likely be snapped before the fall even occurred.

He reflected on his life and how he had spent his entire life trying to build a better world. He wondered if the messages to his team back in the states had been understood. He never expected the extreme commitment of the Bakers. He never expected them to have themselves killed just to protect their daughter. This is what prompted him to take his Midwestern vacation to Des Moines Iowa. His Midwestern vacation had allowed him to access the safe deposit box that was for his daughter. As suspected, he was able to identify how Tim Baker had removed access to the account from him and his colleagues. It also prescribed how they would get it back. He had communicated the name of the individual, Jacob Caldwell, to his associates. Sending the account number would have given all of the keys needed if someone had intercepted and interpreted the messages he was sharing – so he had to hide the remaining pieces, the account number and bank, on the bronze plate. He had asked his colleagues one additional favor as he communicated - to make sure his daughter got his note. How to find the note was also included in his message on the plate. Perhaps his biggest regret was not getting to know her and not being involved.

Did he regret his choices? Maybe he only regretted the one about his daughter. But even that one had enabled him to do great things to change the world. He knew he would die with dignity and pride. But he would die.

Sven stood watching with two guards and Commander Brotoov. Samuel Thomas held the key that was around his neck, the duplicate key to the safe deposit box in Des Moines as Commander Brotoov snapped his neck and dropped him into the pit.

Sven looked in disgust. He loved his country but at the same time, not some of their means. He said, "That is done."

Commander Brotoov said. "Not yet."

He secured Sven. Sven asked. "But why?"

"This whole thing could be an embarrassment to the Kremlin. They will not have that." He then snapped the neck of Sven and dropped him next to Professor Thomas. Washington DC was informed the next day of the "tragic accident" involving Professor Samuel Thomas. The newspaper in Moscow reported how an American professor had tragically died while trying to save his dear friend Sven Choski, an archeologist from the USSR. As almost a footnote, the story indicated how the dig site would be closed temporarily while safety conditions were explored.

The Kremlin ordered Commander Blotoov to catalog and file all of the information and artifacts from the dig site into the archives at the Ministry of Knowledge so that it would not be found for a very long time.

Years later Professor Blovaski, a Moscow University professor of antiquities, came across the set of records on this unique dig site. Of particular interest to him were the plates he found. There were also a few notes associated with attempting translate one of them. He quickly posted a note on an internet bulletin board asking if anyone was familiar with bronze plates in Russia. He also sent a picture of the plates to a colleague in the UK.

CHAPTER 85 – MUSEUM OF SCIENCE AND INDUSTRY

As instructed, the Captain sat at a table just outside the ice cream parlor in the Museum of Science and Industry. He had a red bandana tied around his arm. The museum was very busy. It was a Saturday. A man came by and handed the Captain a phone.

The Captain thanked the man and looked around. It was only a moment later that the phone rang. "Are you the Captain?"

"Stephanie, I am the Captain and I am here. Let's meet." The Captain responded.

He had said enough that she was fairly certain that it really was the Captain this time. Yuri spoke out, "I now have a picture of you and our meeting is inevitable."

The Captain motioned cleverly to some of his colleagues that were watching. "Do you think you will leave the museum alive or even at all?" The Captain was intrigued by this key for a safe deposit box. But other than that he only needed her for a bargaining chip to get at Jim. However, he received word earlier that they had a much more valuable asset to help with that. In his mind, she was now expendable. They kept their obligation to Professor Thomas to ensure she got to the safe deposit box. And good thing or they might not get the additional information at the additional safe deposit box.

"You assume that I am even in the museum. Do you see the family with the phone looking at you? They believe they are recording a film of my elderly father's birthday surprise and yet they are only transmitting a signal to me just outside of the museum. It is amazing what a family will do for $100 bucks." Yuri pointed out to the Captain.

"Aren't you the clever one? So where are we going to meet?" The Captain asked, intrigued by the sequence of events. He saw a lot of the cleverness in Yuri that he had known in her biological father.

"Make your way to the airplane on the second floor. Under the second seat is a GPS device. It is programmed with your first four destinations. Before you go after these, make a stop at locker 24 in the lobby. The key will be taped to the GPS device. There are several pairs of sweats and t-shirts. Find the size that fits you and change in the men's bathroom. Bring only the GPS device and your car keys with you. Leave the phone. Come to the first location for your next set of instructions."

After the Captain got up, Yuri stood from a table about three tables away and made her way to the lobby where she would have to wait a little while. She had snapped a picture of the woman that he had motioned to when he thought Yuri was in the building. Once the Captain arrived in the lobby she noticed him talking to a man that she did not recognize. He handed him the GPS device and went into the bathroom to change. It was not long until he came out, got the GPS device back and made his way to his car.

Yuri now had pictures of three of them, whoever they were. When you are pursuing someone, you will often switch who is doing the pursuing so as not to draw attention to yourself. If you are being pursued and you do not know your pursuer, this can be used to your advantage. Yuri started the day with only a voice and now had three pictures of three different individuals, including the man behind the voice.

The Captain drove up Lake Shore Drive to downtown Chicago. He parked underneath an L-train and made his way into a cell phone store. "Can I help you?" A young woman asked from behind the counter.

"I was sent here by a friend." The Captain said.

"Are you part of the scavenger hunt? The nice lady said you would be by sometime." The young lady was blushing a bit as she was looking at the GPS device. "I might actually get on TV."

The Captain looked at her, "You probably will. Do you know what I am supposed to pick up here?" He said impatiently.

"Of course I do. I didn't know you wouldn't know. Here you go." She handed him a new phone and a set of car keys. "I am supposed to get your car keys from you and keep them."

The captain handed her his keys and took the phone. Once out of the store, he called the only number programmed into the phone. Yuri picked up the phone. "Okay Captain, you still with me?"

"So far, but how long do we keep up this charade. Do you think you will shake all of my operatives or are you just trying to identify them?" The Captain knew the game, he had played it many times himself.

"All of the above, but at least trying to keep a way out for me. Now take the new car to the prescribed second location. Call me when you get there." Yuri was very specific.

This drive took him well out of the city onto the freeway into the far north suburbs. He exited on Willow road and made his way a few miles into local department store's parking lot. He was in Glenview, but he was not familiar with Chicago and wasn't sure exactly where he was. He did not get out of the car but called Yuri. "Okay, now what?"

"I will not be seen with a man in sweats. Go pick out five slacks and five dress shirts that will fit. Try each on and when you find the one that fits best take the tags off and keep the clothes on. Buy a belt, socks and shoes. Buy all of the clothes you tried on. You can pay for it under the account 'Captain Hook'. Save the receipt, the amount you paid will adjust your next coordinate on the GPS." Yuri then hung the phone up.

The Captain was nearly fed up. He followed the instructions, picking out clothes, belt, socks and shoes. He would not try on every piece of clothing. He would try on the one that he knew would fit and be done with it. The lady in front of the dressing room told him they did not usually let that many items into the dressing room—but in his case they would make an exception just so he checked them out with the attendant when he came out of the changing room. He chose the stall that was designed for the handicapped because it was larger and it would give him more space than the others.

Just as he got his sweat pants off, the door was pushed open. Yuri stood right in front of him, gun pointing directly at him. "So we meet Captain, or shall I say Mr. James Corso." She looked at what she saw as a pathetic old man half undressed sitting in the changing room at Kohl's. It was as dignified as this man deserved, she thought to herself.

The Captain looked at her. "How did you get my . . ." He stopped himself mid-sentence. When I left my clothes in the museum bathroom you had someone pick my wallet. Clever."

"I told the boy to keep the money but leave everything else. But he better come out with your name." Yuri finished how the scam was set up.

"I think in the end you are no more than a two bit scam artist" The Captain concluded. "Did you bring the key with you?"

"No. But I will give you the coordinates when I am safely out of here, assuming I get the answers I want." Yuri explained.

"And how do I know that I will live at the end of the answers?" The Captain countered.

"You don't. My parents were killed because of a few petty thieves." Yuri said in disdain.

"A petty thief walks out with under a million dollars. This theft is worth billions, more than you can imagine. This isn't petty, this is big." The Captain said. "You have personally killed for far less than this. And we didn't kill your parents. They had themselves killed."

"Because you threatened my life." Yuri countered.

"It was their choice. We would have preferred them to participate in this petty theft. I would prefer that of you. I can give you the equivalent of what your parents were offered." The Captain continued. "Which, just to be clear, is worth considerably more now than it was then. The portfolio has grown quite a bit since your father was Jim Conrad."

"Why were my parents involved in this in the first place?" Yuri asked. She understood that she had less than ten minutes until store security or the Captain's associates came through the door. She was not worried about the store security.

"They aren't here to ask. I don't know why. I am not the one who invited them into the endeavor. The real question is whether you will choose to be part of it now?"

"Why wouldn't I just shoot you right now? I could be done with the whole thing. I have plenty of money for the rest of my life." Yuri said raising her gun.

"You may decide to kill me but there a couple of reasons why I think you won't, even though revenge is high on your thoughts." The Captain said.

Yuri walked closer putting the gun, silencer and all, right against his forehead. It wasn't as deadly but just felt more intimidating. "You better speak soon."

"Stephanie, I am your only real connection to all of the parties. The others that assisted today are merely hired henchman. I know all of the players from the beginning. If you want the full story you need me. Second, even if you are set for life this has to be a little tempting to you. In one shot you could make more than you have made in your entire career as a criminal. Imagine the power that brings. I know it is a little tempting." The Captain took a little breath, mainly because he needed it. This was the time for a cigarette if he still smoked. "Also, have you checked your accounts? I think you will find you are nearly broke. That would be restored as well as your huge payment."

Yuri looked extremely disgusted. "What do you need from me?"

The Captain looked up less nervous than he was a few moments before. He felt he might walk out alive now. "We just need Jim Conrad. You just need to bring him to us alive. That is the only way we need him is alive."

"I will think about the offer. I will get back to you on this." Yuri exclaimed. "One more thing – who did I kill at the Palace of Versailles? I like to know the name of the people I kill."

"Leland Faremont. One more question for you, where is the key?"

"I will text its location once I am safely clear." Yuri said.

The Captain had saved his ace in his pocket for last. "I have just one more thing for you to consider before you devise an elaborate plan to double cross me."

Yuri didn't like the smug tone, not when she was holding the gun. "What is it?"

"You do not have much family, maybe none really. The closest thing you have to family might be Amir. He is currently my guest here in Chicago. I would hate to see an accident happen to him while he is visiting. I am sure his family would like to see him again." The Captain said.

"You will get Jim. Amir better make it home safely." Yuri grabbed a heavy jacket and a ball cap and slipped both on. She looked a like a man trying to look hip and not doing a very good job at it as she stepped out handing a stack of clothes to the attendant. She was then gone before the Captain could even get his sweats up.

CHAPTER 86 – DRIVE TO CHICAGO

Jenny found it hard to believe that Frank was the mole. However, Jim would not have any reason to lie. She did not know the other agent that was riding with them and she wasn't even sure if he was an agent. If he was, she wasn't sure where he stood. She only knew that he was directly behind her and that was the least safe place for her if he was on Frank's side.

They talked for a while about general topics including sports, the weather and even a few CIA war stories. Frank knew he controlled the situation. When he was ready he just abruptly changes the subject and said. "Jenny, we have figured out who the mole is."

Jenny must have been surprised by his comment and she was anxious to hear his theory. At least this open admittance to a mole did clarify the position of the agent in the back seat. "Okay, who is it?"

Frank kept driving on the interstate towards Chicago. He glanced in her direction as he said. "I am the mole that you think is in the agency."

Jenny pulled her gun and pointed it directly at Frank's head. She had another gun ready to shoot through the back of the seat at the other agent. He also had his gun out. Jenny said, "Pull over and let me out or this could get ugly."

Frank smiled. "Relax Jenny. I couldn't tell you over the phone and I needed clearance before I could tell you in person." Frank paused for a moment. "That is why I wanted you to ride with me."

Jenny looked at Frank inquisitively. She didn't have to ask a question. It was clear she needed to hear more.

"This whole operation is legitimate. We are doing exactly what we said. But there is a second operation that Tom does not know about." Frank continued.

"It looks like an operation to get money from where I stand." Jenny said, putting a few cards on the table.

Sensing the tension relaxing a little, the agent in the back seat put his gun away. This helped relax it even more. Jenny lowered her gun so it would not be visible from outside of the vehicle, but she kept both guns trained on both individuals.

"It is about money, lots of it." Frank explained. "You see in the 1980's we stole lots of money from drug dealers and known terrorists. Terrorists existed long before 9-11 and this was one way to put them out of business or at least reduce the activity. You didn't hear about terrorism nearly as much in the Reagan years."

Jenny was listening. "So where is all the money supposed to go?"

Frank continued to explain, "The money was to be funneled to an account where it could be used by the US government and other international agencies to fight against drug and terrorist organizations. But something went wrong."

"Clearly." Jenny responded.

"Yes. Tim Baker, an agency man, was undercover as Jim Conrad and was the central point in collecting the money. The terrorist found out about his second identity and killed him."

"And that is why Jacob Caldwell was the only option for Jim Conrad, he was biologically related to him." Jenny continued the thought.

"Exactly. If we just move the money to another account where the agency can access and use it then we can continue with this operation and several others can move forward." Frank concluded.

Jenny brought her guns down more. This made sense to Jenny. She needed to verify how Jim knew that Frank was the mole, but if it was reasonable and fit with the story then she was inclined to believe this over the alternative–a group of rogue CIA agents trying to make a quick buck. "Can I verify this?"

It was a permission question. The other operation had been run on top of this one. That meant that at least a senior director in Langley had ordered it. They did not typically like to share information on any of their operations. Frank replied. "He will be expecting you to verify this. You know how to call the office and verify an agent?"

"Yes." Jenny said.

Frank found the next exit and pulled off into a gas station. Jenny stepped out. "I need a name."

"Sr. Director James Corso." Frank responded.

Jenny called a number from her phone and got a secured operator in Langley. She asked for a verification of her credentials. After giving the appropriate information and verification she asked that she be connected to the verified Sr. Director James Corso. The double verification system ensured that two agents that needed to speak could. They would also be assured that they were talking to the correct person. It did not need to be used often, but was a useful tool when it had to be used.

The line was secured and the operator dropped. "Hi, this is Sr. Director James Corso. How are you Jenny?"

"I am fine sir. Do you have a few minutes?" Jenny asked respectfully.

"I anticipated your call. I can verify Frank's story about a second operation, but ask your specific questions. I have a few minutes." The director said.

"I understand that you needed the account number from the bronze plate, but why involve Yuri?" Jenny asked.

"That may have been our biggest mistake. We needed it out of Russia and she had connections. We thought it would be a good win for Tom's operation to snag her also. We didn't know until after she had been engaged that her parents had been agents. We didn't know Yuri was a 'she' when we contacted her. But she has been nothing but trouble. Turns out that apprehending her is no longer the best option. You understand."

Jenny knew that it was, in essence, a kill order on Yuri as the first option. "Yes sir."

"She has single handedly disrupted this operation more than it should have been. She has killed innocent people and an agent. She is more than an arms dealer to terrorists, she is a despicable person." The director commented.

"She killed an agent? Was it one on Frank's team?" Jenny asked not sure of everything that had happened.

"Leland Faremont, he was on my team. He was killed trying to apprehend Yuri. This whole mess was avoidable when the operation was started if it had been executed properly." Corso responded.

Jenny continued, "Sounds like this thing got out of hand about twenty years ago. How did you get involved sir?"

"Some bureaucrat screwed this up. I am sent in to pick up the pieces. You know how it goes." Corso explained.

"Yes, and I have to help." Jenny commented.

"It's appreciated by very few, you know that. But that is the job." Corso said empathetically.

"Thank you sir." Jenny concluded.

CHAPTER 87 – NEW ARRANGEMENTS

Jim knew Chicago pretty well. It was his home town. He found an out of the way hotel where he gave a fake name and a fake home address. He paid in cash. His biggest concern was if Jenny had been able to break away from Frank safely. He didn't really have a clear way to know this for sure. He was truly scared for the first time since he had been dragged into this mess. Even more scared than when he was shot at.

He also knew that if he used the phone issued to him by the CIA they would be able to trace him pretty easily. He called Jenny from a pay phone more than twenty miles from where the hotel was at.

Jenny explained, without being too explicit over an open line on the payphone that it was safe. She explained that as his business manager, she arranged for a large sum of money to be transferred to a "good cause" that he would approve of. She encouraged him to come in so they could work out the details of the donation.

"Okay, as my business advisor I trust you. But the banks do not open until Monday. I will stay where I am until then and we can meet at a local bank to complete the transaction." He paused.

Jim wasn't sure if Jenny had all of the information or not. But she seemed convinced. He wanted one more conversation with Yuri first and needed a little time. Then he figured how to buy time without causing suspicion. "And while we are there, maybe we could talk about medical miracles and demonstrate how people can quickly and somehow publically come out of a coma or something like that. I will call tomorrow to find out how that might happen."

Jenny seemed disappointed. "Okay, we can do that." The phone conversation ended. She had hoped he would want to stay on and perhaps continue with their adventure. But it was clear he was looking for his old life back.

Jim stopped to purchase a laptop and a few burner phones with pre-paid minutes. He wasn't sure how many he would need but didn't want to trigger some obscure law enforcement tracking by buying too many. He had some research to perform on the internet. He decided that he would make his way north towards Wisconsin stopping at Wi-Fi hot spots to perform the internet searches. He would not spend more than 30 minutes in any location. If someone was tracking his internet activity then he hoped he would be able to avoid someone pinpointing his location by moving around frequently.

On the way to his first location he called Yuri. "Who is this?" The voice asked on the other end of the phone.

"This is Jim. How are you Yuri?" Jim asked.

Yuri was surprised to hear from Jim but pleased. "Are you calling for a second date?"

"Something like that." Jim responded.

"I am in Chicago, it might take me a little while to meet you depending on where you are." Yuri answered.

Jim responded. "I am in Chicago also. Do you go to church?"

"I have been to church before." Yuri said. It was not a lie, she had been in many churches as part of a cover or just simply to find a place to think. She had not been to a church service, except when she was undercover, since her parents were alive. Then, they only attended on rare occasions.

."Let's meet to attend Sunday mass at 12:30 at the Holy Name Cathedral off of Wabash." Jim suggested.

"That doesn't sound like much of a date." Yuri said teasingly.

"It might be, you will have to come and see." Jim concluded. He was not really looking for a date, but for information. Yuri had an agenda of her own. Her options were open as of this moment. She would decide after church.

Jim arrived at his first Wi-Fi hot spot at a coffee shop. Booting up the computer he searched for "Professor Samuel Thomas". There were a few archived Washington Posts articles that Jim would have to pay for. He did not want to risk using a credit card at this point. He found a reference to Professor Samuel Thomas at the University of Maryland. It indicated that he had died in the field in the USSR while on sabbatical from the University of Maryland. That was something significant in Jim's mind.

After about 20 minutes, he picked up his laptop and moved to the next location. Jim pulled into an apartment complex. He was able to find a network that did not have security. He accessed the internet and typed in the next name "James Corso". There were a lot of references but no way to tell who it was. Even limiting it to James Corso CIA returned over 200,000 items.

There were too many cars going by in the apartment complex. Jim was paranoid that he might not see someone coming. Jim moved into a nearby neighborhood where he found an unsecured network.

"Frank Warner" returned too many results. He tried the names together and found no information. He continued to move about every 20 to 30 minutes. He looked for Heidi and Interpol after searching a little bit found a profile on Heidi Spellard. He found out that she worked in law enforcement in the Washington DC area in the 1980s. She was actually American and moved to Europe in the late 1980's where she continued in law enforcement and eventually worked for Interpol.

Finally he looked for "Leland CIA" figuring there was no chance of finding anything. To his surprise, there was a story from the day before of an agent killed in the line of duty in Paris. There were no suspects in the shooting and no details as to the nature of what he was working on.

Jim went to one more location, created a new email account and sent a message to jimconrad2@gmail.com. It stated the following:

Jim and Jenny,

According to Tim Baker, five names of those involved in the original incident:
1) Professor Samuel Thomas – died in Russia about that time.
2) Frank Warner – involved in current operation
3) Leland (CIA Leland died in Paris this week–coincident?)
4) James Corso – no information
5) Heidi Spellard – worked in DC at the time, now works for Interpol. Claimed to by Jim Conrad Sr. Wife
        Where are they now?

Sincerely, A Friend

Jim hoped that Jenny would know it was from him. Nobody but the bank, Jenny, and he had the email address. He knew that she would get the email notification on her phone. He just wanted her to say it was still safe to meet on Monday.

CHAPTER 88 – JENNY DOES EMAIL

Jenny didn't check the message until she was safe in a hotel room. She easily figured out who sent the message. Her response was simple. This latest piece of information made the picture much clearer for Jenny. "Thanks. It is a trap so just stay away."

Jim would not get the email until after his encounter with Yuri. He would respond and hope that only Jenny would see his response.

CHAPTER 89 – SECOND DATE

Jim lived in Chicago many years and never once visited the Holy Name Cathedral in Chicago. He always admired the architecture from the outside. It was a unique icon amongst the towering skyline of Chicago. He loved the fortress like beautiful stone structure with high windows. In his mind, it was not so different from the Water Tower in Chicago–although an expert architect might disagree. But he thought it had a similar charm about it. There was a huge decorative round window above the main entrance. All of the doors were heavy wood with exquisite hardware.

Jim walked the perimeter of the building a couple of times before going inside for the early mass. He wanted to know his exit options and nearby businesses and transportation just in case he needed an escape from his date with Yuri. It amazed him that there would be such a magnificent structure in the United States. It may not have been as eloquent as Notre Dame in Paris, but it was beautiful in its own right

Finally making his way into the cathedral, he stopped to glance at a book on the table that described the history of the church. Originally it was not even a cathedral, just a small Parish built in 1843. He assumed it was built as a cathedral but in fact it became one as more Catholics immigrated to the Chicago area. It had been destroyed in the great Chicago Fire and then rebuilt from donations from across the country. There were recent pictures of another fire that destroyed much of the roof. He could have read more, but his purpose was to ensure his own safety for the later encounter with Yuri.

The service had not started but Jim was surprised by the number of people in the main hall. The hall was long. The windows as seen on the outside were more vibrant stained glass from the inside and lined the main chapel area. The center piece was a cross with a statue of Jesus behind the pulpit. He had hoped for a crowd, for safety. Now he hoped for a slightly smaller crowd so that he and Yuri could have a pew near the rear where they could quietly talk for a few minutes during the service and hopefully not disrupt it.

As he looked across the room, several people were conversing. The prelude music was playing in the background. He noted the exits and tried to correspond each to what he saw from the outside and which street and businesses would be nearby. He noticed a lady, near the front, talk to someone that looked a little like Yuri, but she was in the distance and he couldn't be sure. Making his way to the front to find her he had to go around a few people. When he was nearly half way up the pastor/father stood and started to welcome the congregation. This was the invitation to sit down and quicker than anyone could imagine, the congregation began to be seated.

Jim lost sight of the lady and decided his best course of action was to head to the back of the chapel and exit. He still had a few things to prepare and did not want to sit through two masses on this day.

He walked out the doors at the back of the chapel as the ushers were shutting them. Standing in front of him was Yuri. "Do you always come early for your dates?"

Jim did not anticipate this, neither did Yuri for that matter. "I wanted to pick out the most romantic seats in the church." Jim responded

"I should have asked you for your real name when we were playing the game. I did not realize we were both playing parts." Yuri said without smiling. "You have learned this undercover stuff pretty quickly–I mean staking out a location ahead of time."

They started to take a walk. Jim suggested they find a place for a small bite to eat and maybe skip afternoon services, since they already ran into each other. They started to walk east on Superior Ave towards Michigan Ave. Jim knew the town well enough to get around, at least generally. Anyone who visited Chicago would likely know that the "Miracle Mile" (Michigan Ave) would have someplace to eat.

Jim talked as they walked. "You have learned more about me and I have learned a little more about you."

"Really Jim, or should I say Jacob, what do you know about me?" Yuri asked. Yuri was a master at understanding that it is better to get information from someone else than to share what you know. She learned to listen a lot more than she talked.

"First, the man that you thought was your father is really my biological father." Jim said as though it might be a revelation to Yuri.

"Yes, and I know who my biological father is also. You aren't telling me anything that I don't know." Yuri said a little impatiently.

They walked across Michigan Ave to Gino's pizza place. It just opened and they decided to head in and get something to drink.

Jim answered. "I don't know who your father is. Who is it?"

My real father was just some professor at Maryland. He died while on sabbatical in Russia." Yuri continued. "But what can you tell me that is helpful?"

"Professor Samuel Thomas?" Jim asked.

"I thought that you didn't know who my father was." Yuri said a bit angrily.

"I know who Professor Thomas is; I didn't know he was your father." Jim felt a little uneasy. He was not sure how tight the connection was between her and her biological father. "How close were you?"

"I didn't know him."

The waiter arrived and after a brief discussion, Jim decided it was best if Yuri try a true Chicago style pizza. They ordered a small. Yuri was not that interested but Jim was persistent.

Yuri continued, "Jim, how did you know my father's name?"

Jim hesitated, not wanting to give up everything he knew. It might be his only leverage. "I got a list of names of people involved in trying to steal money from Jim Conrad."

Yuri considered the answer. She leaned against the table. "Who?"

Jim was nervous so he put the gun that was in the waist of his pants onto his lap. "I don't think I should tell you that."

Yuri leaned in even closer. "This is one date I will not forget. I know that Jim Conrad was my father that I grew up with and it was not really his money. He worked for the CIA. I suspect that you were recruited by them. Somebody is responsible for their death. I want to know who." Yuri had a look of determination that frightened Jim.

"Your biological father was one of the names on the list, but I will not give you the rest of the list." Jim responded.

"I also know that James Corso's name was on the list." She paused to see if there was a reaction. She could see by Jim's eye movement that she had likely gotten name number two correct from the list. "If you won't give me the remaining three names, then tell me who gave you the list." Yuri was now just inches from his face.

Jim picked the gun up from under the table and pointed it at her under the table. "Tim Baker left a note for me in a safe deposit box in Des Moines with the names." He paused and then said. "I have a gun pointed at you and I think it is time for me to go. We can continue our date another time."

"I will expect flowers and my Chicago style pizza next time." Yuri said. She could easily kill him and could probably disarm him.

But if he got lucky then she might have an injury that was not necessary. So she let him walk out the door.

She was not more than 20 steps behind him. Jim immediately headed for Michigan Avenue where he knew the street would be busier. He had his gun back in his underneath his belt before he got onto the busy street. He immediately turned south looking for a taxi or a police officer. Jim knew that Yuri would not be far behind him.

Jim passed the Disney Store. He was nearing the Omni when he saw a police officer about one block down the street. He picked up his pace slightly and then felt the end of a gun point at his side as Yuri matched his pace. "You may be reluctant to use your gun in a public place but I am not."

Jim slowed to a stop. He looked at Yuri. "I think this is the first date that I have been on where my date pulled a gun on me." He said with a charming smile. He understood it wouldn't help his situation, but it was all he had to offer at the moment.

Yuri responded. "It's not the first time a date has pulled a gun on me, but it might be the first time a date pulled a gun on me and didn't actually shoot at me."

CHAPTER 90 – CHEAP MOTEL

Slowly, Jim started to regain consciousness. He tried to rub his eyes but realized that his hands had been secured to a chair. His legs were also secured. He was not going to move anytime soon. It took Jim a few moments to realize the sequence of events that put him into this position. He hadn't been hit so somehow Yuri must have drugged him.

His eyes were beginning to focus. He could see a flowered pale green curtain that was in constant movement from the fan below. Every once in a while the blowing curtain would open wide enough that he could make out that it was still light outside. He could see the cheap alarm clock from the side but couldn't make out the time. The room was worn and old; the type of motel that likely attracted a much lower form of criminal than Yuri.

The focus of his eyes shifted to the table directly in front of him. There was a makeshift folded piece of paper that had been used as a sign. It simply read "Date 3?". Behind the makeshift sign was a small bouquet of flowers trimmed to fit into the ice bucket. There were two beds in the room. He couldn't get his neck around to see the one directly behind him, at least not very well. On the other bed he saw his computer and his case that had his money and a few alternative identifications for him and Jenny in it.

He was gagged so that he could not scream. The television was off, but he could hear the televisions from other rooms. At least he hoped they were watching television since there was someone being tortured. Jim would need to wait for what seemed like a very long time in that position. It was in all actuality not more than thirty minutes.

Yuri walked in the door with a bag of takeout Chinese and a couple of waters. She pushed the flowers to the side. "Oh Jim, you are awake." Jim shook his head as Yuri reached over to remove the gag. "Are you hungry? Lunch out didn't work to well for us so I thought we could eat in for dinner."

"I can't eat unless you untie me." Jim said.

"I need some assurance that you won't run. You see I need you to help out a friend, a very dear friend." Yuri responded.

Jim agreed not to run. He hadn't decided if he would keep that promise or not. As he listened to Yuri over egg rolls, broccoli chicken and rice, he became more convinced that he might need to break the promise. Yuri explained that she drugged him so that she could find his hotel. Finding the car took a while. He parked in a fairly good place for hiding a car. It was the temporary plate that gave it away. He still had a dealers tag on the key chain, so she knew she was looking for a recently purchased vehicle.

Yuri told Jim that finding the hotel was pretty easy once she found the key in the car. From there she had access to the letter, money and his computer. Jim's only bargaining chip had been the rest of the five names and she had those now.

Yuri continued. "I need to just hand you over to them so that I can get Amir back. He may be my closest friend. They need you to access some bank account and steal a lot of money. I don't really care about that. They thought they took my money, but I have plenty stashed that they cannot find. When Amir is safe, I will find the remaining three and kill them."

"They will just kill me when they have what they want." Jim explained.

Yuri had devised a plan, more of a negotiation that would protect him from being killed. There was still a chance, but it was an unavoidable risk in Yuri's mind.

Jim was frustrated. "Why did you tell them about Iowa? If they hadn't come to Iowa then Jenny would be here and we could figure something else out." What he really meant, and Yuri knew it, is that Jenny would not have let Jim get captured by Yuri. Yuri felt the outcome wouldn't be any different, just maybe Jenny would have to be eliminated but she understood his sentiment.

Then it hit her. "I didn't tell the Captain about Iowa. I assumed that you told them or Jenny did."

"No, of course not." Jim hesitated. "Jenny and I have avoided telling anyone that we even had a translation of the codes on the plate. We left the translation with Professor Borden in Switzerland." Jim insisted that Professor Borden was so scared for his life he would not call anyone.

"Amir killed Professor Alto after he translated the plates. It was only the two of us with him when he did. Amir would never . . ." Yuri stopped in mid-sentence. Amir had been close to her for many years. The contact for this job originally came through Amir. Perhaps he made a copy. She kept thinking through the sequence of events in the hotel when the translation occurred. There was time. She could not be sure, but he could be the source. Nevertheless, she determined that even if he were the source, she would need to rescue him just to understand why. She also realized that sacrificing Jim to do that might not be in her best interest.

Jim already devised an alternative plan. Yuri listened and did not believe that it had a chance to work. It was something almost as crazy as what she would come up with. That, of course, made it the perfect plan.

CHAPTER 91 – YURI'S PLAY

Yuri stepped out of the motel room to take care of business. She was paranoid that Jim might just take off, but she had to make her phone call in a place with a little less noise. The outside was nearly as noisy and she went down the street to a park to get a little privacy. She made a few phone calls to arrange an appropriate location before calling the Captain.

Then she called the Captain. He answered "What do you want Stephanie?"

Yuri resented that he would always refer to her as Stephanie. She had been Yuri for many years and reserved the name Stephanie for no one. Maybe if she got married, she would use that name again. "Captain, I have Jim within my grasps."

"That is good news. Is he with you right now?" The Captain asked.

She told the Captain she would have him in the morning for a trade. Yuri described the location of an empty warehouse on the south side where they should meet at 9:30 AM "Bring Amir with you. It is an even trade." Yuri concluded. Then she headed back to the cheap motel.

CHAPTER 92 – UPWARD MOBILITY

Frank and Jenny were engaged in a career conversation, at the request of Jenny, over dinner. She discussed how she hoped her performance and trust on both of these assignments would help move her up the ranks and provide additional opportunities. Frank agreed that it might, but reminded her that she had not been able to reach Jim all day. He was worried and still viewed this as her responsibility.

Jim called Jenny right in the middle of dinner. The phone rang from an unknown telephone number. "Jim, where have you been?" Jenny sounded frustrated and intense. She was focused and did not get up from the table.

The volume was just loud enough that Frank could catch pieces of what Jim was saying. "Jenny, I am truly sorry. I ran into Yuri today—we met and I got the impression that she was looking for me. I am not sure what for. I am away from her now. I am a little worried though. I think that I am safe for now."

Jenny expressed sympathy and then told him that he ought to just come in and they can protect him. Jim was not at all comfortable with that suggestion. He told Jenny that he locked himself in a room and didn't want to come out until it was light outside. Jenny conceded and then told Jim that they could meet at the Chase bank downtown at 9:30 AM.

Jim responded, "Ricardo has set-up another purchase for us at 9:00. I think we should do that first and then go to the bank." After explaining to Jenny that they were to meet in a conference room in a hangar at the Lake County airport, he further explained that they should get one more criminal out of the deal before he went back to accounting. "Besides," he said, "the bank will be open all day. Ricardo's contact has to leave town shortly after the meeting."

Jenny responded in a near whisper. "I don't care, you work for the agency and this thing at the bank needs done first."

"I am going to Ricardo's meeting. Be there." Jim said emphatically.

"You better be at the bank." Jenny responded. Jim just hung up on her.

Frank looked at Jenny. "Where do you think he will go?"

Jenny said, "Oh he will be at the bank. He better be at the bank."

Frank wasn't so convinced. "Look, I will go to the Ricardo meeting and make sure it goes fine if Jim shows up there. You go to the bank."

"Trevor can handle things at the Ricardo sight." Jenny pressed.

Frank thought for a minute. "Without your guidance at the negotiation table he might get in trouble. It is probably best for Trevor and me both to be there. I will get Sr. Director Corso to meet you at the bank. That is primarily his operation anyway."

Jenny let Frank know that she was still convinced Jim would go to the bank, but Frank insisted that they account for any potential contingency.

Monday
Chicago

CHAPTER 93 – LAKE COUNTY

Situated between Chicago and Milwaukee is the reasonably sized city of Waukegan with the Lake County Regional Airport nearby. It has a regional airport that many business travelers use to avoid the congestion of Chicago O'Hare. It is not known for elaborate meeting facilities, but tucked away in some of the buildings are prime locations for a quick in and out business meeting – never having to even leave the airport. If one knows who to talk to then a location can be arranged. Ricardo is familiar with those who could secure meeting rooms.

The conference room was selected at the last minute so that it could be confidential. Ricardo brought breakfast, coffee and juice for the meeting. It was a long room with a single wide table down the middle. Chairs were on both sides. A single chair was at each end of the long table. The wall was decorated with pictures of various small engine aircraft and their owners. Each of these airplanes landed at least once at the airport.

Ricardo sat near the head of the table but not in the end seat. While Ricardo waited, he read the local Chicago paper. A pilot walked in "Sorry, I didn't realize this room was being used." Ricardo motioned as if to say no big deal. The pilot promptly left. The pilot then entered a nearby office that had the blinds shut. Shutting the door behind him he took off his hat and said "Frank, I got the bug in place."

"Nice job Trevor." Frank responded. There were only three scheduled flights before 9:00 AM. Frank was pretty sure they had narrowed down which flight was coming in to meet with Ricardo and Jim.

A private jet registered to Seema Patel was scheduled to land at about 8:45 AM. Seema was from India but worked out of New York City acquiring artifacts from the Far East for use in the US east coast museums, such as the Smithsonian and the New York Museum of Natural History. Her business was completely legitimate. However, she often leveraged her father to get exhibits to tour the US. He lived right in the disputed territory between Pakistan and India. He had become wealthy over the years by playing each side of the dispute against each other. He used connections he made in this conflict to expand his business to other parts of the world.

Trevor was thrilled at the prospect of making a connection with another world criminal. This plan was working better than he thought it might.

Frank tuned the radio in the office into the tower intercom system and knew when the jet was landing. Ricardo waited for his son to bring Seema to the room. Ricky brought her in shortly after landing and it became a waiting game. The breakfast and juice helped pass the time. Seema was patient, but when 9:30 rolled around she began to question if Jim was going to show or not.

CHAPTER 94 – THE WAREHOUSE

Heidi and four other henchmen came to the warehouse almost immediately after the phone conversation the captain had with Yuri. They wanted to ensure that they controlled the situation. If she really had Jim, he needed taken alive and she knew that Yuri was among the most volatile and unpredictable people in the world. They took the time to sweep the room for bugs and to make sure all exits were secured and understood.

Each of the help was strategically placed so that there were clear shots at the primary entrance and to the main part of the warehouse. This is where they would direct Yuri. All of the other potential entrances were chained and locked so that Yuri's only choice was to come through the front door.

The warehouse was huge. It was lit with fluorescent bulbs that were in various states of effectiveness. It was fairly dim throughout most of the warehouse. There were a number of conveyors and catwalks above the warehouse floor. A lot of the shelving was still in place. It still stored a number of old supplies, as if it were a dumping ground for a building that had been dismantled and stored in pieces in this warehouse. There were commodes, piping, door hardware, windows, and just about anything else you could imagine. It was a used parts version of a home improvement store.

Amir arrived at 9:00 AM guarded by one more person. He would be placed in the center of the warehouse strapped in an explosive that would easily kill him and not hurt anyone else in the room. Once Amir arrived they waited.

The phone that Heidi had with her rang at exactly 9:30 AM. She answered. "Yes, who am I speaking to?"

"You are not the Captain." Yuri said.

"The Captain had other business to attend to this morning. He gave me his phone. I am in his place. I assume you are Yuri." Heidi said as she stood next to Amir and a guard.

"I am Yuri. You must be Heidi." Yuri commented. "The captain didn't come personally to get Jim?"

"Like I said, he had another item of business." Heidi responded.

"Okay, we can do business. First you need to remove the bomb strapped around Amir. Then you need to take off your blue blazer, I want to see what type of weapon you are carrying." Yuri explained.

Heidi motioned to the guard with her and he quickly radioed to the others that Yuri must be in the building.

CHAPTER 95 – THE BANK

Jim walked in the bank front entrance at precisely 9:30 AM. Jenny and Director Corso were waiting in the lobby. Jenny said. "I told Frank he would come here first."

Jim looked at them. "Let's get this done. I am sure that I just ticked Ricardo off and that will not make Frank very happy."

Jenny introduced Director Corso and the other agent that was standing there with him before they went back to the conference room. The banking transaction could have taken place nearly anywhere; it just felt better to actually do it in a bank, even if it was a bank that had nothing to do with the actual money and assets that were in play.

A video conference line was open between the banking office in the US and the small Swiss bank in Zurich. Director Corso asked the banker in Switzerland if there was someone there representing Jim in person. Director Corso arranged for one of his operatives to be present. He already knew that the operative was there, they had been trading messages for the last thirty minutes. Hans, the Swiss banker, confirmed his presence. Then Hans said, "For a transaction of this size, we will need verification of identity."

"Of course," Jim responded.

Hans observed as the nurse carefully took a hair sample and then a blood sample. Both were put into a machine to analyze. The results were put onto a memory stick and then sent to Hans over the internet from the bank's computer. Jim also provided the primary account information and the password. He was able to do this over an encrypted connection. Once verified, the transaction was ready to begin. The nurse was excused. The local banker insisted on being present for the transaction. He did not want the appearance of anything shady going on in his bank.

Hans began. "Jim Conrad, are you sure you want to proceed?" He asked wanting to make sure that he understood the consequences.

Jim nodded and then said, "Yes. Let's get this done."

Hans pulled up the portfolio screen with the summary. Remembering the interaction from a few days ago, he quickly switched the currency to US dollars. The amount was just shy of $92 billion dollars. "Looks like we lost a bit" Jim said.

The local Chicago banker's mouth just dropped to the floor. This was much more than he ever thought possible for one investor. It certainly made Jim one of the richest men in the world.

Hans looked disappointed. "The markets fluctuate. It is a temporary setback I assure you."

Jim was not really concerned about a few hundred million when they were talking about billions, he was actually just joking. However, he realized it might not be the best thing to joke about with a banker who takes great pride in his work. "Hans, my quick calculations say you lost considerably less than the market as a percentage. I think you have done fine."

Hans looked relived. "Thank you Jim. This is your total portfolio. You understand that these assets are in multiple bank accounts and investments around the world. Your primary account just gives you one place to manage these assets. But this primary account does control total ownership of these assets."

"I understand. If I transfer the primary account to Mr. Corso

here, then he controls all of the assets associated with that account."
Jim explained back to Hans just so there was no confusion.

Hans replied. "You are correct. Would you like to drill down
into the portfolio and see the relationships?"

Jim looked at Director Corso. Director Corso indicated that would
not be necessary. He told Jim that the amount seemed about right and
that they should proceed with the transaction. Jim spoke to Hans. "I
think we are fine. Bring up the primary account like we discussed."

Hans went to the account. He looked at the video monitor and
said. "I need to know what account to transfer ownership to."

Director Corso pulled out a piece of paper that had a routing
number and an account number on it and the words "Friends of the
World Charity Fund" and handed it to Jim. Corso then said quietly
to Jenny, "We have to put the money someplace where others can
access it."

Jim typed the information into the screen with the title of the
charity. Hans looked at the people on the video screen and then
glanced at the man next to him. "Jim, I am doing this because you
have requested it. It is your account. Are you sure you really want
to do this?"

Jim hit enter. He was prompted again for a password to confirm
the transaction. A message popped up on the screen. "Your account
and all associated accounts have been successfully transferred. Your
balance is $0."

Hans concluded. "The transaction is completed exactly as
requested. The account and all of its associated accounts has been
moved to the 'Friends of the World Charity Fund'. We are sorry to
see this part of our portfolio go."

Director Corso received a message from his operative at the
Swiss bank that it all looked fine. "Thanks for your help Hans."

Hans just said. "We hope to have future business with you Mr.
Conrad." The conference call was ended and the room was vacated.

Jim asked for a ride to the hotel from the director because he
had taken a taxi to the bank. Director Corso agreed. It fit better with

his plan anyway. As he got in the SUV he received a text from Frank. "Something is wrong at the warehouse. On my way." The director instinctively asked Jenny to drive. Jim sat in the back with the other agent. The director sat in the front sit next to Jenny.

The director asked Jenny to drive to a warehouse in town. He put an address into the GPS device so she would have directions. Jenny glanced over at the director and asked. "Why don't we just take Jim back to his hotel?"

"There is a colleague in trouble we are going to help. I believe Yuri is involved." Director Corso responded.

CHAPTER 96 – BACK IN THE WAREHOUSE

Heidi kept looking around the building trying to discover where Yuri might be located. She slowly removed her blue blazer and revealing a holster with a gun under the left arm. Then she walked over to Amir and removed the explosives from his body placing them at his feet. If exploded, it would not kill him but would likely cripple him. She wanted to do what Yuri asked but did not want to give up her superior position. Then, not using the phone she asked, "Where is Jim?"

Yuri spoke quietly into the phone. She did not want to give up her position if she didn't have to. Through the scope in her rifle, she could see that Heidi was holding a trigger switch for the bomb in one hand and the phone in the other hand. She knew where the trigger switch was but that didn't give her an answer as to how to avoid the bomb going off. Her main goal was to take out Heidi. It didn't matter to her if the rest of them lived or died. She wanted Amir alive if she could get that, but that was not even necessary at this point. Two shots would give her position away.

Heidi repeated impatiently and this time in the phone. "Where is Jim?" Her scanning the room had narrowed the best locations for Yuri down to about four. She was hoping that her operatives would be drawing the same conclusions by this time.

"Not until Amir is safe." Yuri responded. "Take your hand off of the trigger and move the bomb away from his feet.

"I can't do that until I know you have Jim." Heidi responded.

Yuri opted to use her first shot. The guard next to Amir fell first to his knees and then flat faced onto the floor. The shot helped Heidi narrow Yuri's position to two likely locations. She knew that if Yuri were alone, other than Jim, then Yuri was now in trouble. The other operatives would be narrowing in their shots to those locations and perhaps even moving in physically to that location. "The next shot is aimed at you Heidi."

"Amir will either die or be seriously injured if you do that." Heidi said now focusing in on the specific areas where Yuri was likely to be.

"Amir betrayed me. I only want him alive so that I can personally kill him. But maybe shooting you is a better two for one deal." Yuri countered.

Heidi understood that if Yuri wanted a two for one deal, the show would be over already. But she also understood that conditions change and Yuri may opt for that condition sooner. Time was not on Yuri's side and she seriously doubted if Jim was at the warehouse. "Where is Jim?"

Yuri had given enough time for everything else to get into motion and simply said. "Jim is not here. I am here to kill you."

With that, Heidi began to move back behind metal shelving unit. Amir started to run for the exit and was shot by one of the operatives. Yuri took advantage of the opportunity and shot at Heidi just as the explosives went off. The shot missed Heidi and revealed Yuri's location on scaffolding above the catwalk in front of Heidi. Heidi sent a quick text to Frank that she was in trouble and he had better get there as soon as he can.

Yuri was now exposed and knew that she needed to move or she would be trapped. She was in a great position and could hold it for days if nothing changed. However, she could not cover additional people coming into the warehouse through the front door. Hence, she was certain that things would change. There was a roof exit that was her last resort and she was in a position to get to that with little damage to herself.

She knew the layout and about where each of the four operatives started. She had made her way into the building a few hours before they arrived the night before and observed their sweep of the building and their positioning. She could easily take out one of the operatives but that would cut out her only viable exit through the roof. However, she would also have Heidi pinned in a way that she could not get out. She opted for the move down to the catwalk and onto the top of an office area that had a cement block barrier built up.

On the way to her safe zone, she took a clean shot hitting the operative squarely in the head. Then she was on top of the small office area. Heidi tried to come around the shelf and Yuri placed a shot that nearly hit her. It was a message that Heidi got clearly. The remaining three operatives spent the next several minutes trying to flank and out maneuver Yuri. This was fruitless. They would not be able to get to her and she would not be able to get out.

CHAPTER 97 – CONVERGENCE

Director Corso insisted that Jenny stay out in the SUV to keep Jim safe. Jenny objected and said that she should be able to come in the Warehouse with Corso. The director would not allow it so she sat in the driver's seat. Jim climbed into the front seat while Corso and the operative with him went into the warehouse. Once Corso was gone, Jenny sent a text to Trevor and told him to get down to the warehouse as soon as possible.

Yuri could see the daylight come through as the front door opened. Heidi was relieved. With additional help, she might be able to get a better position or angle on Yuri and might be able to take her out. Heidi could make out two figures walking into the door. One of the three remaining operatives radioed Heidi and said it was Corso. This was great news.

Heidi shouted the location of Yuri to Corso. He spoke back. "Stephanie, you lied. Jim made it to the bank today and completed the transaction. We didn't need you after all."

Yuri responded back. "He slipped through my hands. But I now know who is responsible for the death of my parents."

"You figured out that it was Amir." Corso responded. The other operative had already made his way to attempt to flank Yuri. Corso had moved to a secure but more central location in the warehouse.

Yuri was not sure what to think. "I know it is you and Heidi and Frank. I also believe that the agent I killed in Paris was also involved. And so was my real father."

"You think you have learned a lot, but you don't really know anything." Corso yelled back to Yuri.

Again the door to the warehouse opened. Heidi could see two more figures come into the warehouse. The voice radioed to Heidi that it was Jenny and Jim. Corso continued. "But you didn't know it was Amir who planned the actual murder."

Corso was just buying time so that everyone could get into position. He saw Jenny and Jim approaching. "What do you need? I told you stay out in the car. We are about to get Yuri. It will be a great feather in our cap. You can get credit if you would like, just get Jim out of here." Jim pulled a gun and aimed it right at Director Corso. "What are you doing?" Corso asked.

Jenny had her gun pulled also. She was facing out looking for anyone that might come towards them. She spoke loudly next. "I have Corso. Who wants him?" She said as she disarmed the director.

He responded quietly. "I hope you know what you are doing."

"I am arresting a thief." Jenny replied.

Heidi did not want to say anything. One of her operatives radioed and said he had a shot at Jim. She gave the go ahead to shoot Jim. He fired and Jim went flat onto the ground. It only hit his leg, but he had never been shot before and the pain was excruciating. Jenny returned fire while Jim scooted to the edge out of the line of fire. Corso ran around the shelving unit and could no longer be seen.

Jenny wasn't sure where all of the players were. So she asked in the only way that would keep most people in the room wondering whose side she was on. "Can anyone tell me where Yuri is? She has ticked me off for the last time."

Heidi felt this was the opportune time. She described exactly where Yuri was located. Then Yuri spoke up, which is what Jenny really wanted. "You can get behind the goons trying to kill me starting with Heidi." Then Yuri proceeded to point out where each of the marks was except the new one that had come with Corso.

Jenny told Jim to stay put. He had a gun and was ready to shoot in any direction. She made her way around the shelf carefully. Then getting into position she had one of the marksmen in her sights. Aiming carefully she took a shot that wounded the man in the abdomen area. He was still able to shoot, but his mobility had been reduced to almost zero. Another man popped up and took a shot at Jenny. He came a little high and Yuri was able to get a shot off that hit his gun. It fell from his arms and to the ground. He was able to pull a hand gun from his holster but not before Yuri had a chance to get back to the scaffolding and have a better position. She quickly made her way back to the scaffolding and was ready to shoot anything that moved.

Jenny made her way to the end of the shelving unit, partially looking for Corso and partially looking to get a good angle on someone else. She could see Heidi and knew that if she could coerce her out a little then Yuri would likely have a shot. Jenny took aim and shot, hitting the shelving near Heidi's head. Heidi stepped further down the aisle to avoid another shot that might not miss. Jenny adjusted and again took a shot that just missed Heidi. Heidi moved a little further down the aisle to avoid Jenny's fire. It was a little too far. Yuri shot her square in the back.

Jenny moved quickly into Heidi's spot. This gave her a clear shot at one of the operatives. She shot and one fell from the catwalk all the way to the cement floor. If the shot hadn't killed him, the fall surely did.

The man that had come with Corso had flanked Yuri. When he had a shot, he took it. Yuri was hit in her arm but was able to turn and get a shot off knocking the man to the ground. She was deadly accurate with her gun.

Corso had made his way back around to Jim. Jim was caught off guard and quickly disarmed. Corso pulled Jim up onto his one leg that wasn't shot and put the gun to his head. He then sounded off. "I have Jim. Who wants him?"

Jenny was now somewhat trapped by the man with the hand gun. Yuri, however, now was free to move around the warehouse. She made her way quickly past the injured operative and snapped his neck. Then she came down to the main floor and stood facing Corso and Jim. Her pistol was pointing right at Corso.

"Have you come to save Jim?" Corso laughed a little.

"No. I came to kill you." Yuri said. Corso kept the angle as such so that Yuri would have to shoot through Jim in order to hit him. He would shift a little each way every time Yuri made a slight move.

"You are every bit as good as your parents were. Only they were noble people–misplaced alliances, but noble. You are a common thief." Corso said in disgust. In spite of the pain and a gun to his head, Jim just thought of the irony of Corso's statement. Who was the thief? Jim knew who it was.

The remaining Operative had made his way down and was about to take aim at Yuri. Yuri was not able to shift her position quickly enough. A shot whizzed by her from the other direction and the final operative was lying dead on the ground. Yuri glanced to look at Jenny. "Thanks." Then she turned her attention back to Corso.

Jenny also had an angle on Corso. Only he knew that she wouldn't shoot unless he shot first. Corso knew that he had no chance and was not ready to answer the questions that he would be asked. He figured that if he didn't die here, it wouldn't be long after that someone would kill him. As he let Jim fall face first to the ground, Yuri said "You killed my father!"

She shot him directly in the chest. Blood came out his mouth. He dropped to his knees and looked up at Yuri. "You have no idea." Then he fell backwards and died.

The warehouse door opened again. They could see one figure coming into the room. Yuri ducked behind a shelf as Frank walked into the view of Jenny and Jim. Frank saw Corso on the ground and didn't hear any sounds at all. He wasn't sure what had happened. Jenny had her gun pulled and it was aiming in Frank's direction. Frank looked at her and said. "Either use your gun or put it away."

Jenny didn't hesitate; she shot Frank in the right leg.

"What are you doing? Are you crazy?" Frank barked back.

"You conceived this whole thing over 25 years ago and now it is costing too many lives and for what? Money." Jenny said looking disgusted at Frank. "Call Tom. Tell your boss what this is really all about."

Frank looked at Jenny with disdain and anger in his eyes. "This is not about money. This is about principle. I would do it all again if I had to."

"You promised to uphold the law, not kill innocent people." Jenny said. She was almost crying as she said it. It was the moment that Frank had hoped for. He pulled his gun and got a shot off hitting her in the shoulder. He kept his gun up. If she lifted her gun again he would kill her.

From behind the shelving unit a shot was fired hitting Frank's shooting hand. His gun fell to the ground. Yuri stepped out from behind the shelf and fired hitting him in the left leg. "My father, my mother. You and four others killed them. Yes, they took their lives to save me. Now I have nearly avenged them."

The warehouse door had opened again and three shadows were walking towards them.

"Yes. Professor Thomas asked us not to threaten your life. But Corso felt it was the only way." Frank said as he struggled to even sit up as the blood came out of his body. His left hand was on his gun now but he had not lifted it up yet. "And the only way to get an accountant to leave his comfortable life would be to arrange for his family to be in a tragic accident."

Jim took notice and picked up a gun. "You murderer."

He aimed the gun but could not bring himself to pull the trigger. Yuri grabbed the gun in his hand and pulled the trigger with him. She then looked at him with her big blue eyes and kissed his cheek. "Now we are both avenged." The bullet hit Frank squarely in the forehead.

The approaching men pulled their guns. Trevor came into view with two other agents. Trevor caught a side view of Yuri as she disappeared around a shelf. He walked over to Jim and carefully took the gun from his hand. "I will take this. It might be difficult to explain with your fingerprints on there."

Jenny looked at Trevor. "We have a lot more to explain than just the gun."

CHAPTER 98 – REPORTING BACK

Director Tom Sportsman was already on a jet from Washington DC to Chicago. He would land at Midway, delaying several passenger planes in the process. They would never know why they were delayed. He wanted to be onsite before the scene was completely cleaned up.

Jenny and Jim were both treated by a doctor that had been brought on site. Director Sportsman asked that no one still living leave the scene until he arrived. Trevor knew that would be easy, very few were still alive. Amir had a serious enough injury that he had to be taken to the hospital. In spite of being under heavy guard, Amir never made it to the hospital. The facts and details behind his disappearance remained vague.

Jenny and Jim found a couple of old lawn chairs that they pulled out to sit on. Jim only hoped they would not fall apart when they used them. They sat drinking a cold soda brought by one of the clean-up crew. Several other agents, including Trevor sat with them.

Trevor was under strict orders not to debrief until he arrived. It was a long few hours.

Finally Tom Sportsman walked into the warehouse. He had an additional twelve agents with him. Even though he was older than any of the other agents, he briskly walked several steps in front of them. When he arrived to Trevor, Jenny, and Jim he excused everyone else except those three and the other two agents that had come in with Trevor at the end of the shootout.

"What are all of you doing here? Frank is dead and I am told two other agents are dead. So is some former agent who is with Interpol, Heidi, is also dead. Then there are these two other guys that have no identification on them. Then there is the one suspect we had got away on the way to the hospital. And worst of all Sr. Director Corso is dead, a simple advisor to the CIA now– emeritus status and all. I just don't understand how these things happen. And maybe worst of all, you let Yuri slip through your hands." A man gentle in words on most occasions added to his tirade with a few choice words.

Trevor wanted to jump and say that he could explain, but he couldn't. Tom helped, "Okay Trevor you start. What went wrong?"

Trevor explained that they had a planned meeting to discuss purchasing artifacts with Seema Patel at the beginning of the day and Jim did not show up. Frank and him were set and were monitoring but Jim and Jenny were not there.

"Then where were you two?" Tom asked looking at Jenny.

Jenny was about to explain the trip to the bank when Jim jumped in. "Director Corso brought us to the warehouse. Frank asked him to. I think, and I am not an agent or anything, that Heidi must of tracked Yuri here. It was a last minute call to miss the meeting and Heidi thought she might need us to identify Yuri since we had seen her."

Jenny figured it might be a better explanation than trying to explain the bank. She knew that at some point that would need explained, but now it would just complicate everything.

Trevor interjected, "It didn't seem that Frank was shocked that they didn't show. Then he left with a pressing engagement pretty quickly. He probably thought he could handle it and didn't need me. Then Heidi sent a text saying that it was urgent I get here."

"Well, did you come quickly?" Tom asked.

"It is a long way from Waukegan to the warehouse in Chicago, but we were already on our way to the city, so we got here pretty quickly." Trevor responded. "As I walked in the warehouse I saw Yuri shooting Frank."

Tom stood up and walked the interior of the warehouse and then up to the catwalk. He looked around where Frank's body had been and then where Heidi was killed and finally the resting place of Director Corso. He came back to Trevor and looked at him and Jenny and then at Jim. He was talking to each of them, but particularly looking at Jim. "Frank will be buried an American hero, but none of this happened on American soil. There will be too much red tape if it happened here. Am I clear?" They all agreed, including Jim. Then Tom continued, turning his attention to Trevor and Jenny. "Is the character of 'Jim Conrad' compromised?"

Jenny looked at Jim then at Trevor and finally back to Tom. "No, we will need a cover story of why we were here, but I do not think we could be connected to either side of this shootout. I am not even sure if one of the dead agents isn't who shot Jim."

Tom looked at Trevor. "Is Ricardo compromised?"

Trevor thought for a minute. "He is ticked, very mad. But I do not believe he is compromised."

Jim knew otherwise but did not speak up. He had personally told Ricardo the entire operation the night before in order to get his cooperation in setting up a fake deal in the morning at the Waukegan Airport. He would tell Jenny about this consequence of his plan as soon as they left the warehouse.

Tom simply said. "It sounds like we are still a go for this operation. Trevor, you are on point. Consider it a field promotion. Send Jim and Jenny back to the hotel. I already called for the company Limo. Have dinner with Ricardo if he will come to send your sincere apologies. Then have Jacob come out of his coma in the morning and send him home." Tom turned and started for the exit of the warehouse. He stopped just a few feet away and turned back around. "Jim, or rather Jacob, thanks for your service. You have done an incredible service for your country." Then he turned and headed for the door and was gone nearly as quick as he came.

Trevor simply said. "Looks like I have taken over for Frank."

CHAPTER 99 – THE DRAKE AGAIN

An onsite agency approved doctor and nurse attended to their wounds while they waited for the limo.

As Jim and Jenny stepped out of the warehouse a black stretch limo was waiting at the door. They climbed in to find a small metal case with some money and a few alternative identities for each of them. The driver told them that the hotel arrangements and the dinner appointment had already been arranged. He then shut the window for privacy. There was a dress on the hook for Jenny and nice slacks, shirt and sports blazer hanging for Jim.

Jim looked at Jenny. "Can you avert your eyes?"

Jenny laughed as she quickly got herself dressed. Jim looked to the side.

"I am serious." Jim said.

Jenny turned around and said, "I know you are."

They soon arrived at the Drake Hotel in Chicago.

Jim stood next to Jenny near the check-in counter of the hotel holding only the metal briefcase. The check-in clerk said, "Ah, Mr. and Mrs. Smith, your suite is ready. I have provided you and Mr.

Smith with the normal amenities. We are pleased to have you back."

Jim and Jenny turned and headed for the elevator. Jim once again looked through the closets and found the same familiar clothing. Jenny excused herself into the next room to see if Ricardo had dinner plans. She knew that there was no cover story that he would buy, not since Jim had shared the whole operation. But she needed dinner with him so that she could go back and explain to Trevor that the operation was over.

Jim stepped out of the room and went down to the lobby where he found a house phone that he could use. He borrowed a phone book from the front desk. He ordered a Chicago Style pizza and flowers. He had them sent to a cheap, sleazy motel. The card with the flowers simply said. "Truly a second date to remember." He wasn't sure if she would get it or if she was long gone.

Jim showered and then put on a tuxedo before they headed down for dinner. Arriving at the restaurant the attendant said. "Mr. and Mrs. Smith, we are pleased you have joined us again for dinner. Can we start you with water and an order of our jumbo shrimp cocktail?"

Ricardo arrived a few minutes later. They stood and greeted each other. Jim thanked Ricardo for what he had done. After ordering the main course, Jenny did not waste any time. "Ric, thanks for having dinner with us. Actually meeting with you will make it easier to explain why we can't continue the operation. We will just tell them that your reputation was hurt and you don't care to business with us at this time."

Ricardo took a bite of the shrimp as he listened to Jenny. When she finished, he jumped in. "Do you know I have been here probably over 100 times and never tried this. It is very good."

Jim jumped in. "I agree. We order this every time we are in town."

Ricardo continued. "We will eat here next time I find an artifact that you wish to purchase. Seema is anxious to show you a few. I am sure I can get her to come again or we could go to New York."

"Ric." Jenny interjected. "I am not sure how much Jim told you, but when we close this down we will likely hand you over to the feds."

Ricardo laughed. "Jenny, I am a businessman. If I do not break the law then there will be nothing to hand to the feds. And as long as I get to work with you and Jim, I can do this for years."

Jenny looked at Jim and then at Ricardo. "What if Jim is longer involved? What if it is just me?"

Ricardo looked a little disappointed. "Jacob would come out of his coma?"

"Yes." Jenny responded.

Ricardo smiled. "Then I would have my daughter bring Jacob to dinner and get to know him. She would love that. Maybe you would come sometimes also, after one of our business deals."

Jenny was impressed. She wasn't sure if Ricardo was crazy or an extremely brilliant business man. He would now know all of the surveillances the CIA was doing on him and probably figured that meant other agencies would avoid him also. Either way, the operation could continue. Dinner was as good as it was the week before, only this time Jenny was sad to see it end.

Jim and Jenny returned to their hotel room. Jenny explained that she was going to call Trevor and let him know everything was a go for the operation. She would also see what the arrangements were for his miraculous recovery that was sure to happen within the week. Jim interrupted. "Jenny, what if I want to stay in?"

Jenny smiled as she dialed the phone. "Trevor, this is Jenny. Ricardo is still on board if he can deal with Jim and me together." There was a brief pause as Jim heard some loud talking on the other end of the phone. "Jim is on board. He is willing to stick this out for several months or more if needed." There was another brief pause not quite as loud. "Yes, he expects the normal pay and he will tell us if he wants out." Then a final pause before Jenny finished. "Since you took Frank's place you will need to call Tom."

When she hung up the phone she said "I am going to like working for Trevor."

Jenny went into the bathroom to get ready for bed. Jim changed in the main room. Jenny came out with a long t-shirt on and climbed into bed. Jim pulled up a blanket and a pillow on the couch. Jenny looked over at Jim from the bed and said. "Goodnight Mr. Jim Conrad."

About an hour after they had gone to bed, Jenny's phone went off. She had received a text. She checked it and then turned back to Jim. "Jim, are you still up?"

Jim said in a slightly hoarse voice. "I am now."

Jenny said. "Text for you. It says 'Jim, You were right, it is great pizza. I have a place to suggest next time.'"

Jim smiled and was glad that she got it.

Jenny didn't ask about the text, but had figured it was Yuri. However, since they were up she continued. "How does it feel to be back in the poor house again?"

Jim smiled. "I am Jim Conrad. I will bounce back."

Jenny looked at Jim across the dim room. "Yes, still my Jim. I just hope that Tom can find someone to trace the money you sent to the 'Friends of the World Charity' or whatever that was."

Jim sat up a little. "Jenny." Then he was silent.

Jenny looked at him playfully. "Yes Jim."

"Do you think it is a good use of taxpayer dollars to go hunting after $100 sent to some world charity fund?" Jim asked slyly.

Jenny pulled her phone out and looked at her email. "You didn't?"

Jenny looked at the email from the small Swiss bank "Jim, we are sorry to lose your account of $100 and all of the associated assets for a total account value of $100. We appreciate your continued business. With today's European markets your account value is once again over $92 billion. I hope the US market does as well. Your Banker, Hans."

POST SCRIPT

Professor Arthur Borden was questioned and then released with regards to the murder of his wife. The murderer was never found.

Jim Conrad let him keep the bronze plate on loan for a while. The professor also received an anonymous donation of the second plate a few weeks after the initial incident.

The professor taught one class over the next year. It was nearly a sabbatical for the professor. He spent most of his time attempting to translate two interesting plates that he had in his possession. He kept in contact with Dragos on his progress. Dragos came to visit him in the UK on several occasions.

With the help of a brilliant Hebrew scholar who was also a grad student on loan from Harvard to Cambridge and only 23 years old, the professor was able to crack the translation of this text that clearly had strong elements of ancient Egyptian and ancient Hebrew.

The first plate was an account of the flood. It was close enough to existing ancient records available that, once Arthur understood this, it became a basis for the complete translation of both plates.

As he completed the translation of the second plate, the history became clearer.

I am Obedi son of Aaron son of Ephraimi descendent of Ephraim, true king of Israel forsaken by our brethren of Juda and attacked by Assyria. We have taken what is left of the ten higher tribes northward out of harm's way. I leave this plate as a marker for our captured brethren, if it be God's will they are set free. May god be with us and with you. We will go east until we find water or an impassible mountain. Then we will leave another marker. Perhaps we will wander until we are no more. God watched over Moses and our brethren may he watch over us as we wander in the wilderness. There are many to feed and little time. We will not rest until we feel God is among us again.

The reference that Dragos found in blood on the one plate, Kings1131, became clear now. It was not about a king that lived in the year 1131 BC or AD. It was a scriptural reference to 1 Kings 11:31.

And he said to Jeroboam, Take thee ten pieces: for thus saith the LORD, the God of Israel, Behold, I will rend the kingdom out of the hand of Solomon, and will give ten tribes to thee.

www.ingramcontent.com/pod-product-compliance
Lightning Source LLC
Chambersburg PA
CBHW071051250626
47159CB00002B/442